CW01073064

ALL SHOOK UP

WILLIAM BEDFORD

ALL SHOOK UP

MACMILLAN
LONDON

First published 1992 by
MACMILLAN LONDON LIMITED
a division of Pan Macmillan Publishers Limited
Cavaye Place London SW10 9PG
and Basingstoke

Associated companies in Auckland, Budapest, Dublin, Gaborone,
Harare, Hong Kong, Kampala, Kuala Lumpur, Lagos, Madras,
Manzini, Melbourne, Mexico City, Nairobi, New York, Singapore,
Tokyo and Windhoek

ISBN 0-333-56963-6

A CIP catalogue record for this book is available
from the British Library

Typeset by Macmillan Production Limited
Printed by Billing and Sons Limited, Worcester

Acknowledgement is due to the editor of *Panurge* in which
parts of this novel originally appeared.

For Greg and Gill Evans

CONTENTS

PART I

None of the Cadillacs was Pink

ONE

We moved from the coast in the spring of that year. For my father, the move was a promotion. After spending several years with the police in the fishing port where he was born, he solved a murder in which a nightclub singer battered her mother to death and then tried to get rid of the body by setting fire to it with a can of petrol. She left the charred remains out on the sand dunes. My father spoke to the singer for hours, getting her to sing her favourite songs while he kept time with a pencil and took down her confession. He asked the duty sergeant to complete the crime reports and prepare the hearing. The singer had grown up in the same streets as my father, and once the confession was signed he refused to have anything else to do with the case. He said her breath smelled of acid drops.

'Acid drops?' My mother smiled, looking up, interested.

'Yes, acid drops.'

'I wonder why she liked acid drops.'

'Does it matter?'

He went on to tell us about the gruesome condition in which the police found the body, and the publicity photograph the duty sergeant had got the singer to sign before she was taken to the cells. It had been taken by one of the photographers who worked the fairgrounds and promenade all summer, offering family portraits to the tourists.

'What did she sing?' my mother asked suddenly.

My father glared at her, rubbing the side of his nose with the back of his hand. He had rough, clumsy hands, the fingers gnarled with arthritis from the years he had spent on the trawlers before the war. He was always irritated by my mother's vague interest in the things he told her, her casual surprise.

'Sing?'

'What songs did she sing?'

'How should I know?' he said tensely.

'I'm just interested.'

'In what?'

'What songs she sang!'

He sighed and stared out of the window, gritting his teeth.

'I sometimes wonder about you,' he said. 'Make us a cup of tea, Stephen.'

I got up and filled the kettle.

We were sitting in the kitchen. The door was wide open into the yard. My mother was shelling peas, filling the colander and humming to herself quietly under her breath. My father was cleaning his boots, daubing the toecaps with polish and gobbing onto them to make the polish shine. He knew this irritated my mother. When they got married, she told him he should clean his boots in the yard, and offered to clean them herself. But she poured water on them the first time she tried, saying she refused to spit for anybody. After that he always cleaned his boots in the kitchen, threatening to use the living room if she kept up her complaining.

I made the tea and my father worked angrily over his boots.

He was an awkward, clenched-fisted man, hard and stockily built, under average height for a policeman. They took him because he was tough enough to look after himself. He had square, hunched shoulders and grizzled grey hair, cropped to the skull. His stubble was white if he went for too long without shaving. He was still not forty. His face was cracked with lines, hardened by years of sunlight. He had worked the northern fishing grounds when he was on the trawlers, and during the war volunteered for the minesweepers with the Murmansk convoys. His eyes were blue and grey like the sea. He met my mother when he was stationed at Lowestoft where she was working as a waitress in a café.

I poured the tea and watched him.

He wanted to tell us about his promotion, but was too cussed to say a word until my mother asked him. She went on blithely shelling her peas. She wasn't being difficult. She just didn't notice. We would end up with enough peas for a fortnight before she realised what she was doing.

I drank my own tea and thought about the job I had.

I was helping casually on the fairgrounds, waiting for a permanent job on the fish docks. I had worked the fish docks for the past two winters, the fairgrounds since I was thirteen. In the morning I was supposed to help strip the paint off the Wonderland shutters and start the new undercoat. I thought I might go to bed and get an early start.

4

My father got up when he was finished with his boots and put the cleaning rags away.

'We're going to Fulnar,' he said abruptly. 'It's an American camp about thirty miles from here. Being developed for nuclear missiles. I'm going to be the station officer.'

He closed the cupboard door and left the kitchen before either of us could speak, and we heard him slamming the front door and whistling cheerfully as he went up the narrow drive beside the house. He would be going to the police club for a drink and game of darts.

My mother and I were left staring at each other over the peas.

It was three or four days before my mother was able to persuade him to tell us about the promotion.

In fact he was going to be responsible for a large rural area and an enormous American airbase that was being upgraded for nuclear missiles. There were seven villages on the beat and some of the richest farming land in the country. The nearest market town was about nine miles away, the cathedral city more than twenty.

He could hardly hide his excitement.

'It's what you always wanted,' he kept telling my mother.

'What I always wanted?'

'You're always going on about living in the country.'

My mother had grown up in the countryside, in the fens not far from Wisbech. She hadn't been back for twenty years.

'Black Fen,' she said bemusedly when he showed her the camp on the map. 'That's what I mean by country.'

He smiled warily, looking puzzled, irritated.

'What's that, woman?'

'Black Fen, where I grew up.'

'It's still countryside, isn't it?'

'Black, for the peaty soil. Dark, flat land.'

'Monotonous,' he said brusquely.

He wasn't in the mood for my mother's sentimental stories.

He kept telling us how wonderful it was going to be, living on the base.

He took us to see the house three times before we eventually moved.

The police house was situated two miles from the nearest village

5

and immediately opposite the United States Air Force camp on the main coast road. From the front of the house you could see the guardroom and the hangars of the camp. The bedroom I was going to use overlooked concrete runways and fields shimmering with dust and heat. In the kitchen there was a Yorkist range, its black polished doors surrounded by delicate green tiles. The garden ran straight down to open fields, and there was a water butt in the yard.

'What am I going to do?' I asked on the first visit as they walked round planning how they were going to arrange the house.

'You'll love it.' My father laughed.

My mother hardly seemed to notice I was there. The more she thought about it, the more excited she got.

'What *am* I going to do?' I asked her, grabbing her arm as we walked round the empty house.

She touched me lightly on the face, excited, girlish, as if suddenly seeing the house for the first time, realising that she was going to live surrounded by fields and trees.

'Oh, Stephen,' she said, pinching my cheek in her excitement. 'Don't you think it's wonderful?'

She loved the idea of the water butt. She loved the huge garden and the house, and owning a kitchen we could sit and eat our meals in. She started packing our things weeks before we were due to move, and laughed light-headedly when I kept on asking her what I was supposed to do in the middle of the country. In the end, I gave up asking. She seemed too excited to listen. She must have been thinking about her own childhood, living on the farm on Black Fen where her father had been a labourer.

I asked her one night to tell me about the farm, and she glanced at me abstractedly and then sat back on her heels, kneeling in front of a packing case, her hair straggling untidily into her eyes. She pushed it back vaguely with her free hand and shrugged.

'We used to go skating,' she said, rocking backwards and forwards, hugging herself with both arms.

'Skating?'

'On the ice, every winter. Black Fen Field. It was quite famous on the fens. A big field, must have been more than a mile long. It used to freeze over every winter and you could skate quite safely on the ice because there was no water. It was just so wet, an inch deep sometimes, but nothing if you were skating. Hundreds used to come. Travel from all over. My father took me there every year. He used to skate with me on his shoulders. He was a strong man. You never knew your grandad.'

'I know that.'

'He would have loved you, Stephen. He always wanted a boy.' She smiled quickly, matter-of-fact, regretting.

'He was ever so strong. He used to lift the carts if the wheels needed mending. He lifted me up onto his shoulders, and skated across the ice like he owned the world. He called the farm Black Fen. He was the best skater in our village. He bought me a pair of red skates from Cambridge. Went into the market one day and came back with these beautiful red leather skates, with shining steel blades. He taught me how to skate right round the field, and then stood and watched me racing. I was the fastest girl in our village. He said there was no need for him to go on the ice after that because he could just stand and watch me. He hardly ever skated, once I started. He used to stand and watch me with my mother.'

'Didn't she like skating?'

'She was frightened.'

She shook her head briskly and lifted some shoes haphazardly out of one of the boxes, looking at them as if she expected them to have buckles and skating blades. She held the shoes in one hand and rubbed the leather with her apron.

'A man drowned,' she said briefly, smiling at me.

'Drowned?'

'On the ice.'

'How could he drown?'

'He fell through the ice.'

'But you said it was a field . . .'

'He was very unpopular,' she said emphatically. 'And he fell through the ice and disappeared.'

I sighed and got up to go and watch television. 'I don't believe you.'

'It was what my mother told me. That's why she never went skating.'

'It's a story.'

I never knew how much my mother invented. We had hundreds of photographs from the farm, and none of the big field frozen for winter skating.

'Everybody was too excited to bother with photographs,' she said when I asked her why there weren't any.

I gave up asking her what I was going to do on the camp.

As far as she was concerned, living in the country was going to be pure romance and she wouldn't listen to any arguments.

She laughed when I pointed out on the map that the American base was nearly a hundred miles from the fens she had known as a girl.

To me, the move seemed like a disaster.

I was sixteen. I had to give up my job as a barrow boy on the fish docks and forget all about summer work on the fairgrounds. Having failed the eleven plus and spent four years in one of the worst secondary modern schools on the east coast, I was qualified for nothing but labouring. As far as I could see from my new bedroom window, that meant working on farms. I had no ambitions, no talents, absolutely no idea what I was going to do, but I knew I didn't want to work on farms.

On our first day in the house, I sat in the kitchen and listened miserably to the radio while the men unloaded the van.

Pheasants coughed in the fields.

On the radio, they were playing old hits from the charts, 'I Got Stung' and the raucous 'One Night', Presley's voice like a broken knife scraping over sheets of tin.

Restless, I went outside.

Under vast skies, American cars thumped along the dusty road: Buicks and Oldsmobiles, Chevrolets and brightly coloured Cadillacs. Unlike Presley's famous collection, none of the Cadillacs was pink. In his office, checking the stationery, my father waved and gave a thumbs-up sign. A beautiful white Mustang turned slowly into the camp entrance. From its radio I could hear the hit of the previous year, 'To Know Him Is To Love Him' by the Teddy Bears, aching in the dry air.

It seemed just right that they should be playing the hits of another year.

I felt as though I might as well throw myself under the wheels of one of the giant-finned cars.

TWO

It was early in the afternoon when Matthew cycled up the drive.

I found him talking to my father.

'I'm Matthew Frohock,' he said, holding out his hand and blinking awkwardly into the brilliant sunlight. 'My father's a technical sergeant on the base. We heard you were coming.'

'Did you want something?' my father asked, bemused by Matthew's steady handshake, cheerful authority.

'I thought I'd show Stephen round the camp,' he said, noticing me and grinning broadly.

I scowled back.

My father raised his eyebrows. He was wearing shirt-sleeves rolled up to his elbows, the sweat marking the shirt underneath his arms. His hair was plastered down with Brylcreem.

'You know my wife's name as well?' he said unpleasantly.

'Sorry.' Matthew grinned, apologising. 'I'm always showing off. It's nerves.'

'You should be in the police.' My father frowned.

'Wouldn't have me,' Matthew said airily. 'Short-sighted. I wanted to be a pilot but I failed the eye-test. Rockets will never replace fliers.'

I started to go back into the house, but Matthew followed me, turning his back abruptly on my father and still talking about the state of his eyes. I went straight down the garden to avoid him, but he took his glasses off to polish them and followed me.

'You've got a great garden,' he said as we stood in the shambles of weeds and broken sweetpea canes. 'You could grow anything here.'

Back on the coast, my father had grown all our own vegetables, weeding the neat rows of lettuces late at night or early in the morning, working the allotment he hired from the council at weekends. He rubbed his hands with pleasure when he saw the size of the new garden.

'This is wheat country,' Matthew said, nodding towards the huge yellow machines lurching up and down the fields which surrounded the house. 'You know what they're doing?'

'No, I don't.'

'Drilling spring wheat. Big sugar-beet area as well, and potatoes. They had kale in this field last year for sheep grazing.'

I grunted and stood with my hands in my pockets.

'My friends in the village use kale for pheasant cover. You'll get pheasants in these fields. They'll probably come in the garden.'

I heard the coughing sound again as the massive engines churned to the far end of the field and began their clumsy lurching process of turning round. As if to prove Matthew right, two enormous pheasants shot up out of the ground and fluttered helplessly towards our ramshackle garden fence. Their feathers shone purple in the blinding sunlight. I couldn't remember a hotter April for years.

'Hens,' Matthew said with a self-satisfied laugh, as if the pheasants settled some argument we hadn't been having. 'Come on, I'll show you round.'

I glanced at his filthy grey trousers and white shirt, and thought about the red jeans I'd just bought at the coast and probably wouldn't be able to wear in this desolation. The jeans were drainpipes and had gold studs down the outside of each leg. The fly-buttons were the same gold studs. I was going to wear my black shirt with the jeans, the shirt with the cut-back collar and red silk edging. With electric yellow socks and thick-soled brothel-creepers, I'd have dazzled any pheasant Matthew could have brought along.

I followed him reluctantly down the garden to the kitchen where my mother was crashing and banging about with the crockery, unpacking the wooden cases and washing the pots as she emptied each box. She was hammering at one of the packing cases when Matthew walked into the kitchen.

'You don't do it like that,' he said pleasantly, leaning in the doorway and watching her.

She blushed, startled and annoyed, pushing her disordered hair back out of her eyes.

'What did you say?'

'You don't do it like that,' Matthew explained politely.

My mother stared at him.

I could tell she was tired. She was determined to have the house organised before the morning, even if it meant working all night.

'But what's the point?' I asked her sullenly when we arrived and she launched straight into the unpacking.

10

'People might come.'

'We don't know anybody.'

'It's a police house.'

'Then they won't be interested in the furniture.'

'Shut up, Stephen.'

My mother looked at Matthew now as if he was mad. She massaged her hands for a moment and then went on hacking determinedly at the case with her screwdriver.

Matthew shook his head patiently, and glanced at me.

'You need a claw-hammer for that.' He smiled. 'We've got one at home if you like . . . '

'I can manage, thank you,' my mother said, trying to smile.

'But . . . '

'I can manage.'

Matthew shrugged.

'You get used to moving in the RAF,' he said after a pause. 'We've moved seventeen times. They have a special ceremony. They march you in, with the housing officer. Not literally march you in, but that's what they call it. They just have to check the inventory, get you to sign before you take over. Same when you leave. Everything's provided. Absolutely everything, and it's all identical, cups, furniture, sheets. You have to have the basic furniture. You can use your own sheets but most people don't bother. Just take them down to the camp laundry and get a fresh set every week. Saves bothering. You can have your own things if you like, but you have to pay for the packing cases. And when you get moved so often . . . '

My mother caught the edge of her hand with the screwdriver and threw it down on the floor. She glared at Matthew.

'You wouldn't like to move now, would you?' she said.

I turned and walked out of the kitchen and round to the front of the house. My bike was leaning against the wall where the removal men had dumped it.

I could hear Matthew saying goodbye as I pushed the bike towards the gate, where there was a big sign for the local constabulary. My father's name had already been painted in temporarily, until they could find a signwriter to do the job properly. They had spelt Godard with two *d*s in the middle. I leant against the white gate and glared at the dusty road. The post office stood next to the police house. There were queues of American servicemen standing outside the post office, laughing and talking, waiting for their wives. The servicemen were all incredibly young. They wore pale blue shirts and blue trousers with knife-edge creases. Enormous cars were parked in neat rows at the front of the post office.

'She's very beautiful, your mother,' Matthew said, catching up with me outside the gate. 'I like her.'

'Do you.'

I took a deep breath and pushed away from the gate, cycling straight across the road in front of a giant, swaying Oldsmobile, and making for the wide gates at the main entrance to the camp. As the driver of the Oldsmobile blasted his horn and waved his fist, Matthew cycled after me and pointed down the road I was already making for.

'We go down here,' he said.

'I know,' I shouted, glaring at him over my shoulder as another car bounced past us, hitting the kerb and sending Matthew skidding across the grass verge in a cloud of dust. Loud music throbbed from the open windows of the Buick and the driver pipped his horn, looking back in his mirror and waving his hand in apology when Matthew got back onto the road.

'I'll show you Nemesis,' Matthew shouted, his glasses grimed with dust and his white shirt smudged with filth.

'Right,' I shouted back.

I didn't want to admit I had never heard of Nemesis.

'Past the guardroom,' Matthew instructed, drawing level and beaming now that he was back in control.

'Won't they object?' I asked.

'They know me.'

'They don't know me,' I said.

'You want a bet?' Matthew laughed.

At the guardroom, two military policemen lounged outside the white building, staring up into the sun as it climbed from the east. To the east was the sea. I thought briefly about the coast, the sands packed with visitors, the fairgrounds just beginning to get busy. I could have had my summer job back on Wonderland now and be working the big dipper or the fruit machines. I could have been listening to rock 'n' roll on the juke boxes. Instead, I was cycling past American military policemen who waved cheerfully as Matthew yelled an obscenity and gave them both an energetic finger.

12

'That told 'em.' He grinned delightedly as we skidded round a bend in the road and cycled in front of the Naafi and across the grass towards the huge hangars.

'You'd have got your face punched where we lived,' I told him, slowing up as we approached the first of the green-roofed concrete cathedrals.

'On the coast.' Matthew nodded smugly.

I glared at him.

'You should have been in the police.'

'My father used to drink with the previous bloke.'

'Did he?'

'He used to tell him things,' Matthew explained.

'I worked on the fairgrounds,' I said, trying to make it sound exciting.

'And the docks.'

'That's right.'

'We did a project at school on the fish docks,' Matthew said, drawing up outside the first of the hangars and taking his glasses off to give them a wipe. His handkerchief was nearly as filthy as his shirt. He blew on the glasses and blinked at me. He was sweating. His face was white, despite the brilliant sun. His eyes were grey and sarcastic. He rammed the glasses back on his nose and smiled straight at me.

'I left school years ago,' I said, ignoring his friendliness.

He just shrugged. 'That's rough.'

Out beyond the hangars, we could see the vast emptiness of the runways. The plateau stretched for miles, the blue hills in the distance climbing out of the sky, the coast thirty or forty miles away to the east. To the west, the flat countryside followed the line of the limestone ridge for about five miles, and then there was a gentle plunge down to the wheat plains, hundreds of miles of flat countryside with some of the biggest cornfields in the country. Up above us, the sky was cloudless, electric blue, the hot air throbbing with skylarks.

'Out there,' Matthew said quietly, pointing to a mound of earth surrounded by barbed wire. Security jeeps patrolled backwards and forwards outside the wire, and I could see more military policemen, standing in the heat, chatting or walking their dogs. The dogs appeared to be Alsatians. I could see nothing at the top of the mound of earth.

13

'That's Nemesis,' Matthew said flatly, staring into the heat, gripping the handlebars of his bicycle.

'Is it?' I muttered, angry that I didn't know what he meant. My father had never mentioned anything about Nemesis.

'Greek goddess of retribution,' Matthew intoned solemnly. 'The punisher of crime.'

I nodded, waiting for him to continue.

'I looked her up in the classical dictionary,' he said. 'The Americans don't know, but she was originally envisaged as allotting to men their share of happiness and unhappiness, chastening the over-fortunate. Seems appropriate, don't you think?'

'Why?'

'Chastening the over-fortunate. Just right for Americans. If anybody's over-fortunate, it's them. And they don't even know it, do they?'

'I can't see anything,' I said after a pause.

Matthew fidgeted on his bicycle and nodded. 'That's because she's underground,' he said, 'in a concrete bunker. Took them months to build. It's reinforced with steel.'

I stared into the scorching sunlight, watching the empty mound of earth, the guards with their black Alsatians. One of the jeeps drove slowly towards us, and then veered lazily away.

At my side, Matthew waited patiently.

'Why is it underground?' I asked.

'In case of attack.'

'Attack?'

'Well, you never know.'

'Who'd want to attack it?'

'The Communists,' he suggested with an ironic laugh.

After a few minutes, we left the hangars and went for a long ride round the camp, Matthew explaining all the offices and facilities, waving and shouting to people he knew.

I had never seen such a flat, desolate landscape.

THREE

We went back to the house for tea and sat outside the kitchen, eating scones thick with strawberry jam and drinking scalding hot tea.

My mother chattered happily about the kitchen. 'There's a Yorkist range,' she told Matthew proudly, showing him the delicate green tiles and the black polished doors. 'They're ever so expensive.'

'And hard work,' Matthew said.

My mother smiled at him shyly.

She kept offering him the plate of scones and going back into the kitchen to get on with the unpacking. My father sat on the doorstep and smoked his pipe. He was still wearing his uniform trousers and blue shirt. He was always complaining about the way the starched collars chafed his neck. He was nearly sixteen stone, red-faced and tight-skinned from all the steamed puddings and fried breakfasts my mother kept cooking him, muscular from long hours gardening or working down on the docks.

'You don't have to eat it,' she said if he complained about the food.

'Your dad with the project, Matthew?' my father asked as he took another of the scones.

Matthew told us what he knew about Nemesis and said that the Americans couldn't manage without technicians like his father.

'Does he like the work?' my father asked.

'He wasn't given any option.' According to Matthew, technicians needed for the rocket programme had been told that either they volunteered or their services would no longer be needed.

He told us that they'd just arrived back in the country from Egypt, where his father had been in charge of maintenance work on Lincolns. Here at Fulnar the Americans were using their own transport planes, and there was only one aircraft left on the base, an ancient Anson.

'I've been to fourteen schools,' Matthew said finally, swallowing his tea and wiping his mouth on the back of his sleeve. 'I expect it's just the same in the police.'

'Can be,' my father agreed. 'I've been lucky.'

15

'You haven't moved around?'

'Only in the war,' my mother told him.

My father got up lazily and yawned, staring down the ramshackle garden.

'Plenty to do there, Stephen,' he said, nodding towards the weeds.

'I could do it for you,' Matthew volunteered.

'No thanks, lad.'

My father went back to the office to get ready for the morning, and when we'd helped with the washing up, Matthew suggested a ride down to the villages.

'You won't be late?' my mother asked ridiculously.

On the fairgrounds, I'd often be working until gone midnight.

'What do you think's going to happen to me, Mother?'

'You don't know the country.'

I ignored her and followed Matthew down the drive.

'She's a good cook as well,' he told me as he leaped onto his bike and pedalled off along the main road. 'You are lucky.'

'Can't your mother cook, then?' I shouted.

'She's dead,' Matthew called back over his shoulder.

We cycled up the main road to the edge of the limestone ridge and then turned south along the cliff road. The countryside spread westwards beyond us for miles, the yellow farm machines still busy drilling seeds, smoke rising from the farmhouses that were spread out in isolation as far as you could see. The sun was already burning dark red down to the horizon, and smoke rose from a cluster of lights which must have been the nearest town, a market town where the police had their divisional headquarters. The county headquarters were twenty miles south in Lincoln.

We cycled along the top road and then down a narrow lane through an old wood. The trees on the top road were mainly beech, the smooth metallic-grey bark shining in the last of the sunlight, but the wood was almost entirely ash, with a few oak trees covered with ivy. Matthew said ash grew most vigorously on limestone. The woods were full of pale purple violets, early primroses shining pale yellow through the trees. There were hundreds of bluebells, and the air was heavy with the scent of wild garlic. At the very bottom of the hill, where a stream ran along the edge of the wood,

16

the ground was brilliant with the great yellow stools and bosses of marigolds.

At the bottom of the hill we cycled between the tiny cottages, pale yellow limestone warm in the evening light, the church squat and sheltered in the lee of the hill. The church bells were ringing as we cycled along the narrow lanes, the hawthorn hedges so high we couldn't see into the fields where sheep were grazing the thick grass.

A road ran along the bottom of the cliff for several miles, joining the isolated villages together. Turning north again, Matthew said we could cycle along to Fulnar and have a drink in the Plough. He said their cider was still kept in the barrel, and was stronger than anything he'd ever drunk in his life.

I had never been out in the countryside before, not like this, cycling through the twilight, lost among the strange smells of flowers and trees.

I would have known every scent down on the fish docks.

Matthew recognised everything. 'My father used to be interested,' he told me.

'Used to be?'

'He isn't now,' he said irritatingly, as if I was trying to find out something he didn't want to talk about.

I cycled behind him, refusing to speak.

The fields at the bottom of the hill were sown for kale. Sheep grazed on the far slopes, and I could see cottages almost hidden by the trees, the squat tower of the church.

We cycled past a vast crumbling ruin, which Matthew said was early eighteenth century. 'One of the landowners.' He laughed. 'Got rich out of enclosures.'

I didn't know what he was talking about.

In those early months, I hardly ever knew what Matthew was talking about. I kept quiet, and resented his endless information. I thought it was a kind of boasting, always having to know the names of things, but he was surprised if anybody ever said so. He cycled everywhere frantically, his saddlebag full of *Observer* books of birds and trees and flowers, his mind crammed with his latest reading. He was a year older than me, and already suffering eyestrain.

On that first night, we cycled along the bottom lane to the village. A freshly painted maypole stood in the centre of the village green, opposite the church, and we could hear singing inside the pub. We left our bikes propped against the low church wall inside the graveyard, and went into the single room of the pub. The bar was a tiny dark counter in a corner, and several farm labourers were standing round a dartboard, laughing and shouting at the man playing. Older men sat on the trestles along the wall.

'I'll get the drinks,' Matthew said. He seemed to know the landlord, and nothing was said about our age. 'They don't bother much round here,' Matthew said. 'Last policeman said he was too busy chasing poachers to worry about drinking laws.'

With our backs against the wall, we sat and drank our pints and munched through packets of crisps.

The lights from lamps shone and flickered through the glasses, and I didn't argue when Matthew went and bought two more pints and a thick wedge of Cheddar cheese and bread to help the drink down. The men playing darts were getting louder, furious, and the old men watching argued about the score and the different darts the players were using.

'I like it here,' Matthew said as we lounged in our seats and drained our glasses. 'You don't get the men here.'

'Men?'

'Servicemen. Americans. They go to the Naafi.'

'Yes?'

'Subsidised booze. It's a club, so they can do what they want. Make their own rules.'

'Just like here.' I grinned.

'More or less.'

I closed my eyes and enjoyed the taste of the cider. The fairgrounds would be getting busy by now, the music loud and the rides screaming and throbbing through the darkness. Hundreds of visitors packed into the fairgrounds at night, and there were fights and drunken attacks, girls giggling and fooling about, the juke box booming with the latest rock 'n' roll.

I wanted to go back. I didn't want to be here in this remote village, watching farm labourers play darts and old men argue about harvests.

I could hear them arguing bitterly about a local farmer.

I didn't want to know anything about farming.

18

At midnight, we walked out into the cool air and I slumped against the church wall, vomiting into the graveyard.

Matthew stood behind me, looking up at the weather-vane on the tower.

'Warm tomorrow,' he said vaguely.

'Warm?' I belched, the vomit running down my arm as I tried to wipe my face clean.

He looked at me, dark, bemused. 'Warm,' he said, as if I was an idiot, and glanced up towards the weather-vane.

It was a cockerel, dull gold in the moonlight.

'Better get you home.'

I said I could manage, and took the skin off my ankle, clambering over the church wall.

My hands were yellow with lichen.

We trudged up the hill through the village pushing our bikes. We passed a cottage surrounded by an apple orchard, and the blossom seemed to sway in a great silent mass like the sea, rocking and moving in the delicate light of the moon. An owl flew low over the narrow lane, and I glanced up, peering drunkenly into the darkness, the sky suddenly brilliant with millions of stars.

'An owl,' I said through my thickened lips, my mouth moving awkwardly, my brain throbbing and stumbling for the words.

'An owl,' Matthew agreed at my side, and suddenly laughed with delight, punching me on the shoulder when I managed to focus on him.

'An owl,' he said more seriously, when I tried to move his hand from my shoulder.

Through the sodden warmth of the alcohol, I tried to tell Matthew I could find my own way home. He seemed to be laughing all the time.

Back on the cliff top, we cycled in huge wheeling circles along the main road, and shouted to the guards from the base perimeter, the Land-Rovers parked outside the barbed wire surrounding Nemesis, the dogs barking distantly across the deserted runways. On the camp, a mass of lights flickered from the houses, the hangars and the all-night bowling alley.

Far away, a car blasted its horn, and we could see the beam of the headlights swivelling across the empty sky.

FOUR

I learned a lot about Fulnar from Matthew.

The RAF had been stationed at the camp since the beginning of the First World War, and they still had more men on the base than the Americans, but with the arrival of the new weapons, the Americans had taken over. There was a British group captain technically in charge, but it was the American commanding officer who made all the real decisions.

'Like when to press the button,' Matthew said gleefully. 'Like when we're all going to expire.'

The camp itself was built along both sides of the main coast road, a vast area of two- and three-storeyed buildings like a giant prison or hospital. To the south, where the police house faced the main gates, were the officers' mess and living quarters, the large houses built round a green, the mess buildings surrounded by cherry blossom trees that were dense with pink blossom throughout the spring. Civilian personnel attached to the project were also quartered round the green, the larger detached houses being thought more suitable for the families of the scientific experts.

The civilian personnel were all Americans: engineers, physicists, technicians, administrators.

According to Matthew, you could tell the scientists from the forces personnel by the cars they drove. The scientists preferred the Lotus Elite, MGA, Triumph TR3A, Austin-Healey 3000 and Jaguar XK150. The officers preferred Cadillacs, Oldsmobiles, Buicks and Mustangs.

'You know why?' he said cheerfully.

'They're more patriotic,' I suggested.

'They're moronic,' Matthew said. He also insisted that you could tell the scientists and the officers apart physically.

'Don't be ridiculous.'

'You look. See for yourself. The ones with brains are all sallow and preoccupied. That's because they're intellectuals. They read all the time. The uniformed men are athletic, sunburned, mean-mouthed and full of fundamentalist piety.'

'What's that?'

'They evangelise.'

The scientists certainly stuck together. Several of the physicists had become friends when they were students or doing graduate work at the Massachusetts Institute of Technology or the Institute of Advanced Studies at Princeton. They played tennis and went to endless drinking parties with each other's families. Their wives had coffee mornings and ran the clubs on the camp. They did social work with the problem families.

'It's like a Mid-Western university campus,' Matthew said when he was showing me round.

'Is it?'

'You know the sort of thing.'

'No.'

'Beards and pipes.'

'My father smokes a pipe,' I said.

The main part of the camp was to the north side of the road, a vast area of cheap terraced housing, tennis courts, the Naafi, cinema, sports facilities and administrative offices. The Naafi shop sold everything you could get in town but at a ten per cent discount for camp personnel. My mother immediately started shopping there. There was a youth club on Saturday nights, and a family club near the main gates, where the Anglicans and Roman Catholics both had churches. The priest from the Roman Catholic church rode round the camp on his bicycle, selling apples for church funds.

The Americans had improved the cinema, built the all-night bowling alley in one of the hangars, started a branch of their own PX stores, which sold goods and food we had never even heard of, and subsidised Carlsberg Special so that it was soon the most popular drink for miles around.

'That's why the Plough's always empty,' Matthew explained.

I couldn't imagine a drink stronger than the barrelled cider.

Every Saturday afternoon you could see groups of men playing netball out beyond the hangars, and a large area of disused land was being cleared for baseball.

According to Matthew, the Americans insisted on coming to Fulnar when the Nemesis contract was awarded to a British company. The first weapon had actually been delivered to the USAF as far back as 1956, the year of 'Hound Dog' and 'Blue Suede Shoes', but not adopted by the RAF until the following year when it entered service with some twenty squadrons of Bomber Command.

'But you said it was British,' I pointed out.

'British scientists.' Matthew nodded. 'Not the same thing at all.'

'Same thing as what?'

'Bomber Command. They needed persuading.'

I didn't believe a word Matthew was saying.

'How would you know?' I insisted.

'From my father.'

'He's a sergeant.'

'A technical sergeant,' Matthew said, stressing the technical.

At great length, Matthew explained the different ranks. 'With the RAF, you have aircraftsman, leading aircraftsman, senior aircraftsman, corporal, sergeant, flight sergeant, warrant officer, pilot officer, flying officer, flight lieutenant, squadron leader, wing commander and group captain. The technical ranks my dad belongs to are the same, corporal technician, sergeant technician and chief technician. Chief technician is the tops.'

'Why isn't your father a chief technician, then?' I asked.

Matthew shrugged. 'He's got the brains. He just hasn't got the character.'

In the USAF, the Americans used army ranks: private second and first class, corporal, sergeant, staff sergeant, master sergeant, second and first lieutenant, captain, major, lieutenant colonel and colonel.

'I could type it all out for your father,' Matthew suggested, but when I checked in my father's office he already had the rankings pinned up above his desk to help him fathom the visitors to the station.

He also had the actual names of the senior officers, Colonel Richard Grainger, the American commander, and his seconds-in-command Lieutenant Colonels Lawrence and Beck. It was Lieutenant Colonel Lawrence who drove the beautiful white Mustang. His first name was Gene.

'Like the cowboy,' Matthew said, raising his eyebrows.

'Cowboy?'

'Christ, you're ignorant!'

Like the scientists, the higher ranks all lived in the big detached houses round the green.

'The privilege of rank,' my father said flatly.

'The privilege of *empire*,' Matthew preferred to say. 'Eventually, we'll have three missiles,' he explained. 'The same as all the squadrons in Bomber Command. Probably sixty missiles around the country. It's an occupation. It's an American empire.'

My father scoffed and walked out of the room whenever Matthew started talking about empires.

By the time we arrived at Fulnar, Nemesis had already been fully operational for three months.

'They could rule the world,' Matthew claimed derisively. 'They could destroy Yugoslavia. If she was any good.'

'She?'

'Nemesis!'

'I thought it was a joint operation,' I said sarcastically.

'Not really.' Matthew smiled.

I refused to ask him how he knew.

Half the time, I gave up listening to Matthew.

As we settled into the house and my father met the men he was going to have to deal with, I gradually got used to the sight of American servicemen and the wonderful American cars they drove around the camp.

It was like living in an isolated fragment of America.

Detachments of a technical training squadron had been the first to arrive on the camp with the rockets. They were followed shortly afterwards by a strategic missile squadron and the civilian personnel who were going to look after the actual missiles. The base had been made nuclear at very short notice, and the Americans in the technical training squadron were working to get the RAF personnel ready.

The first rockets arrived by air in the early spring, together with the huge flying transports that brought in the excited families of the servicemen. Each transport came loaded with household goods and furniture, wives and screaming children, American flags and handsome rocking chairs.

Homesick abroad, the Americans simply brought their way of life with them. Their government guaranteed to create little Americas wherever they went, so every week air transports rumbled from the skies to deliver deep-freezers, washing-machines, record players, furniture, exotic carpets and clothes that could be ordered from a Sears Roebuck catalogue. On the camp, you could have been in deepest Ohio.

There were Americans everywhere. The men were young, soft-voiced and incredibly polite. The wives laughed and shouted and said, 'Hi,' to shopkeepers. They wore jeans to visit the market in Gainsborough and took all the parking places, behaviour which led to local people getting up a petition of complaint to their commanding officer. Colonel Grainger issued a reprimand. In their massive Oldsmobiles and Chevrolets, the wives took no notice, parking their cars in the middle of the street and going off for hours to drink coffee. The servicemen simply nodded and apologised.

In the narrow lanes around the camp, glamorous American cars and expensive uniforms soon became a familiar sight, and Saturday night fights a ritual at all the dances. With their greased-back hair and ravaged complexions, the local teddy-boys had absolutely nothing going for them.

Like everybody of my generation who had ever heard 'Heartbreak Hotel', I longed to be American.

On the base, the girls had a ready supply.

'They're welcome,' Matthew said acidly. He didn't like Americans.

The implications of all this for my father were actually minimal. The Americans had their own military police, and they kept a tight control of American personnel. Such additional crime as existed was mainly due to the increase in RAF personnel, rancid working-class louts who were far worse behaved. The Americans seemed to be perfect gentlemen, and I soon got used to being called sir by twenty-two-year-olds in charge of enough nuclear power to destroy half of Leningrad. They called everybody out of a pram sir.

For my mother and myself, the chief effect of the new arrivals was a constant stream of visitors to the house seeking alien permits. American servicemen were not required to register with the police, but their wives and families and any civilians attached to the missile programme needed proper authorisation. The usual procedure was for an office to be made available on the camp one day a week and for new arrivals to register there, but this didn't prevent the endless enquiries at the house. Within days of arriving, my mother and I realised that being attached to the police station was going to involve more than living our own lives.

To begin with, it seemed funny.

'Is it true they don't carry guns?' a crew-cut master sergeant asked my mother one morning when she was trying to explain that my father was out.

'He never found he needed one,' my mother said nervously.

'And his wife and kids on the station?' the sergeant said in amazement. 'Back home, you'd be taken hostage.'

My mother slammed the door in his face.

Another morning, when I was eating breakfast, a young airman came up the drive with an axe.

'You take me in or I'll kill her,' he shouted when I answered the door, tears running down his cheeks.

'What?'

'You take me in, man, you take me in.'

I had to tell him my father was out looking for poachers, and he walked up and down the drive, brandishing the axe and weeping while I telephoned for help from the division.

When my mother came through from the kitchen and saw the man crying in front of the house, she nearly fainted.

I could hear her in the breakfast room. 'There's a man in the garden with an axe,' she kept saying. 'There's a man in the garden with an axe.'

'He says he's going to kill her,' I shouted down the telephone to the switchboard at division.

'Kill who?' the duty officer shouted back.

By the time a patrol car arrived, the airman had gone back onto the camp and the policemen in the car suggested we ring the military police. The man was charged with assaulting the police and threatening my mother, but when she refused absolutely to testify they had to drop the second charge. The man's wife flew back to America.

My mother was up at dawn every morning. From my window overlooking the fields, I could hear her singing in the kitchen, hanging clothes on the washing line down the garden.

'It's beautiful,' she said when I complained about being woken up at five o'clock in the morning.

'It's flat.'

'You've no imagination, Stephen.'

The birds seemed to agree with her.

I spent hours sitting in my room, listening to my record collection or trying to read some of the books Matthew lent me.

With Fats Domino and Little Richard on the turntable, I struggled through *Lord Jim* and *The Old Man and the Sea*. I gave up on *Moby Dick* within a dozen pages.

Matthew seemed to think I was missing the sea.

I hadn't heard a herring gull for weeks.

I was surprised by how simple I found Hemingway.

A few days after our arrival, the superintendent in charge of my father's division visited the house. He was brisk and red-faced, his voice booming inside the small office. He kissed my mother on the cheek and shook my hand.

'I bet you're proud of this lad, Norman,' he said to my father.

'I am, sir.'

'Going to follow your father, Stephen?' The superintendent beamed at me.

He had the smallest eyes I'd ever seen, green and expressionless, dangerous with good humour. He crushed my hand, refusing to let me go.

'I'm not sure.'

'That's the ticket, lad, that's the ticket.'

'You should call him sir,' my father said when the superintendent had gone.

'Why the hell should I?'

'Respect.'

I'd heard a great deal about Watters. He was the youngest superintendent in the force, and one of the most unpopular. He enjoyed humiliating men, catching them out and ridiculing them on parade. He had favourites and my father seemed to be one of them since solving the murder with the nightclub singer. His breath stank of stomach ulcers and bile.

'He's nothing to do with me,' I said to my father, and walked out of the house, slamming the office door behind me.

At night I wandered round the camp with Matthew, watching the antics of the Americans. Matthew never seemed to want to go home. We sometimes stayed out all night.

To the wail of Conway Twitty's 'Only Make Believe' or the erotic frenzy of Presley's 'I Need Your Love Tonight', unmarried servicemen would stagger out of the bowling alley at dawn and shout obscenities to the waiting military policemen. The British MPs were stolid and humorous, the Americans dangerous with their steel-capped boots and wooden staves. They had orders to make sure their own men behaved.

'Or keep them on the camp,' Matthew said sourly.

Far out on the runways, beyond the enormous hangars, the site was still being prepared for the first testing of Nemesis, and the security lights shone weirdly through the hot dawns. I could see them from my bedroom window.

The testing was on a Saturday morning. I couldn't believe it when the rocket emerged from the ground, shining white in the bright sunlight, the rounded head black and gleaming. From a mile away, we could hear the fire engines and smell the fumes of diesel. At my side, Matthew shouted the stages. The rocket was fuelled and then the dummy head was connected. The order to fire was given, and the liquid oxygen was released. The whole horizon seemed to vibrate to the pressure, the clouds of white oxygen thundering and blazing round the rocket, the fire engines disappearing in the hot vapour, the tannoys echoing and the sirens wailing until the all-clear was given. At fifteen seconds from termination, an operator had to throw a switch and the rocket closed down five seconds before firing. The liquid oxygen simply evaporated.

When the testing was finished, we sat stunned at the perimeter, watching the fire engines circle the rocket, the military police scurrying backwards and forwards in their jeeps.

'They've got them in Alaska too,' Matthew told me.

'Alaska?'

'Nearer to the Soviets. The range is only two thousand miles. Wouldn't do much damage from here.'

On that first day, there were hundreds of cars parked on the roads and narrow lanes round the camp, watching the American rocket, watching Nemesis.

Several people cheered.

On long bicycle rides round the camp perimeter, I used to sit and watch the excavators at work.

Because the spring had been so dry, the air filled with pollen, and I was driven to bed with a blistering attack of hay fever, my nose bright red and my eyes swollen and aching with sties. I had never had such an attack before, and complained bitterly about ever leaving the coast. The sties came every year because I couldn't stop rubbing my eyes.

'You'll get used to it,' my mother said blithely.

'I need to see a doctor.'

'A few more weeks . . . '

'Mother!'

'The pollen count's down anyway.'

I sat in my bedroom, watching the men with the excavators, the technicians busy installing the rockets.

But I had to have some kind of job of my own.

FIVE

My father's jaw clenched when he was angry, his face knotted with fury.

'You're mad if you think I'm going in the police,' I told him, but he went on eating his breakfast, steadily shovelling the cereals in as if he couldn't care less what he was eating, frowning into the newspaper he was pretending to read.

'What are you going to do, then?' he sneered, a vein at the side of his head pumping angrily.

'I don't know.'

'You couldn't get an apprenticeship.'

'I know . . . '

'You left school without any exams. You haven't any qualifications.'

'I know,' I shouted again, 'you don't have to keep telling me.'

I glared at him across the table, my hands sweating, my eyes blurred, resisting him, bewildered. All the time I was at school, he ridiculed the work they sent home to be done, laughed whenever I got into trouble. He said school was a waste of time. He thought the school-leaving age ought to be brought back down from fifteen to fourteen, as it had been when he left school.

Now he was attacking me for not having done the work.

He finished the cereals and pushed the dish across the table.

In the kitchen, my mother was listening to the farming programme on the radio. She said that we had to be interested in what was going on now that we lived in the country. She quoted things from the programme every morning.

'You'll be lucky if they even take you,' my father went on angrily, sarcastically. 'Acting clever.'

'What do you mean?'

' "Are you going in the police, son?" ' he mimicked. ' "I haven't made my mind up." '

'I didn't say that.'

'You think jobs fall off trees?'

'I already had a job.'

29

'On a fairground!'

'I had a job.'

'You want to learn how to behave,' he shouted suddenly, his shoulders hunched over the table, his fists clenched in abrupt rage. 'You want to learn how to speak to people.'

He got up and went into his office, leaving his breakfast, slamming the door behind him.

I could hear him talking on the telephone, then using the typewriter, hammering methodically at the keys. He had taught himself to type, thumping the typewriter every night for hours. He set his mind, and went ahead and did things. He clenched himself into concentration, forcing himself to walk into crowded rooms, tackle the things he hated doing. He seemed to live in terror of disorder. He seemed to need his routines and spotless uniform. I thought suddenly about the photograph my mother kept in one of her albums, a school photograph taken when he was thirteen. He sat hunched on a bench, glaring miserably into the camera, an elbow showing through his jumper. His fists were clenched on his knees.

'I hated it,' he once said when I asked him about the photograph. 'I hated it.'

I felt desperate, shaken. I knew he was upset. He wouldn't speak for hours. Sometimes he ignored us for days, his contempt lost in his job, slamming through the house, eating alone in the kitchen. I could feel the blood pounding in my ears. My hands were trembling. He always had more important things to do than argue with me or my mother. In his office, I heard the telephone ring again. I went through to the kitchen for some more tea.

'It's a good job, Stephen,' my mother said quietly, sitting at the open door, smoking and balancing a cup of tea on her knee. She was wearing a blue dress and her hair shone in the sunlight.

'I know, Mother.'

'And a good pension.'

My parents had both grown up through the thirties. They had a terror of unemployment. On the coast, my father would take casual work on the harvesting or down on the docks when he had finished his eight-hour shifts. He did the gardening and the allotment after he had finished the casual jobs. He was often grey with exhaustion. My mother had a job in a bakery from four thirty until seven in the morning, and then worked all day on the steampresses in a laundry.

30

The early-morning job was so that she could see me off to school with a huge cooked breakfast. At the end of her long hours at the laundry, she frequently came home badly scalded, her arms a lurid yellow from the ointment they used for burns. On Saturdays she worked in a bread shop.

But I was sixteen. Two years before I left school, one of my father's friends was attacked on the fairground where I was working and badly injured. After some weeks in hospital, he was transferred to a psychiatric ward, and eighteen months later took early retirement. Judging by the stories my father told me, I didn't think I would last eighteen months. Working on the fairgrounds, we were protected by the bouncers. In a police uniform, I would be the one doing the protecting.

And in any case, I wasn't old enough for the police. Or qualified. You had to be nineteen, and you had to have some sort of academic qualification, or pass an entrance examination.

I stood in the yard and breathed the pollen.

My eyes were running and sore, and the only relief I could get was from drinking tea. The tannin seemed to help. I had to keep going to the toilet I was drinking so much tea.

My father walked into the kitchen and went straight to the sink. He poured himself a cup of tea and told my mother she shouldn't be smoking.

'I've had a word with headquarters,' he said abruptly.

Headquarters was where the training department for the county force was based.

'They say you'd better go to college,' he went on, draining the cold tea and frowning at my mother. 'Do some sort of course. You can go into the cadets until you're nineteen.'

'I'm not going in the police.'

'You can't until you're nineteen.'

My mother blinked, smoke getting into her eyes.

'That's wonderful, Stephen.'

'I want to go back to the coast,' I said stubbornly.

'You could try the local college,' my father suggested, ignoring anything I had to say. 'Start in the autumn. Get you ready for the entrance exams.'

'I don't want to sit any entrance exams.'

'I'll ask round the farms in the meantime.'

'I don't want to work on farms.'

'Well, we aren't keeping you,' he shouted suddenly, blazing, wild, slamming the kitchen door so that the plates rattled on the shelves and the door vibrated. 'You can keep your bloody self.'

My mother flinched, stubbing her cigarette out on the concrete yard and smiling nervously.

The office door closed with a crash.

'He's tired,' she said, getting up and leaving me in the yard. 'Just tired.'

I stared at the empty fields.

I was tired myself.

We'd been having these arguments for years, all the time I was at the secondary modern learning how to use a lathe and keep out of trouble. Being a policeman's son didn't help there. There didn't seem much point in going one further and actually joining.

'I'm not going in the police,' I said angrily to the deserted fields.

I thought briefly about the boxing lessons my father had tried to give me when I was fifteen. I had ringing ears for days afterwards. I could hear the ringing now.

'I'm not,' I said furiously.

In the corner of my eye, one of the sties throbbed to a head, and I went back into the kitchen to get some hot water to burst it, cursing the pollen-drenched fields.

I walked to Matthew's house and rattled the letterbox.

A post van passed me in the road.

It was just after eight o'clock.

Matthew's father was sleeping on the settee, his mouth wide open and the stubble on his face black. He didn't move when Matthew turned the radio down. He was a small, aggressive man, loud-mouthed and always arguing. He had a thin moustache which looked blue above his selfish mouth. When he went out drinking with his friends, he wore expensive suits and blue silk shirts.

Matthew nodded towards the radio. He always listened to the Third Programme. He was already dressed, waving his breakfast spoon in my face and holding a book in the other hand.

'Vaughan Williams,' he explained.

He hardly ever noticed what the music was they were broadcasting.

'So what?'

'Listen!'

'I don't want to listen.'

He turned the radio off and went on with his cereals.

'The thing about the Welsh,' he said theatrically, 'is that their language has a rhetoric beyond their achievement.'

'I'm not in the mood, Matthew.'

'You listen to the rhetoric, you imagine they're the greatest poets and composers in the world, but where's the evidence, where's the actual poetry, the symphonies and sonatas?'

'What's that?' I asked, slumping down at the table and nodding at the book he was reading.

'The college I'm going to.' He grinned.

'College?'

'Finish my A levels.'

'What are they?'

'For college.'

'Jesus . . .'

'For university,' Matthew tried to explain quickly.

I was too impatient to listen.

I got up and stood at the sitting-room door, glaring at his father snoring in the front room. Saliva dribbled out of his mouth. He had bits of food stuck in his stubble.

'Are you coming?'

'Do I look as if I am?'

'*What?*'

'God, you are in a foul mood.'

Laughing, Matthew followed me out to the front of the house and got his bike from the shed. He was still carrying the spoon and college prospectus.

'Why the fuck should I go in the police?' I said angrily.

'I don't know.'

'Why should I?'

'I told you, I don't know.'

'Just because my father says so?'

'Dostoevsky,' Matthew suggested.

'What?'

'You should read him.'

'Who?'

33

'*Crime and Punishment.*'

'Why the hell should I read *Crime and Punishment?*'

'To find out what you want to do.'

'I want to go back to the coast.'

Matthew sighed and pushed the prospectus into his saddlebag. He stuck the spoon into his jacket pocket.

'You should do what you want.'

'I had a job on the coast.'

'Then go back.'

We cycled between the rows of cheap terraced housing and past the Naafi shop. A butcher's van followed behind us, ringing a bell for the women in the houses. Mobile vans visited the camp every day, the baker's, the greengrocer's, a wet-fish man on Friday mornings. There were several thousand servicemen on the camp by now, as well as the civilian scientists. A special petrol pump had been put into the camp for the American gas guzzlers, and already another pump was being demanded. We cycled past the tennis courts and headed out of the camp.

At the guardroom, the guards had a table outside in the sun and were drinking coffee, playing cards. They waved to Matthew and one of the rough-looking military police blew him a kiss. The men all roared with laughter. One of them waved his wooden stave after us and rubbed his hands up and down it as the other men yelled and jeered.

'Raskolnikov's interrogator,' Matthew said blithely.

I glared at him, daring him to go on, my eyes watering with the heat and grit and pollen, the inside of my mouth bleeding as I clenched my teeth to stop myself getting upset.

'I can see you as Raskolnikov's interrogator,' Matthew shouted, following me as I pedalled furiously towards the cliff road and the narrow lanes down to the villages.

I refused to ask him what he was talking about.

By the time we reached the village, I was gasping for breath. Tears poured down my face from my swollen eyes. The broken stye wept into my eye, and smarted when I tried to clear it with my handkerchief.

Eventually Matthew caught up with me and we sat outside the church and watched the weather-vane glinting in the sun.

'Seriously,' Matthew said.

I glanced at him.

His voice was tentative, quiet.

He shrugged and grinned awkwardly.

'Go to college.'

I looked away.

I was ready to hit him, then suddenly too upset to listen.

'Go to college,' he said patiently.

'And then?'

'You might learn something.'

'And then?' I repeated nastily.

'At least you'd have some choice. Work in an office. Be a journalist.'

'I don't want to be a fucking journalist.'

I thought instinctively of the way my father talked about journalists. Second-rate unreliable drunkards, who spent their lives boozing and writing lies about the police. Supercilious, overweight little men who liked nothing better than to shop a bent policeman.

'Have you read *The Sun Also Rises*?' Matthew asked.

He knew I was going to lose my temper.

'It's a great book,' he protested, holding his hands up. 'About a journalist. You should read it. You should go to college. We could go together on the bus. You should see some of the girls on that bus in the morning.'

He was laughing, fiddling with his saddlebag and glancing at me as he spoke. He got off his bike and finished fastening the saddlebag.

'What are you going to do?' I asked him.

I think it was the first time I had ever asked him anything.

He got back on his bike and beamed at me.

'I'm going to be a writer.'

'What kind of writer?' I sneered.

'Sportswriter.'

'How do you do that?'

'Write about sport.'

'You don't know anything about sport.' I laughed.

'Motor racing,' Matthew said with a firm nod. 'I know a lot about motor racing.'

We were both laughing now.

We cycled out of the village and along the bottom lane past the church and stream, the overgrown verges thick with dandelions and poppies, cow parsley and nettles.

'Sportswriter,' Matthew insisted, wobbling into the hedgerows on his bike and waving at me with his spoon. 'Sportswriter of the year.'

SIX

The job my father found me was on a chicken farm. Twenty-six thousand hens, housed in three huge batteries. The noise and heat were unbelievable. We worked six days a week, from seven in the morning until late afternoon when the eggs were washed, packed and loaded ready for collection. Saturdays we finished at twelve.

The stench was incredible, tons of faeces and urine and broken eggs falling through the wire cages onto the conveyor belts which ran underneath the chickens and then off the conveyor belts down into concrete pits which ran at right angles across the buildings. At the end of each day, we had to open wooden trapdoors at the end of the pits and shovel the blood, feathers and excrement out into another massive moat which ran the length of the building outside, like a giant fly-infested midden. The farmer used the dried manure for his fields. On days when the pits inside got blocked, we had to climb down in our wellingtons and shovel the slurry manually through the wooden doors.

There were two labourers working in each of the batteries. The man I worked with hardly spoke. He was tanned a hard mahogany from years of working in the fields, and resented working in the batteries. He had eight children.

Silently, he showed me through the routines of the day. He worked all the overtime that was available, and seemed to be the only man on the farm who cared about the state of the hens. At tea-breaks, he sat and smoked his foul-smelling cigarettes while the other men made filthy jokes about the hens or told each other about their wives.

Frank ignored the other men.

'Don't mind,' he said when I asked him what he thought of them.

I found him one morning standing in front of one of the cages, wringing the neck of a distressed bird.

There were tears in his eyes.

The chickens were fed on layer mash to keep them laying. Sometimes they pecked out each other's entrails. When the entrails dripped through the wire onto the birds below, frantic hens would start pecking at each other's eyes, excited by the taste of the entrails. Broody hens would stab at our hands as we collected their eggs.

'T'ent right,' Frank said bitterly, sitting down to light a cigarette. He smoked to try to disguise the smell.

On my first morning, Matthew cycled with me to the farm.

It was seven o'clock. As far as you could see, there was nothing but fields of wheat and barley. Towards the coast, the blue hills of the wolds climbed coldly out of the clouds. Sheep grazed in the fields.

Apart from the green-roofed hangars, we could have been anywhere in the remote English countryside.

Then a giant-finned car slid from the camp entrance and raced past us, throwing up clouds of dust. From the car radio, Little Richard's grating voice murdered 'By The Light Of The Silvery Moon', boisterous with a raw joy. Outside the officers' quarters, an American flag fluttered on a white flagpole.

'I thought about getting a job,' Matthew said as we cycled slowly towards the farm entrance.

Beeches and horse chestnuts surrounded the farm, so that you couldn't see the ugly batteries. At the gates, a giant yellow chicken held up a welcome sign.

'Why didn't you?' I asked.

'I've got to get these exams.'

I couldn't see how he could fail.

'Do the reading,' he explained.

'You read all the time.'

'Not the right books.'

'Well, read them, then,' I said impatiently.

'I can't.'

'You're a prick, Matthew.'

I cycled up the drive past the yellow chicken.

Why the fuck should I care about Matthew's exams?

I dumped my bike outside the first battery and went inside. Frank was tipping feed into a sack ready to go round and fill the feed troughs. He nodded bleakly. He wore a thick check shirt and baggy trousers. A cigarette dangled between his lips and his cloth cap seemed stuck to his head with Brylcreem.

He showed me what to do and I took a broom and began sweeping down the narrow path between the cages where he had just filled the

38

feed troughs. The birds screamed and went mad as I knocked into the cages. I could feel the heat drying my mouth. The brush was heavy and clumsy in the narrow space between the cages. I stopped and wiped my face, listening to the thousands of hens. They looked thin and emaciated to me. At the end of each year, the farmer sold the hens as broilers.

'Mornin'.'

I turned and found another of the labourers watching me. He offered me a cigarette. He was wearing the same sort of cloth cap Frank wore, but jeans and a red shirt.

'Want a cup of tea?'

'All right.'

I followed him down the row between the cages. At the end of the cages was the pit where the bird droppings collected. It was three feet deep. Another labourer was checking the machinery that drove the conveyor belt. As I stepped onto the wooden plank across the pit, the man stepped back and bumped into me, winding me with his elbow. His friend turned round and grinned, colliding with me when he stopped and making a grab for my arm as I went down on the wooden slats. I slipped straight off the edge, jarring my back against the edge of the slats, and then losing my grip and sliding backwards straight into the pit.

It was the man in the red shirt who grabbed my arm before I went under, and I only realised they were laughing when they dragged me up the side of the concrete pit, taking the skin off both my hands. Helpless with laughter, they washed me down with a hosepipe, and told me that was the traditional welcome for all battery workers. Down at the far end of the battery, Frank was still pouring layer mash into the feed troughs.

'They do that to you?' I asked Frank when we were taking our break mid-morning.

He shook his head.

'Why didn't you tell me?'

'Won't hurt.'

'Shit?'

He looked at me over the cigarette paper he was licking.

His eyes were very blue, and he seemed to be laughing. He shook his head again and rolled the cigarette.

'I got to work with 'em,' he said, taking a long drag at the cigarette.

'Thanks.'

'They're all right. Don't know any better.'

We spent the mornings feeding the birds and then cleaning the concrete floors, shovelling everything into the pit. After a break at eleven o'clock, we emptied the concrete pits. If the filth caked at the mouth of the pit, Frank climbed down and forced it through with a huge wooden shovel he'd made himself. Sometimes he had to loosen the muck first with a garden fork.

After lunch, we began collecting the eggs, wheeling barrows up and down the cages and putting the eggs into cardboard egg trays. When the barrows were full, we took them back to the centre of the building, wobbling over the wooden planks that crossed the pits. In the main part of the battery, we had to wash the eggs in buckets and then pack them ready for collection.

Late afternoon, when the eggs were all washed, packed and stacked in thousands against the walls, we had another break and then refilled the feeder troughs.

The troughs were nearly empty.

'They feed all night?' I said wearily as we dragged fresh sacks of feed from the store.

Frank nodded.

'Don't they sleep?'

'Lights are kept on,' he said.

'I don't believe you.'

He shrugged and wheeled another load of food out to the cages.

My head was thumping with the noise.

My clothes had dried out from the hosing, but I stank. My hands were caked with egg yolk and shit. I kept washing my hands, but the muck stuck under my fingernails. My hands were yellow. My hair felt stiff, congealed to my head.

At four o'clock, Frank told me to clear off.

'See you in the morning,' I said.

He nodded. 'That's right.'

I got my bike and started to cycle up the road between the batteries.

The metal rim of the wheels grated in the dust, and it took me half an hour to get the tyres pumped up again. When they were firm, I saw the young labourer in the red shirt standing in the doorway of his battery, watching me. He grinned and shouted something to me, but I couldn't hear for the din of the birds. I cycled up the drive to the giant yellow chicken and found Matthew waiting at the gate, sitting underneath the chicken and reading a maths textbook.

'I thought I should suffer,' he said with a weak, apologetic smile.

'Suffer?'

'You look as if you have.'

'Bastards,' I said under my breath.

'What?'

'Bastards.'

I felt my eyes filling with tears and rubbed them furiously. I could smell the stench on my hands.

Getting up, Matthew went to his saddlebag and handed me a silver flask. I unscrewed it and drank the iced lemonade. I handed the flask back.

'It's my father's,' Matthew said.

'Thanks.'

'You need it more than him. You smell, do you know that?'

We cycled back to the house and sat in the yard while my mother made some tea and told us about the Americans who had called at the house during the day.

'There was an officer,' she said, bringing a chair out of the kitchen to sit down with us. 'Major Windmuller. They've got such strange names. Major Donald Windmuller. And Captain Carmine, Floyd Carmine.'

'Sounds American.' Matthew laughed.

My mother wasn't listening.

'They have such lovely manners.' She sighed. 'And the uniforms! I don't know how they get such creases in their trousers. If your father had trousers like that, he wouldn't know what to do with them!'

I closed my eyes and listened to the radio.

It was 'Stuck On You', Elvis Presley's latest. He hadn't made anything decent for years. He had even recorded an album of hymns. Matthew said he was the new Mario Lanza.

'I love Mario Lanza,' my mother said. 'And David Whitfield.'

I sneezed, the dust and pollen of the fields getting up my nose.

41

My mother seemed to take it for granted I would come home unable to speak. She felt like that after every day at the laundry. She made some sandwiches and asked Matthew if he was stopping for tea, and then went back inside to cook a meal. I wanted to lie down on the grass and go to sleep.

'Do you think it's a song about masturbation?' Matthew asked when the record ended.

I opened my eyes and saw a bright red tractor lurching down the side of the field towards the police house, the man in the seat bouncing up and down and waving his free hand in the air. As the tractor roared past our garden and out of the field onto the road, I could hear more music throbbing in the afternoon heat, and the man chanting the words as he disappeared up the side of the house.

On the radio, some putrid woman was wailing about love.

SEVEN

The giant yellow chicken had to be washed two or three times a year.

'You can do that,' the foreman told me one morning when I arrived at the batteries.

He was a remote, stiff man, hard-eyed and contemptuous. He drove a Land-Rover slowly round the different farms belonging to the company and took his cap off when he was talking to the owner.

I thought he was joking.

I took a stepladder and bucket of water down the drive and stared at the huge plastic chicken. It was covered with bird shit. The beeches and horse chestnuts that surrounded the farm were swarming with crows, and there were dozens of ring doves nesting in the old barns. I propped the stepladders against the concrete stand on which the bird was fixed and took a drink from the flask. The heat was dry, arid, and the bird stared across the flat fields towards the distant hills as if thinking about taking off. In an hour or so the heat would be unbearable, the sun high above the plateau and the hot cloudless skies burning down on my bare head. I could breathe the pollen, floating in thick clusters from the rampant hedgerows. I climbed up the ladder and started to wash the giant bird's beak. I thought the job would take me minutes, but the shit was dried and plastered onto the plastic like concrete glue, and the water in the bucket was filthy within two or three minutes. There was no water near the gate. I had to walk all the way back up the drive to the batteries and fill the bucket from the tap.

'Can't I use a hose?' I asked Frank, slumping down against the wall and watching him pour the mash into a feeding trough.

'No.'

'Why not?'

He shrugged.

'I don't know.'

'Foreman said the hosepipes had to stay in the batteries,' one of the other labourers told me.

I felt the top of my head. It was hot. 'I'm going to ignite.'

'Give us a shout,' Frank told me.

He went back into the battery. The hens screeched and squawked as the trolley crashed into the cages. I filled a bucket of water and poured it over my head, then filled my own bucket and walked back down the dusty drive between the barns and batteries.

At the chicken, a dozen starlings fluttered and pecked in the water I'd spilled on the ground. There had been no rain for weeks and the water from my bucket stood in puddles in the thick ruts of mud. Fresh bird shit spattered the chicken's head and beak as I worked.

I threw the bucket of water straight in the chicken's face and trudged back to the tap in the battery.

'You going mad?' Matthew grinned when he cycled up later in the morning.

He'd never been during the day before.

The girl with him had blonde hair knotted in tight curls round her cheeks. I had never seen hair such colour. It was like honey, catching the sun. She was tanned dark brown. She looked older than either of us, seventeen or eighteen. She was wearing jeans and a white T-shirt. Her eyes were a steady, good-humoured blue and her round face was covered with freckles.

I was sitting astride the head of the yellow bird, chipping at the thick coating of dried slime with a paint scraper. My hands were numb with the water and the constant scraping. I had a deep cut on the palm of my left hand where the blade had slipped. I tossed the scraper to the ground and sat and stared at Matthew.

'This is Barbara.'

'Hello.'

'Hi.'

She was trying not to laugh. She rubbed her nose with the back of her hand and glanced at Matthew. She had a small, upturned nose.

'You look busy,' Matthew said cheerfully. 'Cleaning the chicken?'

Barbara snorted and looked down at the ground.

Matthew took a bottle of orange squash from his saddlebag and passed it to me.

'Have a drink.'

'Thanks.'

The girl was staring absent-mindedly across the fields, trying not to watch me on top of the bird.

44

'This is lovely,' she said pleasantly. 'You have such a beautiful country.'

'It's not ours,' Matthew pointed out solemnly.

'I've read your Thomas Hardy,' Barbara went on, smiling at me. 'And your romantic poets—'

'Stephen doesn't read poetry,' Matthew interrupted.

'No?'

I stared at them.

'No.'

I felt stupid, angry, embarrassed.

I closed my eyes and drained the orange squash from the bottle.

'Thanks,' Matthew said. 'That was for our picnic.'

'Go to the Plough,' I said furiously.

'We came to invite you,' Barbara began, but I jumped down from the chicken and got the bucket and scraper.

I began walking back towards the farm buildings.

'I've got work to do,' I shouted.

'Tonight,' Matthew called.

'Fuck off.'

I could hear Matthew coming after me.

I turned and held the bucket in both hands. It was full of filthy water, bird shit and feathers.

'Stephen . . .'

As he drew opposite, I lifted the bucket and hurled the water into his face.

I could hear Barbara's gasp.

I walked back to the battery and went inside without looking round.

'Am I disturbing you?' the foreman asked when he found me late in the afternoon, straddled on top of the bird and fast asleep, exhausted.

I woke up with a start, my face red raw from the sun, my left eye closed with pus from a burst stye.

'What time . . . ?'

'Three fifteen.'

'I'm sorry . . .'

'You're nearly finished,' he said sarcastically.

'I was just finishing,' I began to explain, but he stabbed the chicken with his finger, scraping a lump of white shit from the

45

plastic feathers and holding it up for me to see like a dollop of lemon-flavoured cream.

'A whole day?' he said with his cold sneer.

'It won't come off.'

He pointed to the bucket of cold water.

'You boil it.'

'I've been scraping—'

'You boil it,' he said again icily, speaking slowly so that I would understand the words.

I started the climb down off the bird and slipped on the sides which were slippery with all the water. I jerked my back, the pain jarring up to my neck. I gritted my teeth and climbed down more carefully.

'Take your time,' the foreman said.

He got back into his Land-Rover and drove up to the yard.

I wasn't going to ask Frank.

It should have been obvious.

I felt the tears filling my eyes. I didn't want to work on the fucking farm in the first place. I gave the bucket a savage kick and sent it crashing into the hedgerow, bouncing down into the ditch full of dandelions and weeds.

In the evening, I sat in the yard by the water butt.

I had a pot of tea on a tray beside me, and a flannel soaked in cold water over my eyes.

In the kitchen, my mother was listening to the radio.

'I used to work on a goose farm,' my mother said, standing in the kitchen doorway and lighting a cigarette.

I took the flannel off and poured another cup of tea.

'Used to be a lot of goose farming down south,' she said. 'Huge herds. That farmer had nearly three thousand. Rats was the problem.'

I closed my eyes and breathed the tannin.

Was it possible to breathe tannin?

'Men used to tie string round their trouser legs,' she said. 'In case there were rats. Huge ones sometimes. Buck rats. Frightening. I don't like rats.'

'These fields must be full of them,' I said nastily.

'Don't be silly.'

'You can hear them.'

'That's pheasants, silly.'

'Frank says it's rats,' I insisted.

She stood for a long time, smoking her cigarette, listening to the radio. I put the flannel back over my burning eyes. Every spring I had this trouble, but this year was worse than ever. My eyes were red, as if I'd burst a blood vessel. The sties throbbed. If I touched them the pain was agony, and they itched all the time, driving me mad. The only time I was free from pain was when the cold flannel soothed and protected them from the light. It would be late summer before the attack cleared.

'I've seen rats,' my mother said.

'Here?'

She ignored me.

'I went down the field one morning, help with the feed. There was an old farm hand, David Gostelow, carrying the sacks. He stopped at the gate. Said I should go back. I didn't know what he was talking about. I was only fourteen. I climbed up on the gate. The field was moving. I thought it was the wind. Blowing the grass. I stood on the gate, and he climbed up beside me. I thought he was going to be funny. You know. He climbed right up onto the top bar and left the sacks. It was the grass moving. Thousands of them. Crossing the field. Thousands. They were going for the abattoir. Never bothered with our birds. Went straight through them. You couldn't hear a sound. We sat on that gate nearly an hour, in case they came back.'

I took the flannel off my face and looked at her.

She was completely white, the cigarette burnt down in her fingers, the box of matches in the other hand.

'You're making it up.' I tried to laugh.

'No, I'm not.'

'You are.'

'Why should I make something like that up?' she said angrily, then laughed. 'Why should I?'

She went back into the kitchen and I could hear her filling the kettle.

I could hear somebody coming up the drive. I soaked the flannel again and put it back over my eyes. I knew it would be Matthew.

'Hurting?' he said, sitting down on the chair and helping himself to some tea.

47

'What do you think?'

'Must be horrible.'

'Yes.'

He drank his tea and sighed.

'Sorry about this morning,' he said quietly.

'That's all right.'

'We didn't mean anything.'

'I was hot.'

'What?'

'I was hot.'

I took the flannel off and touched my eyes. My face was cold from the water.

'Your skin's gone white,' Matthew said with his laugh.

I touched my face and forehead. The skin was cold and wrinkled, as if I'd been in water for a long time.

'I can't stand that place,' I said suddenly, looking out over the fields, blinking my eyes against the soft twilight. 'I can't stand it.'

'Leave,' Matthew said.

'I have to have a job.'

'Do something else.'

'I can't find anything else.'

I could hear a pheasant calling at the far edge of the fields.

A long way away, an owl hooted.

'You want some egg and chips, you two?' my mother shouted from the kitchen.

'Egg and chips.' Matthew sighed with pleasure, shaking his head.

'Don't you like egg and chips?' my mother asked, watching him from the window.

'I love them, Mrs Godard.'

'Well, then.'

I sat alone in the yard while Matthew took the chair and tray inside.

When the food was ready, I went into the kitchen and washed my hands.

In his office, my father was busy, laboriously typing out his reports.

EIGHT

I'd never heard 'Mystery Train' played so loud, or 'Blue Suede Shoes' or 'My Baby Left Me', 'You know she left me,' wailing in the immense heat of the hangar. The ghosts of fighter pilots watched from the shadows, blue stubble on their faces and scarves round their necks, their eyes flinching from the relentless music, the raw throb of Presley's voice. At the bar American servicemen sat and drank bourbon, which they could buy from their PX at twelve shillings a quart. One of the wives, a girl called Willa, leaned on the counter and made lewd remarks to the young servicemen, leading them on and then laughing with surprise when they tried to kiss her, ask her out for a drive.

I sat and ate giant hamburgers with Barbara and Matthew, watching the tight-jeaned airmen laughing and performing in the polished bowling alleys, listening to the music that they seemed to have playing day and night, whatever the hour.

'But you must hate the idea,' Barbara shouted above 'Hound Dog', and then closed her eyes as the slurring voice lurched into 'Don't Be Cruel', the throbbing cry yearning into the vast rafters of the hangar, the long heat of the fluorescent light.

I didn't bother to answer.

'I want him,' Barbara said with a shudder, laughing at herself when she opened her eyes. 'I want him.'

On the fairgrounds, I'd once seen a girl faint when somebody put 'Don't Be Cruel' on the juke box.

Barbara sighed and smiled ruefully, finishing her drink.

'You must hate it,' she said again, watching one of the airmen take a long swing with a ball.

'I do.'

'Then why do it?'

She thought I was insane, working on the farm and doing what my parents told me. She had no idea about life without exam results. She had no idea what I felt about my father.

'You do what you want,' she said as if there was no problem. 'Surely that's obvious?'

49

'He won't listen,' Matthew told her.

'Then he must want to be miserable.' She shrugged.

'He doesn't.'

She lit a cigarette and shook her head.

'I don't understand,' she said, smiling and watching the bowling.
'Jesus, look at that guy.'

She was from New York. Everywhere she went on the camp, she was followed. She told me her parents were getting a divorce, which was why she was staying with her uncle on the camp. Her uncle was Lieutenant Colonel Beck, the officer in charge of security. He was a tall, grey-haired man, with a slow smile and careful eyes. He wore his uniform like a skin, and watched one afternoon while Barbara thrashed me at tennis, coming up afterwards and shaking my hand as if he ought to apologise for Barbara's bad behaviour.

'You boys know how to behave with a lady?' he said with his flat, humourless smile.

'Yes, sir,' Matthew said, nearly saluting as he mocked the Colonel's rasping, hard voice, bleak, vacant eyes. 'We know all about ladies.'

'Good,' the Colonel said after a long silence.

He walked away and reversed his car right up to Matthew's bicycle where it was lying on the edge of the grass. He saw the bike, and lifted his hand briefly from the steering wheel, pretending to be surprised, and then drove off in a great cloud of dust. His exhaust nearly choked us.

'You want to know what my father's like, look at him,' Barbara said as we walked away from the bowling alley.

'He's not that bad.'

'Don't get on the wrong side of him.'

'And your mother?'

'She's like me, only degenerate.'

'Barbara!'

'I'm joking, I'm joking.'

We walked out of the bowling alley and breathed the night air.

Out on the runways, the security lights round Nemesis were blazing, and a jeep lurched speedily towards us, its headlights shining in the darkness. The air was cool after the bowling alley. The jeep screeched past us, its headlights picking us out and then swinging away towards the guardroom. The driver dipped his lights and sounded his horn.

' "She walks in beauty",' Matthew said straight away, and Barbara burst out laughing.

'Fool.'

'They seem to think so.'

'They've got the hots.'

'I'm not surprised,' Matthew said.

'American boys all have the hots,' Barbara said dismissively. 'Should I know that?'

'What?'

'Romantics, right?'

'Byron.'

'Should I know him?'

'He'd have thought so.'

'Do you know him, Stephen?'

'Stephen's reading Hemingway,' Matthew said sternly, as if I wasn't there.

'He's great,' Barbara said. 'I read him in fourth grade.'

'What's fourth grade?' I asked, watching a crowd of airmen walk arm in arm towards the Naafi, singing and stumbling across the rough grass.

'Infant school,' Matthew said solemnly.

At the police house, the light was still shining in my father's office and I could see the lamp shining in the sitting room. The windows were all open. Beyond the house, the countryside stretched darkly for twenty miles until the cathedral city. Behind us, the Americans had built their own glittering, shining city. The sky blinked like a dome, shimmering above the deserted countryside.

Barbara leaned against the gate and rested her arms on the top wooden bar.

'You know you really ought to do what you want. And nobody else can tell you what that is. But you must know. You must know if you actually *want* to wear a uniform, like these guys, like your father. I wouldn't do what my father wanted just to keep him happy. He isn't the one going to live with that decision. I am. You have to think the same way, Stephen. I don't think you can rely on your parents to know the right thing for you. You have to make your own decisions.'

'I've been lending him Hemingway,' Matthew said ridiculously, nodding his head in the darkness.

51

'I beg your pardon?'

'*The Old Man and the Sea.* He misses the sea. They do, you know, seafarers. A kind of mourning.'

They walked off together, and I went into the house.

'We'll see you in the morning,' Matthew shouted in the darkness.

'Right.'

'After Communion.'

I could hear them laughing as they walked up the road, Barbara asking about Communion, Matthew hooting his derision. Barbara had told us she was Roman Catholic and didn't understand the English services.

When I got back to the house, I made a coffee in the kitchen and went upstairs before my mother could come out of the sitting room. Every Saturday, she bought sweets and chocolates and liked to sit in the evening watching television, munching through the sweets. I usually sat with her, and she looked disappointed when Matthew called at the house with Barbara. In my room, I lay on the bed and tried to concentrate on *A Farewell to Arms*, but I kept thinking of Barbara, her long blonde hair and blue, carnal eyes. I turned off the light and lay in the darkness, wondering how long she would be on the camp, when she would be returning to university. Downstairs, the house was silent.

' "In a summer season, when soft was the sun," ' Matthew chanted as we walked between the hawthorn hedges and across the open green towards the little Catholic church where Barbara had told us to meet her. '*Piers Plowman,*' he explained when I asked him about the quotation, and claimed that we were on our own pilgrimage, like Chaucer's pilgrims walking to Canterbury.

'You keep showing off,' I said when he'd finished. 'You keep trying to make me look stupid.'

'Not really.'

'Then why do it?'

'Part of my vocabulary.' He shrugged. 'I'm better educated than you.'

'You've read a few books.'

'I've read everything.'

'Is that why you keep failing exams?'

'Yes,' Matthew laughed, 'as you would understand if you'd ever taken any.'

The church was in a converted prefab, and we could hear voices inside as we lounged in the sun, leaning against the white walls, our feet soaked in dew from the grass.

' "In a summer season," ' Matthew sighed, ' "when soft was the sun." '

'I'm not impressed.'

'It's a beautiful poem.'

'I'm still not impressed.'

We could hear a bell ringing inside.

The priest intoned and Matthew translated the Latin.

'This used to be a beautiful country,' he said quietly.

I pushed away from the white wall and kicked aggressively at the earth, speedwell and buttercups thick in the dense grass. I could hear the priest's quiet voice, and resented the strange language, the silent communicants, Matthew's irritating voice. His eyes were dark and sardonic, watching me destroy the grass, crush the flowers to a black mess.

'Beautiful,' he repeated. 'You can learn that from poems like *Piers Plowman*.'

'I can learn it from opening my eyes,' I sneered.

'But you don't even know the names of the flowers you've just kicked into the ground,' he said.

I laughed, glaring at him. 'Fuck off.'

'You don't know the names of anything.'

'Fuck off.'

Inside, the priest raised his voice, and I glanced angrily at the prefab windows. 'You think they know everything?' I said, hating the families inside, the strange sounds, the bells and foreign language. 'You think they're so clever?'

Matthew stood up, nervous, smiling sarcastically.

I bent down and picked up a handful of pebbles from the gravel path in front of the church. I hurled the pebbles at the door, furious at Matthew as he flinched and refused to move. I picked up another handful and hurled them at Matthew's feet, jeering as he danced out of the way and then turning and walking back across the huge open green towards the guardroom at the camp entrance.

NINE

'You have to meet them, Stephen,' my mother said to me one evening, cycling with me down to the village and handing me a basket of eggs as we left our bikes outside the cottage.

The cottage was at the bottom of the hill, surrounded by a rambling apple orchard that ran all the way down to the meadows and the beck before the huge open sweep of the wheat plain.

'Come in, lass,' the old man said, holding the door open for us and showing us into the tiny parlour, sunk into the earth so that the windows seemed full of wild flowers, the garden outside sloping down as if coming into the narrow room. An enormous grandfather clock ticked in the corner of the room, and two armchairs and a sofa crowded round the range fire. On the coals a kettle was boiling, and flames from the fire danced and shimmered on the coal scuttle and brass fender. There was a pot of goose-grease above the fireplace which my mother told me Wilfred used to prevent colds, and over the fire herbs from the fields and gardens were drying in neat newspaper packets, something her own mother had done when she was a child. She said being in the cottage sometimes made her feel as though she was a girl again.

'Hot water with cider vinegar and honey,' Wilfred explained, nodding to the kettle and offering my mother a chair. 'Only cure for arthritis. This is the boy, Emily,' he told his wife, shouting slightly and pointing at me.

'Sit down, dear.' The old woman smiled.

She must have been in her nineties.

My mother told me afterwards that she was thirty years older than Wilfred, and had been the district nurse for decades, cycling round the village lanes in the days when there were no cars, acting as midwife and doctor and making jams for the church fêtes. She had trained in London, at a great hospital overlooking the river, and married her husband when she was too old to have children.

'Lot of nonsense, children,' she told my mother mischievously. 'Lot of sentimental nonsense.'

Wilfred had been the vet, visiting the remote farms on a horse, clattering through the village in the middle of the night to help with a foaling or visit one of the outlying farms. He had spent his life trying to perfect pheasant poaching, and usually had a string of pheasants hanging in the outsheds waiting until they were ready to eat.

My mother talked easily to Emily while I sat and watched the flames of the fire. The kettle boiled and Wilfred made a pot of tea, and then showed me round the orchard while we waited for the tea to brew. We walked between the trees, and he told me the apples were Orleans Reinette, the best late variety for this far north. He said there was a man in the village who had planted a whole orchard of James Grieve, a daft tree for this climate, prone to apple scab and canker, the pale yellow fruit soft and easily bruised.

At the bottom of the orchard, we stood and listened to the beck. There were purple bellflowers at the top of the orchard, and the last of the wood garlic gleamed white in the half-light. The ground near the beck was rampant with meadow-sweet, the sickly smelling air heavy with pollen. He told me the names of all the flowers, pointing to them with his knotted walking-stick, leaning on my arm as we stood at the edge of the shallow beck, the fast-flowing water clean and cold, sky-blue forget-me-nots tugging and dancing against the current.

'You're not from round here, then, boy?' he said breathlessly as we made our way back up to the cottage.

'No.'

'Not from the country?'

'No.'

I had never lived anywhere other than the coast.

'Not like your mother, then,' he said emphatically, nodding and stopping at the cottage door. There was an old water pump outside the door. He leaned against it to catch his breath. His hand was covered with deep tanned wrinkles and dark patches of skin like stains of varnish. His eyes were slightly swollen, brimming with tears which he wiped away automatically. He wore tiny gold glasses, exactly the same as Emily's, and a huge red-wool knotted tie.

'Tea's ready,' Emily said with a smile when we sat down by the fire.

She held herself very erect, her grey hair tied back behind her ears, her eyes grey, amused, watching me as if she half expected me to do something outrageous. When she spoke, her voice was firm and precise, but her hands shook gently, clenching a walking-stick that seemed to be the same as Wilfred's. She was wearing a black dress with a knitted shawl, and her feet tapped restlessly on the carpet in front of the fire.

'You shouldn't let him bother you,' she said very clearly, nodding at me and waiting for Wilfred to pour the tea.

'That's all right, Mrs Starr.'

'He has nobody to talk to,' she explained. 'So he becomes tiresome.'

My mother giggled, taking her tea and touching Emily's hand lightly. The tea was camomile, green as the grass in the orchard.

'Don't be silly, Emily.'

'She can't help being silly,' Wilfred joked, drinking his camomile tea with loud sucks and ignoring Emily's flickering eyebrows.

I knew she was leaving her own tea until after we were gone.

Cycling back to the house, I asked my mother why they hadn't wanted the eggs.

'They knew they were from the battery of course.' She laughed.

'How did they know?'

'Have you ever seen a proper egg, Stephen?'

'They are proper eggs.'

'They knew they weren't proper eggs the minute they saw them.'

'I think that's rude,' I said, opening the gate and pushing my own bike up the drive. 'They could have kept them.'

My mother glanced towards the office.

'You don't understand.'

'Course not.'

'Your father's out.'

The office lights were on, but we could see the empty room, the desk and green filing cabinet, the spare uniform hanging behind the door. There was a map of the area on the wall, and a clock beside the telephone. My father's truncheon and handcuffs were hanging from a hook beside the desk.

'I wonder what he's doing,' she said vaguely as we pushed our bikes up to the house.

I had no idea.

It seemed strange, after all these years, that she should still worry whenever he went out at night.

*

It must have been because of her new friendship with Emily and Wilfred that my mother started keeping chickens. She bought a dozen Rhode Island Reds and a second-hand chicken hut from one of the monthly farming sales. My father and I sectioned off the far end of the garden with barbed wire, and bought metal troughs for the food.

'I'm going to have proper eggs in this house,' she said emphatically when my father told her she was wasting money.

'Taste all the same to me,' he said nastily.

'Do they, dear?'

My mother didn't listen to my father.

She hardly seemed to notice he was there most of the time, and treated him like a child when he started to argue. She was frail and thin, with her pale complexion and untidy fair hair, and her vagueness sometimes drove him wild.

She used up all the kitchen slops to feed the birds, and I bought a bag of feed every month to add to the potatoes and mashed slops. The feed was delivered by the company who collected the eggs from the farm. Each week, an enormous articulated lorry would collect fifty or sixty thousand eggs from the batteries, and then trundle up the road to the police house for the two or three dozen eggs our chickens had managed to lay. My mother signed the receipts with a great flourish, and every month received a cheque from the company. It made the whole enterprise seem real. The eggs we didn't use or sell to the company she sold to people in the village. She gave half a dozen eggs every week to Wilfred and Emily Starr.

She did everything she could to encourage her hens to lay.

They lived in luxury, and became increasingly tame and fat. If we left their gate open by mistake, they would follow us up the vegetable garden. Two of them would come right into the kitchen and eat out of our hands, perched on my shoulder while my father took a photograph.

I seemed to spend my life surrounded by chickens.

I began to dream about chickens.

If we weren't quick to use the tar, a wounded bird could be eaten alive within hours. That was one of the first things Frank warned us about. Out of their cages, they were natural cannibals, and we had to watch them all the time. Then there were the rats. At night, when I

57

went out last thing to secure the hut, a dozen sets of eyes would blink at me in the beam of the torch, rats drawn in from the fields by the smell. I had to protect the hens from the rats, and pretend to my mother that I never saw them.

On a wet Sunday afternoon, Frank came and stood in the garden, checking everything we'd done. He seemed delighted with the idea of my mother keeping her own hens. He went away saying it all seemed fine to him.

When my mother started selling the eggs, I used to pinch the biggest ones I could find from the batteries to add to our supply, carrying them wrapped in handkerchiefs inside my shirt. I took pounds of feed home in my pockets. The farmer was supposed to be a millionaire, and I figured he deserved what he got for the yellow plastic chicken at the gates, the wire cages crammed with screaming birds.

At the batteries, the men ridiculed my mother's hens.

For a joke, one sweltering afternoon, they put a cockerel into one of the cages and roared with laughter when the bird flew into a rage, breaking its neck as it flailed at the thin wire.

Whenever a broody hen pecked their hands, the men used to stand and bombard the cages with fresh eggs, smothering the frenzied hens with yellow slime.

They got nasty if Frank tried to stop them. They seemed to resent the interest he took in our birds.

One night, warned that three Irish contract labourers from one of the farms had been seen crossing the open fields near the village, my father waited until dawn and then cycled to a barn where he thought they might be sleeping. Two of the men were unconscious. The third lay awkwardly in a corner, his left eye hanging from a piece of skin down his cheek. My father telephoned for a car and watched the men being driven away. He got back to the house before six, and sat down as I was finishing breakfast. Drinking his tea, he told me about the Irish labourers who used to work on the docks when he was a boy, sleeping in temporary huts along the quays, cooking their meals on an open fire. He used to go with his friends and listen to the men telling each other stories. He laughed when I asked about the labourers he'd just arrested.

'They're not the same,' he said bleakly, getting up from the table and taking his tea through to the office. 'Not the same at all.'

I sat staring down the long garden.

At the gate, a white Oldsmobile had parked in the road, and an officer was walking up the drive to see my father. My father cycled everywhere on his huge beat, patrolling the narrow lanes on his clanking Rudge bicycle, moving silently through the dense woodlands when he was after poachers. A few weeks after we arrived, he was called to the village pub to a fight and refused to telephone for assistance, using his bare knuckles and truncheon to make sure there would be no more trouble.

'You just have to show them,' he said afterwards, wincing as my mother smeared ointment on his broken knuckles.

'Show them what?' she asked.

'Shut up, woman.'

'Looks like they showed you.' She laughed, but she didn't mean it. He flexed his hands and ignored her. She went on massaging his hands, nervous, restless, and smiled vaguely when she saw me watching her.

TEN

I was so fed up, I took a day off towards the end of June and went back to the coast to visit the fairgrounds. I thought I might even get my old job back. Sleep on the sands and look for a cheap room. Stay in one of the cafés or the storerooms behind the fairgrounds.

In the fields, the wheat was dry and burnt nearly orange. Some of the farmers my father had got to know were already talking about beginning the harvest. It had been the driest spring and summer for decades. I sat on the bus and watched the endless miles of corn, the hawthorn hedges glistening in the sun. I sat next to the driver and told him about working on the farm, the muck they put into the feed compared with the leftovers my mother gave to our chickens. He said he would call in on the way home and buy some eggs for his wife.

'She likes a fresh egg,' he said, coughing through the smoke of his cigarette. 'Boiled egg and soldiers. You know women.'

He drove all the way to the coast with a cigarette stuck to his bottom lip, his eyes bleary with the smoke, his chest heaving as he tried to breathe or sing to the radio. He had the radio tuned to a country and western programme and beat out the rhythm on the steering wheel, whooping to the cheerless choruses, the whining songs of love.

We pulled into the bus station at ten o'clock, and I sat in the transport café for half an hour, drinking tea and chatting with one of the scrubbers who worked the station. She lived in the terraces behind the fairgrounds, and sat in the café every morning drinking tea, watching the crowds of trippers arriving on the buses. She had her hair in curlers under a purple headscarf and kept touching my hand, calling me pet and telling me she remembered my father.

'Terrible feller, your dad,' she croaked, wiping tears from the corners of her eyes. 'Terrible feller.'

Now that I was here, I didn't want to leave the station. The town looked dirty and overcrowded after the countryside. I should have left the visit until the end of the summer, come back in the autumn when I could visit the fairgrounds on my own. Watching the trippers, with their kiss-me-quick hats and blistered faces, Hawaiian shirts and gaudy bingo prizes, I couldn't think why I'd come.

The promenade was packed by the time I left the café.

I walked out on the pier and stood and watched the shipping at the estuary, trawlers and an oil tanker heading up the main channel for port. The foreshore was crowded with people sunbathing, splashing into the sea and screaming at the cold waves, chasing along the sands and queuing up for the donkeys. On the sands, the big wheel was already spinning, and I could hear the music, drifting on the warm air, the girls at the top of the wheel shrieking as the swinging chairs plunged back to earth. Opposite the railway station, the Punch and Judy booth was just opening, and there were three trains at the platforms, hundreds more visitors pouring down onto the sands from the trains.

I left the pier and made my way along the promenade. I bought an ice-cream at a parked van and leaned on the railings, enjoying the sunlight on my face, the salt air lifting off the tide.

At another café I had fish and chips and then caught a tram down to the docks. I walked round the main quays to the fish docks and sat on one of the bollards on the north quay. By late morning, the fish docks were always deserted. A trawler clanged through the lockpit while I sat and smoked a cigarette. I waved to the crew, lounging on the rusty foredeck, and they cheered ironically, blowing me kisses, cursing the deserted quays. In the summer, few of the families came to welcome the trawlers back. The wives would be working or down on the sands. The children would be on the fairgrounds or in the sea. Any of the young fishermen on turnaround would already be in the pubs and drinking clubs. I finished the cigarette and listened to the water sloshing under the wooden slats of the jetty. A fog was drifting in off the sea, and I could hear the fog bell on the buoy, clanging out at the estuary. On the roof of the main market, dozens of herring gulls fluttered and squabbled.

Walking along the sands, I went back to the north end of the promenade and climbed up the great concrete steps to the fairgrounds. The pavements were sticky with candy floss and shrimps, chips and purple toffee apples dropped into the gutters.

I elbowed my way through the crowds, and stood at the main entrance of Wonderland. The tattooed man was still on the doors.

'You been away, laddie?'

61

'Yes.'

'They said you been away.'

He had naked breasts pricked all over his flesh, nipples and cleavages blue and red on his skin, fat bosoms lolling on his stomach and across his shoulders. When he flexed his muscles, tits bounced and trembled.

Inside, the waltzer and rocket rides thundered to the screams of the crowds, the thumping blast of music. They were playing Little Richard's 'Keep a Knockin'', and round the waltzer thirty or forty youngsters screamed and clapped to the music, dancing as the spinning chairs flew above their heads. One of the girls seemed to be in a frenzy, holding her arms high above her head and bouncing up and down to the rhythm, throwing her head right back and swivelling her hips as she danced. As a new record started – Little Richard again, singing 'Lucille' – she pulled her T-shirt over her head, and threw it wildly towards the waltzer, where somebody leaped up and caught it, leaning out dangerously from the car, waving the T-shirt round his head. The girl danced naked on the concrete, and the crowd round her clapped and shouted, cheering as her breasts jumped up and down, her hair swung round her head and her arms punched the heat.

I thought she looked ridiculous.

'Stephen?'

I turned quickly, awkward, embarrassed, as if I was the only one on the fairground watching the girl.

'Sandra?'

'Course it's fucking Sandra.' She laughed.

She took my arm and looked at me as if I was drunk, smiling and squeezing my arm firmly.

'Are you all right?' she asked.

'I'm fine.'

'Shall I get a bouncer?'

'Don't be daft,' I said impatiently.

She blinked, standing back to look at me with mock amazement and surprise. She had huge gold earrings and her hair had been cut very short. She had dusty blonde hair.

'You look incredible.'

I knew she was laughing at my pallor. Two months in the batteries, and I looked as if I had just come out of prison.

She stared at my face, examining me, holding my wrist loosely in her hand. 'Are you ill?'

'I've been working inside.'

'Prison?'

'On a farm!'

'A farm!'

'You look great.'

She was plump and suntanned. Her eyes were dark green.

'I'm surprised to see you.'

'Just a day trip.'

'Come to see your old mates?'

'Something like that.'

'Let me buy you a drink,' she said.

She held on to my arm.

We pushed our way out of the fairground and blinked in the dazzling sunlight.

The crowd round the waltzer were still dancing.

'Show off,' Sandra said when she saw me glancing back at the girl. 'She comes down every day. Got big tits, hasn't she?' She laughed crudely and squeezed my arm.

I thought about Barbara, smiling at Matthew's jokes, her hair almost the same colour as Sandra's, her eyes mocking as we tried to shock her with our wild stories. I wondered what Matthew was doing now.

Down on the sands, we queued up for tea and then sat on one of the groynes and smoked a cigarette. Pools of muddy water collected round the groynes, and crowds of children swarmed around them, paddling and looking for shells.

'What sort of farm is it?' she said, draining her tea and watching me good-humouredly.

'Chicken batteries.'

She shuddered. 'Horrible.'

'Yes.'

'I don't know how you stand it.'

I watched a crowd of children paddling at the edge of the tide, and thought about the arguments I kept having with my father.

I didn't know how I stood it either.

He never listened to a word I said.

I smiled at Sandra and crushed the plastic cup in my hand.

'I might be going to college,' I said abruptly.

'What?'

'In September.'

'I don't believe you.'

I hardly believed it myself.

'No?'

'They'd never take you at a college. They didn't even want you at school.'

We both laughed and I knew I was glad I'd seen Sandra.

She had been working the fairgrounds when I got my first job. She looked after the coconut shy. She had been thrown out of school for breaking a chair over a teacher's head, and left home at sixteen to live with one of the blokes off a dredger. She had a scar at the bottom of her back where her father had hit her with the buckle of his belt. He got three years in Hull prison for that.

'I thought you'd come back for your old job,' she said.

'No.'

'Thought you would have missed us.'

'I do,' I lied.

Sitting on the groyne, I listened to her chatting about the fairground, the new rides and the gangs at night causing trouble, teddy boys from up the coast and young fishermen looking for a fight.

'Your dad all right, is he?' Sandra asked as she munched a mouthful of bread and sausage. Bright yellow mustard ran down her chin, and she wiped it away with her finger.

'He's fine.'

'You going to do that, be a policeman?'

'No,' I said.

'Won't he be disappointed?'

'I suppose so.'

'I bet he is.'

I closed my eyes and tried not to think about it.

I had no idea how I was going to tell him.

When I worked on the fairgrounds, fishermen used to queue at the gun stall every night for Sandra.

'Me fether says I'm man mad,' she used to joke. 'I told him, it's not the fellers, it's the pricks they're hanging off of.'

64

She had shown me how to use the microphone on the housey-housey when I first started on the fairgrounds, teaching me jokes and things to say to the punters.

When my father knew I was working with Sandra, he seemed almost pleased. 'Sandra's all right,' he said. 'She'll look after you.'

It was my father who picked her up from the school after she'd attacked a teacher. He knew her dad, a drunken fisherman who used to beat her up between trips. He warned her when he was due to get out of prison. He spoke up for her when she was put on probation.

'I have to go,' I said, staring out to the estuary where an ore carrier was heading for the main channel.

I stood up and looked at Sandra, waiting for her to say something.

She seemed upset, and didn't listen when I said it was a long bus journey home.

'I was frightened of your dad, you know,' she said suddenly. 'I used to dread him coming down here.'

'He liked you.'

'Did he?'

'Yes.'

'I didn't like him. I couldn't understand why he let you work down here.'

'It was a job.'

'He knew what it was like.'

'It was just a job, that's all.'

'And me?'

'What about you?'

'Working with me?'

She lit a cigarette and flicked the match into the water at the end of the groyne.

'Somebody like me?'

'I told you,' I said quietly. 'He liked you.'

She went on smoking.

She had a tattoo, etched on her shoulder, a blue butterfly with transparent pink wings.

'I'll be off, then,' I said when she refused to look up.

'Yes.'

'See you.'

'Yes.'

I walked back along the promenade and caught the first bus going in my direction.

The bus was nearly empty.

It wasn't the same driver.

Throughout the journey, I thought about telling Matthew about college. I had to tell somebody who would be excited. There was no need to say anything about the police. I could tell my father about that when the course was finished.

ELEVEN

At the camp, I went straight round to see Matthew.

He opened the kitchen door and peered at me from the darkened room. The blinds were down. In the shadows, I couldn't see his face. He didn't want to let me inside, and I could see books spread out on the kitchen table.

'I'm working,' he said nervously, and then shrugged when I said I could do with a cup of tea.

Inside, he turned away to get the kettle, and then opened the blind.

His face was swollen down the left side, and the eye was completely closed, his cheekbone a sickening black and yellow. He boiled the kettle, and sat with the bruise turned away from me once the tea was made.

'How did it happen?' I asked, thinking he'd had an accident with the bike.

He told me there'd been an argument with his father.

'He's drinking more than ever,' he said tiredly, holding his mug of tea. 'He's not usually like this.'

I couldn't understand how his father managed to do his job.

'I thought he was in charge of the rockets,' I said, my own tea going cold on the table.

Matthew laughed and then winced at the pain. 'Slight exaggeration.'

'What does he do, then?

'He orders supplies.'

'Supplies?'

'He's in charge of ordering supplies.'

'How does he manage?'

'Somebody else does it,' he said.

'What were you arguing about?' I asked.

Matthew took me upstairs and showed me his room.

It was the first time I'd seen round the house, and the smell made me feel light-headed. There were clothes scattered everywhere. Plates of food rotted on the landing. The lavatory hummed with flies. I followed Matthew and stood in the doorway of his bedroom.

The bookshelves had been smashed from the wall.

A chair lay in splinters in a corner.

There were books everywhere.

'He doesn't like me reading,' Matthew explained.

Stacks of books stood against the bed. They were all paperbacks, classics, translations. *The Canterbury Tales. The Divine Comedy.* I picked up *Piers Plowman*. On the back of the book, it gave the name of the person who had done the translation.

'I thought it was English.' I frowned.

'I don't read old English.'

'What?'

'Middle English, I mean. I don't read middle English. Fourteenth century . . . my father says I'm too stupid to read them in the original language.'

I was hot, irritable.

I wanted him to stop showing off.

I wanted him to talk sense so that I could understand.

I couldn't stand the small bedroom, the sweltering heat. I opened the bedroom window and went back downstairs.

Matthew followed me, desultory, unhappy.

In the kitchen, he stood by the sink.

He gasped for breath, swallowing air. He was beginning to panic in the hot, locked house.

I could hear the flies buzzing on the window ledge.

There were dead flies in the fluorescent lighting.

'Matthew . . . '

'I don't read . . . '

'Matthew!'

He took a long breath, sucking the air into his lungs, and peered at me through his filthy glasses. The glasses had been mended with Sellotape. He must have been wearing them when his father hit him.

'At least the furniture isn't ours,' he said, his hands trembling. 'I hate this furniture. Why does everything have to be green? Even the sheets are green. Do you realise nobody ever plants a garden because they might be moved on? Just keep everything tidy for the next occupant. My mother used to plant roses. She left roses everywhere we went. I could never see the point. She wouldn't use their sheets either. Queuing up down the laundry for fresh sheets every Friday. She wouldn't do that. We always had our own sheets. But that's all we did have. Sheets and roses. And a few pictures. I don't think we ever saw the flowers. We'd usually gone before they flowered.'

I reached out my hand to stop him. I touched his shoulder.

He looked at me, surprised, and then smiled awkwardly. 'Where've you been?'

He looked away, tears in his eyes.

'To the coast.'

'To see old friends?'

'Not really.'

'I didn't know.'

'Something different.'

'I thought . . . after the chapel . . . '

'Fuck the chapel . . . '

'You wouldn't want to speak to us . . . '

I was still holding *Piers Plowman*. I tossed it flamboyantly onto the kitchen table.

'I can't live without Barbara.' I sighed.

'She thinks you're insane.'

'I can't get her out of my mind.'

'I believe you.'

'I dream about her at night.'

'I bet.'

'I think about her breasts.'

'Shut up.' He laughed, holding his face with both hands and trying to cover his ears. 'Shut up, you idiot.'

'She's got fantastic breasts.'

'American breasts.' Matthew nodded. 'Fantastic American breasts.'

'Superburger giant breasts.'

'Succulent mesmerising breasts . . . '

We were both gasping for breath now, collapsed on the chairs and tears pouring down our faces, shouting at each other to shut up and leave the poor girl alone.

'She's a Catholic,' Matthew said finally, pointing his finger in my face and then wrapping his arms round his ribs to stop the aching pain. 'She's a Catholic, for Christ's sake. They don't believe in breasts. They don't even believe in sin.'

By the time we finished our tea and walked up to the Naafi the civilians on the camp were all finishing work and the traffic was queuing at the gates to get out onto the main road.

'I've made a decision,' I told Matthew as we sat on the steps of the Naafi, watching the beautiful American cars lurch and bounce along the narrow roads. 'I'm definitely going to college.'

'No,' Matthew shouted with delight.

'Definitely.'

'I told you you ought to go.'

'I'm going.'

'We'll be together.'

'And to celebrate,' I said, 'we're going to get drunk.'

'Drunk!'

'Tonight!'

'Tonight!'

With a yelp, Matthew grabbed hold of my hand. 'We're going to get drunk,' he said, pumping my hand vigorously as if the news was his own. 'We're going to get completely pissed.'

In a bright yellow Cadillac, an officer wound down his window and shouted at us furiously to get off the camp.

'Fuck off,' Matthew shouted back, and before the man could open his door, we dodged into the Naafi and out of one of the rear fire escapes.

In the raw heat, huge combines had already started the harvest.

'None of the Cadillacs are pink,' I shouted to Matthew as we ran across the open green towards the fields.

'What?'

'None of the fucking Cadillacs are pink.'

'So what?'

'Just none of them, none of them are pink.'

Later that night, we sat in the Naafi and drank Carlsberg Specials while a drunken American airman played 'Hound Dog' repeatedly on the juke box.

'You guys want to know something?' he growled, slumped at our table and staring morosely at the bright lights of the juke box.

'Go on, then,' Matthew said cheerfully.

The airman squinted at us.

'British, right?'

'Right.' We both nodded.

'British!'

He took a long pull at his drink and glared at the juke box.

'That record, you know, that record . . .'

'Yes?'

'It's fucking rubbish.'

'Right,' Matthew agreed quickly.

The airman waved a finger in his face.

'Not . . . genuine.'

I shook my head, staring into my drink.

'Not . . . authentic.'

'It's great,' I said, still staring into my drink.

The record ended and the airman stumbled back to the juke box and pushed another coin into the machine.

'Hound Dog' came on again.

'I'll tell you,' he said, sitting down and smiling at the empty glasses. 'You want to know something . . .'

'We have to go,' Matthew said, but the airman clamped his fist on Matthew's hand, and pushed his face close to Matthew's.

'You think I don't know what I'm talking about.'

'I'm sure you—'

'You heard Mama Thornton sing that?'

Neither of us answered.

'Fucking great. Fucking incredible.'

'I bet,' Matthew agreed emphatically.

'You know why?'

'She's black?'

'She's black.'

'It's a black song,' Matthew said knowledgeably, looking at me for agreement.

'It's a song that grows out of a community,' the airman said loudly, beating Matthew's hand up and down on the table. 'It's a song that *means* something to a community.'

'Right.'

'They all know who she's talking about.'

'Absolutely.'

'They all know the man.'

'You're hurting my hand.'

'She's singing about a man they know.'

71

'How'd you know?' I interrupted, but the airman ignored me, crushing Matthew's fingers and beating his hand on the formica table.

'I can't stand Presley,' Matthew shrieked, dragging himself free and nursing his bruised hand.

'He's singing to himself,' the airman shouted. 'He's singing to a *studio*.'

The contempt was wild, as if the man couldn't believe anybody would buy the record.

'He's singing into a mirror.'

In the moonlight outside, we had hysterics as we crawled past the guardroom, shouting good night to the guards who came and stood under the porch, making bets we'd never reach the exit.

TWELVE

I had my interview for the college at the end of July.

It was a technical college offering commercial courses for secretaries and examinations for people who'd left school too young for school certificate. It was in Brigg, an old market town north of Fulnar.

The principal sat behind his desk and glanced through the letter my father had written.

'You didn't do very well at school,' he said coldly.

He kept reading the letter when I tried to answer.

'I need some qualifications,' I said. 'I want something better than labouring.'

'You should have thought about that at school.'

He dropped the letter on the desk and sighed impatiently.

'Your father says he can get you into the police provided you have some success here. You'll just have to work very hard, won't you? I don't want these places wasting. There are plenty of people wanting to take them up.'

I got the letter saying I had been accepted a few days later.

'I used to cycle to school every day,' my mother told me eagerly when I showed her the letter. 'I had an oil lamp on the bike and it used to blow out in the wind. I had to leave ever so early. It was still dark, some mornings, and cold, lonely. I had to cycle miles. No street lights then. I used to take a baked potato in my hand and hold it in my gloves to keep my hands warm.'

'I'll be going on the bus with Matthew, Mother.'

'Will you, love?'

'I won't need hot potatoes.'

'Course you won't.'

In August, I switched to an arable farm, helping with the harvest of the spring wheat. The farm still used a horse and cart, and we sat out in the fields and ate our lunch under blazing, cloudless skies. We could have gone swimming in the river which ran along the bottom of the fields, but there was a polio scare that summer and we all preferred to sweat.

73

'You know Frank Bannister?' the old labourer with the horse and cart asked me.

'I used to work with him.'

'T'ent natural,' the old man said, shaking his head and unwrapping his sandwiches. He had beef sandwiches and a bottle of the Plough's cider every lunchtime. 'T'ent right,' he said miserably, 'goin' agin nature.'

At the end of each day, I walked across the fields to the village and had tea with Wilfred and Emily.

Wilfred showed me his library when I told them I was going to college. 'I got this Latin poetry,' he told me, 'for a school prize.' He said I could borrow the volume for as long as I liked.

'I can't read Latin.'

'There's translations,' he explained, showing me the pages. 'Go on, take it.'

We walked to the meadows every evening.

'There's been a fox,' he told me on one of my visits. 'Comes down from the hills for the water.'

A lot of the streams had dried out in the hot summer. Wilfred showed me the paw marks in the mud, delicate footprints treading the edge of the stream. The forget-me-nots still dazzled in the sluggish water, and meadowsweet grew thickly up the banks. The hedges at the bottom of the orchard were brilliant with purple bellflowers. Among the trees, the grass was glowing with yellow loosestrife. The apples hung in clusters from the ancient trees.

'They made a start on the barley?' Wilfred asked me over tea.

Emily sat and listened, smiling, nodding her head.

'Dan said maybe next week.'

'He knows farming, Dan Evans.'

'Like you know apples,' Emily said with her pleased smile.

At the college, I had enrolled for business studies, which meant I would be doing shorthand and typing. The training inspector at police headquarters had told my father shorthand and typing would be very useful.

'For a journalist,' Matthew said blithely when my father was asking about the course.

I could see my father frowning. 'He's not going to be a journalist,' he said unpleasantly.

'He can be another Hemingway,' Matthew said happily, ignoring my father.

'He's not thinking of being a journalist,' my father said again, glowering at Matthew. 'Nobody said anything about him being a journalist.'

'Oh, don't be so silly, Norman.' My mother laughed nervously.

When Matthew had gone, my father went back down the garden to get on with the winter vegetables. He was planting them in straight rows that had been weeded and raked a dozen times. He was out in the garden working for hours, and then suddenly hurled his rake at the ground and came back into the kitchen. I was sitting in the doorway, drinking tea and listening to the radio. My mother was rolling pastry for an apple pie.

'You trying to make me look a fool?' he said angrily, pushing his sleeves above his elbows and washing his hands in the sink.

'Don't do that in here, Norman.'

'Shut up.'

'It makes a mess—'

'I said shut up, woman.'

I stood up, pushing my chair back angrily so that it crashed into the fridge and chipped the enamel. I walked out into the yard.

The heat was like a wall, glowing against my face.

Far away, a car's headlights swept and searched the sky in a great arc, and then raced down the cliff road towards the camp.

My father slammed the pots into the sink and walked out of the house without speaking.

'He's got a lot on his mind,' my mother said tentatively, looking out into the yard, watching me and biting her lip.

'I know.'

'He's got a lot to worry about.'

On the camp, there had been violent incidents at the Naafi and in the American mess. Several airmen had been flown home after disciplinary hearings. The military police had dealt with the cases, but my father had been called in when RAF lads got involved in the fights. The Americans seemed to behave perfectly, and then would suddenly go wild with bottles or knives. My father hadn't faced a knife since his days working the fish docks.

'You got to do what's best for you, boy,' Wilfred told me on one of our walks through his orchard. 'You got to do the thing that's best for yourself.'

Emily burst into laughter when she heard about the arguments with my father.

'You recall my father, Wilfred?' she said delightedly to her husband.

'I do.' He grinned solemnly.

They both laughed, sharing their secret humour.

'It'll all be settled in the grave,' Wilfred said. 'You read that poetry I gave you?'

'I'm getting ready for college,' I lied.

'Don't they read poetry?'

'I suppose.'

'You read that poetry.' Wilfred nodded. 'Nothing changes, you see.'

'Doesn't it?'

'It'll all get settled.'

'I hope so.'

'You'll see.'

It was at one of the parties that I met Caroline.

Dark-haired and thoughtful, she was the daughter of the senior British scientist on the camp, a physicist who had written papers on quantum physics and the Copenhagen theory. Caroline was a few months older than me and so quietly spoken I could hardly hear what she said.

She was back from a year in Paris, in time to start her A levels. She was registered at a private school in Lincoln.

'Matthew says you're going to college,' she said, standing with me on the wide lawns of the house. 'You're going to be a journalist?'

'I don't know.'

'I thought about being a journalist.'

'My father wants me to go in the police.'

She nodded. She made me feel uncomfortable when she spoke, nervous and embarrassed. She said everything with a kind of calm gravity, as if it was all important to her, anything you might say interested her. She looked straight at me as she spoke.

'Barbara said so,' she explained.

'You know Barbara?'

'She's an old friend. I'd much rather be a journalist.'

'Yes.'

'Don't you find it strange?'

'What?'

'That your father wants you to do the same thing.'

'Not really.' I blushed.

I had no idea why I'd mentioned my father.

It was the last thing I wanted to talk about.

'Well, if that's what you want,' she said kindly, trying to understand.

She was wearing jeans and a sweatshirt. Her fringe came down to her eyes, and she had a relaxed, direct way of talking, as if she had known me all her life.

'I'm reading Pasternak,' she said, explaining that he was a Russian poet.

Her father was teaching her the language.

In the other room, they were playing Presley's 'Hound Dog', the electrifying voice echoing in the warm night, the wailing guitars thumping under the hot moon.

'There'll never be anything like those early records,' Caroline said with her soft voice.

I agreed happily, glad to change the subject.

'We were in Washington when he released "That's All Right". Do you know "Good Rockin' Tonight"?'

I told her what the drunken airman had said in the Naafi canteen.

'That's nonsense,' she said.

In the heat, the wailing voice was hiccuping to a frenzy of slapping bass and howling guitar, the chanting of the scientists in the darkened garden.

'We saw him on *The Ed Sullivan Show*,' Caroline shouted above the noise. 'I was thirteen.'

I had read the fan magazines about the famous television appearance, when the cameras never got down to the singer's abdomen.

'He was great then,' she said. 'He was wild.'

Somehow, talking to Caroline, there seemed nothing ridiculous about bringing rock 'n' roll and poetry together.

We went inside, and danced to the mesmerising music.

THIRTEEN

At the beginning of September, Matthew and I started at the college, catching the eight o'clock bus to Brigg every morning and having breakfast at the bus station before walking to the college for the first lectures. Matthew was re-sitting his A levels for university. His grades had not been good enough. I was registered for the commercial studies course.

On the first morning, I found myself in a classroom full of girls. There were twenty-seven of them, all doing secretarial studies.

Next door to the college was the high school, with its daily parade of sporting girls in gym slips and sixth formers in casually debauched uniforms, ties undone, jackets astray, breasts straining against tight white shirts. They mouthed messages through the college windows, did things with their fingers that hinted at raucous filthy delights.

I wasn't sure I could survive nine months until the final examinations.

'You must be our honorary female,' the college principal joked when he came round to introduce himself. 'Our lion among the lionesses.' His name was Leonard Cantor.

The girls all giggled at his humour, and he smoothed his grey hair down, enjoying their laughter, peering at me through his gold-rimmed spectacles. He was a tall, elegant man, with deep lines around his eyes and a perfectly creased charcoal-grey suit. He had a purple handkerchief gracefully knotted in the breast pocket of his jacket.

He introduced himself graciously and left the room.

According to the shorthand lecturer, Miss Timms, he was a saint, 'a martyr,' she said darkly, though it wasn't until I saw him pushing his wife round town in a wheelchair that I realised what she meant.

The course I was registered for involved shorthand and typing but also things like book-keeping and office procedure. Two spinsters took us for shorthand and typing, but when we did English a young teacher came in to lecture us. She was interested in the camp, friendly with Matthew and myself, and soon told us that she had been married to an officer in the RAF but divorced him when they were living in

Germany. She had two young children. She wore tight skirts and stiletto shoes, and sometimes cried when she was reading aloud from Keats or Walter de la Mare. Her name was Liz Maxted, but when Matthew and I were alone with her she insisted we call her by her first name.

It was Liz who took the domestic science classes, and on the first Wednesday afternoon allowed us to join her group because we weren't enrolled for anything. Everybody else was doing liberal studies. She said we could sit at the back of the room and listen while she talked to the girls.

'Provided you don't join in,' she warned us.

'Absolutely,' Matthew protested.

On the first afternoon, when they were doing something called personal hygiene, she asked if anybody had any suggestions for preventing nylons from laddering, and Matthew brought the lesson to an end by saying he always wore gloves.

'That was naughty,' she told him afterwards.

'I won't do it again.' Matthew grinned.

'You promise?'

'I promise.'

As a special concession, Matthew had been allowed to register for some of the commercial courses. He was supposed to concentrate his efforts on getting to university, but when he explained to Cantor that he was thinking of being a sports writer, the principal reluctantly agreed to let him join the typing and shorthand sessions run by the two spinsters.

He sat at the desk next to mine for both subjects.

During the typing lessons, he christened his typewriter Simone, an impossibly exotic name to me, but Matthew thought there was nothing strange about calling objects by real names. His father, after all, was working on the Nemesis rocket.

'Why call a lump of metal after a god?' he said when the lecturer commented on the typewriter.

'God?' the teacher asked stiffly.

'Nemesis.'

'I thought you said Simone.'

'The nuclear rocket my father's working on, that's called Nemesis,' Matthew explained wearily.

'What has that got to do with my typewriter?'

The two spinsters loved Matthew.

Surrounded by girls, he kept up a constant stream of comment, disrupting the speed tests, arguing with the lecturers, teasing the girls. He brought an apple to each of the spinsters every Friday morning and somehow found out their birthdays so that he could send them elaborately romantic cards and posies of wild flowers picked from round the camp.

On the long bus journeys through vast fields of potatoes and sugar beet, he sang obscene songs and tried to persuade girls from the high school to sit on the back seats with us. If any of them ever did, he read aloud to them from 'Prufrock' or *The Waste Land*, dwelling on the typist scene with Tiresias's 'wrinkled female breasts' and the drying underwear from the 'window perilously spread'. On one of the journeys, a tall, aloof girl called Jennifer who lived on one of the great farms sat down on the back seat beside him and offered to show him what they did to the cows when they were milking them early in the morning, and Matthew shoved *The Waste Land* into my hands and fled to the front of the bus. No matter what Matthew or Caroline said about Eliot, I couldn't believe it was anything other than rubbish.

'You have a genuine ear for poetry,' Liz told me after listening to me read one of the Keats 'Odes', and I blushed, embarrassed by her short skirts and shining lipstick, the black sheen of her stockings. She sat on the edge of her desk and flicked through the anthology of poems, avoiding my eyes. Standing near to her, I could feel her warmth, hear her breathing, smell the scent on her neck. I wanted to reach out and touch her. I wanted to feel her hair and kiss her on the mouth. I wanted to tell her how I felt.

She said I reminded her of somebody she had once known, and then pushed me out of the room.

I dreamed about her and then felt embarrassed every time she saw me in the corridors.

She started lending me books, encouraging me to read. I told her all about the books Matthew was endlessly lending me.

In six months I went straight from *Tom Sawyer* to *Crime and Punishment*, from *Swiss Family Robinson* to *A Farewell to Arms*, without understanding any of them.

'You don't have to understand them,' Liz tried to explain.

I nodded.

I thought that was stupid, but she lent me the poems and stories of Dylan Thomas and told me to go away and read them. I couldn't make out what the stories were supposed to be about, and the poems seemed like riddles. I showed them to Matthew and he shrugged lazily.

'You don't have to understand them,' he began, but I threw the book at him and went off for a long ride along the cliff, cycling down to each village and walking round in the late September sunshine, enjoying the deep silence of the narrow lanes, the buried cottages yellow in their sunken gardens.

All round the villages, the farmers were busy in the fields, lifting the potatoes, harvesting the sugar beet for stacking. They would soon be drilling the winter barley.

'You have to take it on trust,' Caroline told me with her calm, wide smile.

I listened to her in her sitting room, the french windows open to the long lawns, her homework spread out all over the floor.

'You just have to wait for the meaning to come to you,' she said.

She had huge, nervous eyes, dark as she sat with her back to the sunlight, pale grey when she smiled, always watching, interested. She was wearing a black skirt and tight black jumper, and had her hair combed down into her eyes. Her face was pale without make-up.

She put her books away and selected a record from the cupboard. Slow, elegiac chamber music filled the room.

The strings seemed to pluck at the air.

The room stilled to a glow.

I had never heard anything so astonishing.

'Read "Prufrock",' she insisted as I left the house that evening.

In my bedroom, I sat and stared at the words, and tried to remember the music. I hadn't asked her what it was called. I flicked through my own record collection and could find nothing I wanted to play. In the fields beyond the house sunlight made the soil shine, the newly turned earth glistening in the last of the twilight. Far away, a pheasant coughed suddenly, rising above the fields. A tractor churned down a lane in Fulnar.

In the mornings, before college, I got up and fed the birds.

The dawn air was chill now in the blue light. Flecks of pink drifted from the hills, and the birds seemed to fill the sky, flying in great swarms backwards and forwards. I let the chickens out of the hut and then filled the feeding troughs with food. Each evening, my mother left a bucket of slops in the kitchen ready for the morning. When the birds were fed, I fastened the wire gate and walked back to the house. I had breakfast alone in the kitchen, or with my father if he was up and about. He rarely talked early in the morning. He liked to drink his tea and listen to the radio.

Some mornings, if there were eggs to be delivered, I cycled down to the village past the silent camp. If there were going to be training exercises, Nemesis might be out of the bunker, the great white rocket pointing to the waking sky, the motionless jeeps parked around the compound. The road would be deserted. Along the cliff top, the hedgerows would be damp with mist, spider's webs glistening where they caught the sunlight. As far as you could see, the earth to the west would be cold and silent, only the blue hills to the east touched by the first light. I would cycle slowly along the narrow road, feeling the damp on my face, enjoying the sense of isolation. A giant Cadillac might pass me on the road, Little Richard raucous in the dawn cold, Fats Domino rocking to the swing of the car. In the village, men would be setting off for work, cycling off down the lanes towards the farms. Wilfred might be in the orchard, poking at the trees, checking the apples for storage. While Emily was still in bed, he would make me a pot of tea and sit in their smoky kitchen, asking me about college and laughing at the things I told him about Matthew.

I never mentioned Caroline.

I was too obsessed to talk about her.

'I can't remember,' she said when I asked her about the music she had been playing. 'Didn't you know it?'

'No.'

'Why didn't you ask?' she said, genuinely puzzled.

She watched me, waiting for an answer, and then touched my arm lightly.

'You are silly.'

She searched through her records and eventually found the music. She put the record on again, saying it was one of her father's favourites. It was the slow movement of Schubert's Quintet in C, and when she told me, the words seemed to be magic, a naming that somehow joined me to the music.

She said she was thinking of studying music.

'I thought you wanted to do languages?'

'I love music,' she said.

Her mother came into the room and scoffed irritably. She was a tall, extremely thin woman, nervous and exhausted, her face plastered with rouge, her lips thick with purple lipstick. She wore very tight suits and high heels, and spent most of her time doing crosswords.

'You won't earn a living from music,' she said with her tight, nervous smile. 'Nobody earns a living from music.'

'Don't be ridiculous, Mother.' Caroline sighed vaguely.

At the Naafi with Matthew, I tried to hum the music so that he could identify the record, but he said I sounded like a diesel engine and we sat for hours, drinking and listening to the juke box until I couldn't remember anything about the record Caroline had played.

At college, Miss Timms used Beethoven for her typing lessons.

'Their and there,' she shouted at us as we tapped rhythmically to the orchestra, a clatter of keys imitating the surge of the music, a thumping of metal that must have disturbed every class in the college.

'Beautiful.' Miss Timms beamed, as we destroyed the glorious music.

'Come on, Simone,' Matthew chanted, causing hysterics among the girls sitting round him. 'Come on, you gorgeous piece of metal.'

I bought myself a portable typewriter with the money left over from the farm, and fixed up a card table in the bedroom. It was too flimsy for a heavy machine, but I sat there for hours typing out long rambling essays about factory farming and life on a nuclear base. I took a shorthand notebook with me everywhere and wrote down what everybody said, bringing most conversations to an immediate halt.

'You want to concentrate on studying,' my father said when he found me reading Dylan Thomas or Hemingway.

'I am studying.'

He took the book out of my hands carelessly and glanced at the cover. 'They tell you to read this?'

'That's right.'

He handed the book back clumsily, tearing the cover.

'Thanks.'

'Buy another, can't you?'

I was too happy to be bothered with his clumsiness.

Every morning, I woke up thinking about the college. On the bus, I talked to Matthew about the books we were reading. I longed for the weekends, when I could see more of Caroline, and then wanted to get back to the studying. In the evenings, I sat and read in my bedroom.

I began to take extra lessons with Liz Maxted. Her office was overcrowded with her desk and two chairs and a big bookcase. She sat on the desk and read to me, or listened to me reading. She said I ought to do some examinations, something better than the typing and shorthand.

I told her I wanted to be a journalist, and she looked surprised.

'It says you're going in the police in the file,' she told me.

I shrugged, blushing suddenly.

'*Are* you going in the police?' she insisted.

I shrugged again.

I didn't want to talk about it. I felt as though the notes on the file were nothing to do with me, nothing to do with my life. I was at college, studying to be a journalist, and the idea of going in the police was something that belonged to my father, something I had said to get into the college. I knew Cantor would not have accepted me simply because I wanted to be a journalist.

When I went to the principal and asked him whether I could change courses, he glared at me and glanced through my file, flicking the pages angrily, slapping the file down on his desk.

'Your command of English is appalling,' he said sarcastically.

I told him what Liz had said.

'So?'

'She said she would give me extra lessons.'

'Did she!'

'I want to be a journalist,' I told him, staring at the thin file on his desk.

He sighed impatiently and stood up. 'I have just told you, your command of the language is appalling. How do you expect to be a journalist when you can't even spell? Get on with the studies you've been accepted for. Do something useful with your life.'

'I don't want to go in the police.'

'Then you shouldn't be here, should you?'

I had no idea what was the matter with him.

He seemed incensed, wild with tiredness.

I told Liz, but she seemed reluctant to say anything.

'You have to understand,' she said. 'He's under all kinds of pressure.' She went on lending me books, but nothing was ever mentioned again about me changing courses.

'He's a saint,' Matthew said.

'What's that supposed to mean?'

'You can't expect a saint to be rational.'

'He was horrible.'

'Saints often are.' Matthew nodded. 'It's a well-known fact. Being saints, they don't get their oats, especially when they're married to somebody in a wheelchair. You are the victim of his lack of sexual fulfilment and wheelchairs.'

When my father received a letter from the college complaining about my lack of application, he shouted for hours, and then didn't speak to either my mother or me for days.

FOURTEEN

In late October I went with Caroline to visit the cathedral in Lincoln.

'We're reading *The Rainbow*,' she explained as we travelled towards the city, the bus lurching and swinging along the narrow country roads, the seats soon filled with women travelling to the market, chattering and nursing huge shopping bags, ignoring the golden fields and softly browning trees. After the long hot summer, the ground was baked dry and the growth looked pale and shrivelled, the hedges hardly any higher than they had been in the spring, the early-morning sunlight shimmering the dew and dancing cobwebs in the hedgerows. 'There's a famous scene in there where the lovers visit the cathedral.'

'You look beautiful,' I told her as we bounced and jostled along the narrow road.

'Don't be silly.'

She was wearing a light blue dress, delicate with small flowers, flared at the waist and shoulders, the neck cut low to show the string of white pearls she had borrowed from her mother.

'You do,' I whispered, and she squeezed my hand and went on looking out of the bus windows, listening to the women chatter.

Taking the old road, the bus headed straight for the cathedral, and it loomed out of the trees in a grey blue haze, darkened by years of smoke and fog, the great twin towers of the west front brooding opposite the castle.

'It's a false front,' Caroline said, glancing through her copy of the novel and making a note on the page. 'The stone used to be golden.'

'It's the factories,' I said, and she nodded, writing something else in the margins of the book. 'Steel works. Foundries.'

'You don't expect them somehow,' she said vaguely.

'Have to have factories.'

'In a cathedral city?'

'Why not?'

We walked up to the great doors and went inside. Caroline put some money in a collection box and unfastened her scarf from round her neck, tying it loosely over her head. She shivered as we plunged into the vast echoing spaces beyond the transept, walking down towards the altar that lifted up to the cathedral roof, soaring into light from the huge windows.

'You can go up the tower,' she whispered as we walked closely together, and her words echoed round the deserted building like a lash of wind freezing the choristers.

'No, thanks.'

'You must.'

'I don't like heights.'

She shrugged impatiently, hardly listening, reading her book.

I thought about the time my mother had gone up the great tower.

It was at the beginning of the war, before I was born. My father's sister had gone with her, pushing her up the slippery stone steps, insisting she see the countryside from the top of the tower.

'I fainted,' my mother told me.

'No, you didn't,' my father scoffed.

'I passed out.'

'You closed your eyes,' he sneered. 'That's all.'

'You were on the convoys,' she snapped back.

'Helen told me.'

'You weren't even there.'

He stared at her, shaking his head as if he couldn't believe it.

'Women.'

'I can't stand heights,' I said again, wanting Caroline to answer.

Sometimes, she scarcely listened to what people were saying to her. It wasn't just with me. I'd noticed when she was talking to Barbara and Matthew. One minute she would be listening to them, asking questions and urging them on, and then suddenly her eyes would glaze, and she would be surprised when they stopped talking, touching them nervously on the arm and asking another question to hide her confusion.

I wanted her to understand about the tower.

'I feel drawn to the edge,' I said. 'I want to jump over.'

She glanced at the notes at the back of the novel and looked puzzled.

'Do you think this is the Angel Choir?' she asked, staring around her at the rows of choir seats, the black candle holders.

'Yes,' I said brusquely.

She stared up at the cold walls.

Out of the darkness, carved faces peered down at us.

'He says they're sly,' she told me. 'He says they winked and leered at the girl.'

'Who says?' I muttered.

'In the novel! Will and Anna in the novel!'

I kept my hands firmly in my pockets. I was cold, fed up, bored with the immense cathedral, the hollow darkness. It seemed dark and old and boring to me. I wanted to get back out into the sunlight. I shivered, and my breath was cold air.

Caroline studied the faces as if expecting them to tell her something, reveal something that wasn't in the novel.

She laughed suddenly, bright, anguished. 'Plump, sly, malicious little faces,' she said excitedly. 'Can't you see them. She's wrong. She's wrong.'

'Wrong?'

'She says they're adorable. She says one of them is a woman. She says the stonemason loved her. But it isn't. It's a man. He's right.'

'Who's right?'

'Brangwen, in the novel!'

I glared at the screwed-up faces. They looked malignant to me, rampant, sexual, vindictive in their cold tower, their rigid isolation. I thought they were ugly.

'They are,' Caroline said with triumph.

I stared at her, startled.

'What?'

She wasn't looking at me. She was staring up at the faces.

'Ugly,' she said. 'Ugly.'

I wanted to leave. She was bewitched.

I wanted to get back out in the autumn air, the freshness, the cold.

'She's wrong,' Caroline said with some deep satisfaction, excited, trembling. 'She's definitely wrong.'

She was scribbling notes all over her copy of the novel.

She wrote with the stub of a pencil, biting her tongue, concentrating on what she was writing.

'Can we go now?' I asked.

'Of course.'

'You don't want to go up the tower?'

'No, you fool,' she said excitedly. 'I can't stand heights either. I can't stand them. They make me quite suicidal.'

Back in the vast spaces to the front of the cathedral, we walked through the arch and stopped to glance back at the mighty towers. Caroline seemed to find them funny, giggling, clinging to my arm. I didn't want to look at them. I felt disgruntled, threatened, as if the weight of the towers was like some huge aggressive authority, some thrust for power lurching clumsily into the sky. I couldn't understand how people thought the cathedral beautiful.

'Matthew says it's a gesture towards heaven,' I told Caroline as we walked down the steep hill towards town.

'Don't you think so?' Caroline asked.

We were walking close over the slippery cobbles, Caroline hanging on to my arm, our footsteps echoing between the medieval buildings.

'He was being sarcastic.'

'Matthew doesn't believe in anything,' she said lightly.

'Do you?'

'I believe in the cathedral.'

I waited for her to go on, and was irritated by her silence.

'You can't just believe in a building.'

'It isn't just a building.'

'I can't see anything else.'

'It's more than that. It's not just functional.'

'It's power,' I said angrily, not thinking about what I was saying. 'It's just power.'

'A kind of power ... '

'Power ... '

'Prayer in stone,' she said pompously, and then laughed when I got angry. 'I'm joking.'

'You don't say what you mean.'

'I don't know what I mean,' she said. 'You don't have to feel so threatened. I'm just studying a novel.'

'You liked it,' I said, feeling bitter and resentful, hating the cathedral and the novel, hating everything about it.

I knew this was precisely how my mother felt.

At the bottom of the hill, Caroline walked off on her own and stood outside a small bookshop. The bookshop was in the basement of a grey stone building, a medieval warren of shops and houses. She stared into the windows at the books, ignoring me when I went and stood beside her.

'My father's a scientist,' she said very matter-of-factly, turning round suddenly and facing me. 'He taught me there are limits to what you can say, actually talk about, in words. That's all I'm telling you about the cathedral. That's all I meant. Now let's go and have a coffee.'

I caught up with her and touched her arm. 'I'm sorry.'

'You don't have to feel so threatened,' she said brightly, walking quickly, looking from left to right in all the shop windows.

'I said I was sorry.'

'Let's forget it, shall we?'

On our way back up the steep hill, after dinner in one of the cheap restaurants overlooking the river, she took my arm again and leaned against my shoulder. The cathedral brooded above us like a black wound in the sky, surrounded by thick cloud. Scudding, wild, the cloud seemed to leak from the cathedral.

We walked past the castle and cathedral without looking at either, and caught our bus home at four thirty.

The bus dropped us off at the police house, and Caroline agreed to come in for some tea. She had never visited the house. She walked up the drive and waved to my father in his office. In the garden, I went to show her the chickens, but my mother was already down there, standing at the wire, fastening the ramshackle gate. We stood in the half-light and listened to her talking to the birds. She was calling them by name, saying good night in a low singsong murmur. When she turned, she blinked and dropped the basket of eggs. Yellow slime covered her shoes, and the basket rolled to one side. She lifted her hand to her mouth quickly.

'Hello, you two.'

'This is Caroline, Mother.'

'Hello.'

'Hello, Mrs Godard,' Caroline said politely.

I could feel her arm through her coat.

She was trembling.

90

The two women stared at each other, and then my mother glanced at her feet and laughed brightly, blaming the cold.

'You startled me,' she said as she scraped the yolk from her shoes and collected the basket. 'I didn't know anybody was there. Will you have some tea, Caroline? I've done some fresh scones.'

'No, thank you, Mrs Godard,' Caroline said quickly. 'I ought to get home.'

I glanced at her, surprised, disappointed.

'My father will be expecting me,' she said. 'I have to write these notes.'

She was still carrying *The Rainbow*.

I walked with her to the gate but she refused to let me come any further. 'Your mother's baked some scones,' she said gently, and I flinched as if she was being sarcastic, quickly examining her face. She looked back seriously, touching my hand and saying thank you for the day. 'We must go again,' she said. 'We must go and see the castle.'

'We could have gone today,' I pointed out.

'You can't do everything.'

As she walked back up the road towards the large houses of the officers' quarters, I leaned on the gate and watched her. She was already thinking about the book. I could tell from the way she walked, how she started so quickly and then drifted into a saunter, stopping at one point and standing for several minutes by the hedgerow, staring into the darkness. I wanted to call out to her, but felt as though she would hate me for it, resent the intrusion. I went back inside as she turned down towards the houses.

FIFTEEN

The November mornings were damp and cold. Rain lashed against the windows and the range in the kitchen roared up the back chimney, heating the walls. Our hens pecked miserably in the mud. The fields were dank and empty, the house lost in dense fog.

At the end of the month, there was a party on the camp to celebrate a successful launching of Nemesis.

A detachment of servicemen from the camp had travelled to America and taken part in the launching of the missile, and several of the scientists decided to throw a party. The launching had taken place on the west coast, at Vanburg AFB, and most of the detachment were still out there, waiting for a flight home, but the local scientists didn't want to delay until their return. They wanted a party.

'I don't see what there is to celebrate,' Barbara said as she cycled with me one morning to deliver the eggs to Wilfred and Emily. 'Why celebrate slaughter?'

'They're scientists,' I said, giving the answer Caroline had given me.

Barbara wasn't impressed.

'Do you have to do this?' She shivered, her blonde hair wet from the clinging mist, her teeth chattering.

'I like it.'

'You live like primitives,' she laughed, turning down the hill into the village after me and free-wheeling past as I tried to balance the eggs on my handlebars. 'You don't even have central heating.'

'We've got the range.'

'All that work.'

'My mother does the work.'

'Exactly,' she said.

The party was held in one of the houses on the green. When Matthew and I arrived, loud music was thumping from the record player, and every room in the house was packed with people shrieking and shouting, talking and dancing to the music, stumbling up the dark stairs.

'When you know that something really repulsive is heading your way at the speed of light, what do you do?' a sour American scientist asked me as soon as Matthew and I arrived.

'I don't know.' I waited for him to tell me.

'You British are all the same,' he said testily.

He stabbed his finger into Matthew's chest, and raised his eyebrows. Matthew had a CND badge pinned to his lapel. It was the early days of CND. Some of the Americans on the camp felt got at.

'We're here to protect you,' the scientist said to Matthew as if explaining something to a four-year-old child. 'We're here to keep the peace.'

'I need a drink,' Matthew said impudently, deliberately ignoring the scientist.

We went inside and stood and watched couples dancing.

'You know they broadcast a lullaby during the countdown for Trinity,' Matthew shouted, spilling half his beer on the carpet.

'What's Trinity?' I shouted back.

'It was the first bomb. At Los Alamos. They played Tchaikovsky's "Serenade for Strings" over the radio.'

'And the scientists danced?'

'Probably.'

'What does your father think?'

'He thinks they're great. He loves Americans.'

'It's a boy,' a tall, greying officer told me proudly, offering me a tray of drinks and glancing contemptuously at Matthew. A boy meant that the launch had been successful. If it had failed, it would have been a girl.

'The bomb they dropped on Hiroshima was a boy,' Matthew said cheerfully.

During the party, an intense scientist from Ohio told me all about nuclear weapons. They got their power from nothing more complicated than an equation, he assured me, awed by the simplicity of it all. 'When a pound of uranium-235 is fissioned,' he said, 'the liberated mass within its atoms is multiplied by the speed of light squared.'

He asked me whether I could imagine travelling at 186,000 miles per second, squared.

I found it difficult.

For a joke, the people throwing the party played Cliff Richard's 'Travellin' Light', and every time the record started they all cheered.

We drank toasts to the boys at Vanburg, and as we left somebody changed the record for Miles Davis's new album, *Kind Of Blue*. I had never heard of him.

'I want to stay,' I argued with Matthew, swallowing my third whisky and listening to the hypnotic rhythm of the music. 'I want to listen.'

In the hall, the scientist from Ohio grabbed my arm and told me that I had to read Norman Mailer's *Advertisements for Myself*.

'It's the book,' he shouted at me drunkenly. 'It's the book.'

Hardly anybody had spoken to Matthew.

'What did you wear it for?' I asked angrily, pointing at his badge, annoyed at leaving the party.

'Show them.'

'You think they care?'

'You don't know Americans.'

'Why should they care? They just thought you were being offensive.'

'They want to be liked.'

'I like them,' I yelled, banging my hands together and giggling as the words ricocheted round the green. 'I love them.'

'Like my father.'

I went back home alone and wrote down *Kind Of Blue* and Norman Mailer.

I lay on the bed and stared at the bookshelf full of books.

My parents must have been bewildered by this new passion. I had spent four years in secondary education being told I was too stupid to read books such as *Wind in the Willows*, and now suddenly I started filling my room with authors my parents had never heard of.

They blamed Matthew, and ridiculed the idea of reading.

He carried a copy of the *Alexandria Quartet* with him wherever he went.

'You take too much notice of him,' my father said angrily whenever I mentioned Matthew's name.

'I thought you liked him.'

'He's a fool.'

'He's my friend.'

My father looked at me as if I had said something indecent.

94

'He's been to grammar school,' my mother said, as if she was having a different conversation. When my father glared at her, she flinched, and went on staring out of the window.

I had the recording of *Under Milk Wood* from the library. Liz had told me to listen to it when I said I couldn't understand the poems. Matthew and I sat up all night at weekends, drinking black coffee and listening to the rich Welsh voices, and then went for long walks through the countryside, talking about what we were going to do.

Matthew was now determined to be a dramatist.

'I have a talent for dialogue,' he said pompously.

'You mean you like talking.'

'I mean I have a talent for dialogue. It just takes time to realise it.'

If he failed to be a dramatist, he would be a sports writer.

I would be a journalist.

I forgot all about working for exams.

At the college, I sat in Liz's room and asked her why the principal had refused to let me change courses.

She blushed, pushing her tightly permed hair back off her forehead and pretending to read the book she held open on her knees. She was wearing a string of expensive pearls, and her breasts pushed against her cardigan, plump and taut whenever she moved. She looked up suddenly and saw me watching her, smiled and blushed again, her mouth slightly open, her eyes shining as if she was upset.

'You don't need exams,' she said, as if we weren't sitting in her study doing extra work for the papers I would have to sit at the end of the year. She shook her head. 'You know what I mean.'

'Not really.'

'To do what you want to do.'

'I want to be a journalist,' I said flatly, puzzled by her smile, the heat in the room. She always had the radiators turned right up. She closed the book and eased herself off the desk, brushing her skirt down over her knees.

I stood up and our faces were close together.

She was trembling.

She handed me the book and told me which passages to read.

A line of perspiration shone on her top lip, and she reached out and touched my arm quickly, blushing again, fiddling with her hair nervously.

Suddenly, there was a quick tap on the door and Cantor walked in. He was carrying a file. He stopped in the doorway, glancing at Liz and then at me. He lifted his hand nervously and touched the side of his face, and then held out the file towards her. Before she could take it, he seemed to change his mind or forget why he'd come. He pushed the file under his arm and glared at me.

'I told you to stop bothering Miss Maxted,' he shouted suddenly. 'I told you to concentrate on your work.'

Liz sat down on the edge of her desk and pretended to be looking through her files. Her desk was always littered with files.

'I think this is the one you wanted, Leonard,' she said brightly, holding a file out to him.

When she spoke, his face drained of colour.

I stood by the radiator and jumped when the hot metal burned my hand.

'It's all right, Leonard,' Liz was saying.

'It is not all right.'

'I was setting some work.'

'It is not all right,' Cantor repeated furiously.

'I'll see you later, Stephen,' Liz said to me. 'I'll see you when you've finished the work.'

On the bus journey home, I sat with the girl who had teased Matthew about the milking, and she told me her father was thinking of going in for pheasant shooting. He had always planted kale for sheep grazing, but this year he planned to use it for pheasant cover. He owned four thousand acres of the best farming land in the country. After high school, the girl was going to farming college.

It was raining when I got off the bus.

'I'm doing cheese on toast,' my mother told me excitedly when I got into the kitchen.

The fire was roaring at the back of the range, and the radio was playing dance music. I dumped my things in the hall and sat down by the fire, trying to warm my hands.

'You used to like cheese on toast,' my mother told me as she handed me the plate.

The cheese was grated thickly and toasted in layers so that it bubbled and crisped under the grill. In places it had browned. I took huge mouthfuls and drank a hot cup of tea. The fire warmed my face and I felt tired and comfortable, sitting in the huge kitchen.

The floor was covered with thick rugs, and the rain lashed at the windows, splattering with gusts of wind.

'I used to do it for you after school,' my mother said, sitting down with her own cup of tea and resting her feet on the fender. The flames shone on the polished brass. The tiles glowed their delicate green. 'I used to meet you out of school and then do cheese on toast and muffins and bread and jam.'

She laughed quietly, staring into the flames.

She had tiny lines round her eyes, and her eyes were dark as if she needed sleep.

'Is your toast all right?' she asked politely, looking up as if she'd just noticed me sitting there.

'It's fine.'

In my room, I played the Miles Davis on the record player.

I glanced through the book Liz had given me, reading the passages she had recommended, but there didn't seem to be anything there, a long-winded description of a shipwreck that could have been rewritten in half the words.

I kept thinking about Cantor's words. I kept seeing his drained, angry expression, his fury at finding me in the room. I couldn't believe he was upset about me sitting with Liz Maxted. I couldn't understand his sudden temper.

I closed the book and listened to the record.

I wanted to go round and see Caroline, but the rain seemed to be drowning the fields, a torrential cold downpour that drummed and lashed across the garden, howled in the bare branches of the trees. I shivered and sat listening to the rain, the radio playing downstairs in the kitchen. In a few minutes, my mother would go through to watch television, and there would be nothing but the sound of the rain.

I sat and had no idea what I was doing, alone in this booklined bedroom, listening to the chilling rain.

I felt like a criminal.

In the morning, Caroline called at the house and helped me feed the chickens.

The ground was sodden.

The chickens came reluctantly from the hut and pecked at the flooded earth. Their feathers were splashed with mud. I poured food into the troughs and watched the hens squabble and flutter round the metal rims. The bird that was our favourite pecked my hand furiously when I tried to lift her to show Caroline, and I dropped her to the ground, kicking her against the trough.

'I thought you might come round last night,' Caroline said as we walked back to the house.

'In that rain?'

'Is that what stopped you?'

In the kitchen, I made some tea and heaped coal onto the fire.

'Where's your mother?'

'She's gone to the market.'

I had to catch the next bus for college.

'I'm not going in today,' Caroline explained, sitting down by the fire and warming her hands. 'I thought we might go for a ride.'

'I've got college.'

'You can miss a day.'

We spent the morning listening to records. She wanted to hear all my collection, especially the early rock 'n' roll records. She made me dance with her to 'Mystery Train' and 'Blue Suede Shoes', stomping on the floor until my father shouted upstairs and made us bring the record player into the front room.

'I love Presley,' Caroline shouted above the music, making me play 'Tutti Frutti' three times because my father had complained about the noise. 'I love your records.'

My father came through and told us he was expecting somebody from the camp. 'Aren't you supposed to be at college?' he asked, controlling his temper because of Caroline. He knew her father. He wouldn't say anything in front of Caroline. 'Studying or something?'

Caroline was delighted by the sarcasm. She made me play 'Hound Dog' just to annoy him and then we went out into the cold and cycled down to the village, eating bread and cheese at the Plough and drinking cider by the open fire.

In the late-afternoon light, we stood outside the church and watched the weather-vane turning.

'You are good-looking,' she said suddenly, turning to me and examining my face as if she had just noticed for the first time. 'You're not at all like your father.'

'He used to be good-looking,' I said.

'I don't like heavy men.'

'He used to look like Spencer Tracy.'

She snorted, linking her arm in mine and turning me away from the churchyard.

'Let's go and see a film,' she said suddenly, squeezing my arm and excited. 'Let's go and see something in town.'

I held her shoulders and kissed her clumsily on the mouth.

Her lips were firm and cold, and she kept her eyes open.

She smiled when I stood back. 'That took you long enough,' she said.

We caught the bus into town and went to the cinema, and it was gone midnight when we hitched a lift back to the camp.

SIXTEEN

An outbreak of cannibalism lost us two of our weakest hens, and on a bleak February morning, Frank had to come from the farm and sever the beaks with a hacksaw. The hens lay stunned in his arms, and I stood in the driving rain and watched, my head soaked, my back rigid and shivering. Frank came into the kitchen afterwards and warmed his hands at the range, drinking tea and listening to my mother's questions about the farm. She said she wanted a job, and thought working with animals might suit her, after her childhood in the country. Frank said he would ask the foreman.

When I woke up the next morning I was sweating, my back and kidneys aching as if I had flu, my throat burning. I could hardly breathe. The doctor came on his way round the villages, and for three weeks I lay in my room, racked by bronchitis and then listless and depressed from the exhaustion.

Matthew came nearly every day. He sat by the bed and, as I gradually recovered, told me about things at the college, about Hemingway dying and the television programmes about Paris and Sylvia Beach and the lost generation.

'How did he die?' I asked when he brought me a second-hand copy of Hemingway's short stories from a shop near the cathedral.

'Maybe I shouldn't tell you.'

'Why not?'

'He put a gun in his mouth and shot himself.'

'You think I'm going to kill myself?'

'You're pretty low.'

'I've had bronchitis,' I said sourly, pulling the sheets up round my shoulders and settling down in the warmth. 'I'm not going to kill myself. Besides, I haven't got a gun.'

During the long hours, I tried to read *Crime and Punishment*.

'You should, if you're going into crime,' Matthew said.

During the fever, I read the chapter about the horse, the frenzy of the drunken men, the whip lashing across the horse's eyes, the maddened cheering crowd, the frightened boy. I felt sick in my stomach, and stumbled across the landing to the bathroom, retching into the toilet. Back in bed, the sheets were soaked. I read on to the scene with the old woman, the axe fracturing and crushing her skull, the blood soaking into the carpet, Raskolnikov's clumsy fingers desperately trying to unfasten the ribbon for the key. And then the other woman, the sister, Lisaveta, lifting her hand to her face, reaching out as if to push the hatchet away, the blow splitting her forehead wide open, penetrating almost to the bone.

Coming in to see how I was, my father glanced at the book. He thought it was a crime novel, flicking through the dense pages. He read the blurb on the back and looked puzzled, throwing the book back on to the bed and asking me how I was. When I closed my eyes, I kept seeing the men my father had found in the barn, two of them sleeping, the third with his eye hanging down his face. My father brought me a glass of barley water and the evening paper, and went down to the office to finish his work.

One Sunday afternoon, Barbara came to visit, bringing grapes and chocolates and flowers and sitting in the bedroom all afternoon, playing the records and searching through my bookshelves, gossiping about the camp and the new families who had arrived for another stage of testing the rocket. When Barbara went downstairs to help my mother with the tea, I lay in the warmth, listening to their voices in the kitchen, wondering why Caroline refused to visit.

'She can't stand illness,' Barbara told me. 'She faints if you even talk about it.'

'Coward.' I managed to grin.

I could hear my mother working downstairs.

I covered myself with the blankets and shivered, suddenly frozen. The sheets were clammy and wet.

I closed my eyes and wanted to cry into the pillows. I felt sick, and exhausted, and then drifted into sleep. I woke up suddenly, I saw my mother carrying the tea things into the room, Barbara holding the door for her. They were joking about me enjoying all the attention.

I went to sleep with Barbara chattering about Brooklyn, pouring the tea and asking my mother endless questions about what it was like being married to a policeman. Occasionally, my mother would ask a question about New York, the words sounding awkward the way she said them.

101

'You'd make a real fine policeman,' Barbara told me when my mother said something about my arguments with my father.

I pretended to be asleep, but she poked the bed with her foot, telling my mother I was nervous.

'He thinks he might not live up to his father,' she said seriously, and my mother shook her head, not understanding, feeling complimented by her interest.

I went to sleep, and Barbara stayed for hours, having tea with my mother and then watching television.

It was Matthew who brought the news about Liz.

Cantor's wife had died, and there had been a scene at the college when he came back from the funeral and burst into one of the afternoon lectures. 'She was talking about Goethe,' Matthew said solemnly. 'About the time she spent in Germany.'

I had never heard of Goethe. 'Who's Goethe?'

'Don't be aggressive.'

'I'm not being aggressive.'

'Yes, you are. You feel humiliated by your ignorance, so you turn aggressive.'

'I just asked who he is.'

'A German poet.'

Cantor walked into the lecture and asked the students to leave.

A girl told Matthew all about it.

'I want to talk to you,' Cantor said to Liz.

'I'm teaching.'

'I need to talk to you.'

'I have to tell them about Goethe.'

'I have to speak to you.'

He was crying.

His black suit was covered with petals from the damaged funeral flowers. They'd disintegrated in the rain. He gestured hopelessly with his hands, the stalks of the flowers blackened and bruised by his pain, the petals scattering on the classroom floor.

He turned and walked out of the room.

'She resigned,' Matthew said finally.

'They'll get married,' I suggested.

'They can't get married.'

'Why not?'

'They were having an affair.'

I thought about her in her room, sitting on the desk, telling me what to read.

'She's going back to Germany,' Matthew said. 'With her children.'

Matthew sat on the edge of the bed, staring out of the window. We couldn't think of anything to say.

'How long is this illness of yours going to last?' he asked after a long silence.

'I don't know.'

'I miss you.'

'Sod off.'

'It's true.'

'Piss off, Matthew.'

'I find you entertaining.'

He went downstairs and I could hear him telling my mother I ought to get up and go back to college. He said something about examinations. My father was in the yard, oiling his bicycle chain. He spun the wheels and then went into the kitchen, slamming the door and going through to the office. He couldn't stand having Matthew in the house.

Caroline came in the third week.

I was sitting in an armchair in the front room, propped up so that I could see out of the window. I was trying to listen to the radio and practise my shorthand. I had never got much further than sixty words a minute, and in the last three weeks seemed to have forgotten most of the forms. I looked up, and Caroline was wheeling her bicycle up the drive. She was wearing jeans, a yellow blouse and a tweed jacket. I waved and she lifted her hand, her dark hair shining in the winter sunlight, her eyes very blue in her pale face. She looked thin and tired.

'I can't stand illness,' she said, sitting down and holding my hand.

Her face was white and her lips were pale with the cold. She went and stood by the fire and then came back and kissed me quickly on the forehead. I could see her nipples dark brown through the yellow blouse, her long neck still tanned from the previous summer. She seemed restless, unsettled, unhappy on the hard chair.

'My parents are both out,' I said, trying to make her sit down.

She shook her head and went through to the kitchen, putting the kettle on to make tea.

'You've been ill,' she said seriously.

'Bronchitis.'

'I know that.'

She seemed to be lost in thought.

'I thought you might come,' I said.

'I told you, I can't stand illness.'

'Bronchitis?'

'It's still illness, isn't it?'

'I suppose.'

'You had Matthew.'

We both laughed, and she flushed suddenly, looking away.

'I heard about the cannibalism,' she said abruptly, walking up and down the room, holding her cup and saucer. She pushed her fringe back, out of her eyes.

'Cannibalism?'

'Your mother told me.'

'It happens sometimes.'

I didn't know why she was talking about it.

'I think it's dreadful,' she said, staring at me, unable to sit down or listen. 'I think you should get rid of them.'

'They aren't mine.'

'She should get rid of them.'

'They're all right.'

'They're not all right.'

'It's natural . . .'

'Don't you understand anything?'

She stood in the middle of the room crying.

I felt my face go bright red and my head aching.

I could see my father coming up the drive.

'I'm the one who's supposed to be ill,' I said.

She left as soon as my father came in for his tea.

'Girls,' my mother said, as if that explained something.

I just wanted to laugh, she seemed so ridiculous, crying when she'd come to see me, standing there and making me feel like death.

I kept thinking about Liz Maxted.

*

Before she left, she wrote me a brief note, and arranged to see me at the college. We sat in the canteen alone. She was wearing a red suit and bright red lipstick. She looked as if she had been crying.

'His wife was in a wheelchair for eighteen years,' she told me. 'She needed somebody with her every hour of the day. That's why they never had any children.'

I nodded, listening, trying to understand.

She seemed to be speaking to herself.

'He had to look after her,' she said, shaking her head and staring miserably at the table. 'He had to feel he was doing the right thing.'

She gestured hopelessly with her hands.

I thought she was crying, but when she looked up, she managed to smile, her face flushed, her eyes bright and angry.

'I didn't like her, you see. I couldn't stand her. She just wasn't a very nice woman . . . '

She stopped again, lifting her hands off the table, shrugging hopelessly.

'She wouldn't have wanted children anyway.'

I wanted to ask her about Germany. I wanted to talk to her about my work and the chance of getting on to a newspaper. I wanted to tell her about the things I had been reading.

'How are you?' she asked after a long silence.

I told her I was all right.

'I could write to you,' she said vaguely, and then shook her head again, lost in her own thoughts.

'I don't know why you're going,' I said.

'No.'

'I thought you could stay.'

She looked up at me. She sat very still, staring down at her cup, looking up again quickly and licking her lips as if she was about to speak.

She touched my hand and then pushed the hair behind her ears.

'I can't think of anything to say,' she said.

She left the canteen, promising to write, and I stayed for a long time at the table, unable to get up and walk away.

It was late afternoon when I left the college.

I hadn't said anything about Cantor.

SEVENTEEN

'You lost a stone during that illness,' the doctor said with some concern, and I exercised furiously to get back into shape. I cycled round the lanes first thing in the morning, and went for long runs when I got back from college in the evenings. I ate steaks and did press-ups, and helped my father dig the garden. I sat for hours and practised my shorthand, and typed like a maniac to catch up with the speed tests. Sometimes, I got off the bus two or three miles from home, and ran along the edge of the road, pounding through the rough grass, jarring my muscles on the road.

Some evenings Barbara joined me on the road, cycling along beside me or running behind in the long grass, chatting as if we had been friends all our lives. I always felt at ease with Barbara.

'You look fit,' I told her the evening she arrived in her tracksuit, her hair scraped back and fastened with a silk headscarf, her eyes shining as she took deep breaths and did some loosening exercises.

'I used to do track,' she told me, and cheered ironically when I raced ahead of her, easily overtaking me and waving as she loped along the road, unperturbed by the rough camber or the cars hooting at her to get out of the way, ignoring the shouts from the drivers.

Occasionally, we ran down into the village, and drank cider in the Plough before making our way back.

'We ought to drink fruit juice,' Barbara pointed out as we drained the glasses of cider and stuffed ourselves with crisps and peanuts. 'We're not really serious if we eat this garbage.'

She was soon running with me almost every morning.

I told her about Cantor's wife, Liz Maxted going back to Germany.

'Poor woman,' she said when I'd finished. 'She must feel awful.'

'I don't see why she doesn't marry him,' I said impatiently.

'Why?'

'If she loved him . . . '

'She might not want to be married. She's got the children.'

I didn't know what she was talking about.

I felt resentful that Liz had gone to Germany. I felt as though

106

she'd deliberately left me behind, forgetting all the talk about my studies, leaving me to sort things out with Cantor.

I gave up the idea of being a journalist.

I would have to argue the whole thing with my father and Cantor, and I felt too confused to explain what I wanted.

At Christmas, there was a card and brief letter from Germany. In the letter, Liz said she was sorry she couldn't help me through my exams, but was sure I would do all right. In the card, she sent her love.

I felt worse than ever after that, and kept them both hidden in my room. I didn't even tell Matthew.

By early April the farmers were out in the fields, drilling spring wheat and sugar beet, kale in the fields around the police house. The woods at the bottom of the cliff were full of violets, yellow with early primroses.

'I thought the winter would have finished them,' Barbara said, thinking about the late frosts.

In Wilfred's orchard, the ground close to the beck was thick with marsh marigolds, and the grass was smothered with daisies. I found him spraying the trees early one morning.

'You got to spray against apple scab,' he told me, tottering on the ladders. 'Spray and water. They like lots of water late spring.'

'Are you safe up there, Wilfred?'

'I am. Water in dry spells. Affects the size of the fruit, you see.'

'I don't think you should be doing that . . . '

'Do it every year. After flowering, so that the fruit isn't too big. They're very prone to scab, these trees, and blossom weevil, you know, caterpillars and greenfly. Like to keep on top. Do it every year. My old dad taught me.'

At the college, Matthew and I sat out on the lawns with some of the girls, pretending to do revision. The girls talked crudely about their boyfriends, laughing about the way they got excited, wanted it all the time. Joanna, a thin, malicious girl with colourless, cruel eyes told us she had been staying with her friend Sheila at the weekend. Sheila was doing another course in the college, a plump, vacuous girl with hot luscious breasts covered, according to Joanna, with horrendous love bites that must have driven her boyfriend to distraction, or her.

Joanna thought it was disgusting.

'Did you do them?' Matthew asked pleasantly.

'Oh, *you*!'

'I just wondered. You've got lovely sharp teeth.'

I went to mass one Sunday because Barbara asked me. I couldn't follow the service, the quickly mumbled Latin. I kept kneeling at the wrong moments, some memory from visits to a different church in the past. In the silence, I could hear Matthew whistling outside, waiting for us to go to the pub. He whistled very loudly. When we left the church, Matthew walked all the way round me, pretending to be looking for my halo.

'It must make some difference,' he said with a puzzled frown when Barbara asked him what the hell he thought he was doing.

'It makes a difference,' she said firmly.

'But I can't see it.'

'Do you have to be able to see everything?'

'Absolutely.'

He went on with his ridicule, angry, resentful, not once looking me in the eye. When I told him to piss off he roared with laughter and shook his head solemnly.

'I'm glad you're all right,' he said. 'I was beginning to get worried.'

'For Christ's sake, leave it, Matthew,' Barbara shouted at him.

'For Christ's sake,' he agreed solemnly.

In the pub, he told us he was going to write a play about a man who worked on a chicken farm and then sabotaged the batteries when he was converted to religion. The climax of the play would have thousands of birds flying around the stage, and the men closing in on the victim, like the rednecks in one of Tennessee Williams's Southern dramas.

I had read all of Tennessee Williams's plays during my illness, along with Dostoevsky and Lawrence Durrell. I could imagine the young man trapped between the cages by the farmhands, a dark-haired, calm girl standing and watching from the shadows, a distant gargle of tractors like the mysterious sounds in Chekhov's *Cherry Orchard*. I had read all of Chekhov as well, wallowing in the long silences, the empty, stunning landscape, sounds carrying for miles.

'I don't get Raskolnikov,' I told Matthew.

'It's about redemption,' he said airily.

'It's about murder,' I snapped.

'Precisely . . . '

'Defenceless old women . . . '

'*Precisely* . . . '

I spent nearly all my time reading. I felt as though I wanted to read everything I'd missed in my years at school. I wanted to read the books Matthew and Barbara mentioned so casually, understand what they were talking about while I still had time. I hardly bothered with the work at college. Without Liz to help, there didn't seem much point, and I began to fail the tests in shorthand and typing. I missed several lectures and had to report to Cantor. He didn't even listen while I lied about doing my best, finding the work difficult. I told Matthew I had changed my mind about being a journalist, and lay awake at night, stunned at the thought of going into the police, incapable of explaining to my father that there was something else I really wanted to do.

He had been happy in the police. He wanted me to have the same security and chances. He had no conception of the kind of life I wanted.

I knew I could never tell him.

At the end of term, we had a debate organised by one of the lecturers. I had to propose a motion that capital punishment should be supported. Matthew opposed. I spoke without thinking, talking about the things my father had told me. I mentioned horrific crimes and abused children and murderers who had come out of prison and committed further crimes. Matthew gave details of cases where the wrong person had been hanged. He talked about human fallibility and our duty to forgive, leaving punishment to God. He read extracts from an essay by Shaw, and mocked my appeal to emotion, which he said was nasty. I lost the vote by ninety to seventeen because the audience loved Matthew's sense of humour.

A week later, when I was supposed to be acting as prompt, I left Matthew stranded in the middle of the stage, until he had to come off and grab the book out of my hand before he could finish his scene with Desdemona. It ruined the play.

'Well done,' he said when he came off.

'I lost my place.'

'I bet.'

'I did.'

109

'Did you see my father in the audience?' he asked casually.

I didn't believe his father was there.

Later, when I saw him leaving the college, I felt numbed with regret, knowing the kind of things he would say to Matthew.

I had my interview for the police when term ended.

'You realise you can't become a probationer until you're nineteen?' the training inspector explained.

I nodded numbly.

He was a tall, dark-haired man, overweight from spending most of his life at a desk, his eyes cold and supercilious, his face greasy and tight-skinned.

I sat the test and was measured for a uniform.

I would have to get my hair cut, but they measured me for a cap anyway. I was shown the kind of uniform I would be getting. I went round headquarters with another cadet, and he laughed when I told him I had been studying at college.

'Waste of time,' he said. 'You want to get stuck in.'

I passed the test and the training inspector told me I would be expected at the beginning of June. I would spend several months in headquarters, and then be posted to a division.

'We can't guarantee it will be the same as your father's,' he said coldly. 'Do you mind?'

'No.'

'No, sir.'

I said the word for the first time.

I felt like one of the young Americans, the servicemen who called everybody sir.

'You don't like living at home?'

'I don't mind.'

'Sir.'

'I don't mind, sir.'

'We'll see what we can manage.'

I caught the bus back to the camp and saw Caroline being brought home from school by her father. She waved and I waited until she reached the bus stop.

'You look miserable,' she said, swinging her satchel over her shoulder and looking at me happily.

'I am.'

'You want to go for a walk to the village?'

'All right.'

'Just let me get changed.'

She went back to her house and I waited in the bus stop. It was nearly four o'clock, and the camp was busy with traffic, music thumping from car radios, servicemen queuing up for the buses into town. A car drew up, and the driver offered lifts to anybody going his way. Four or five servicemen got into the back of the Studebaker, and the car pulled out into the traffic, leaving me alone in the shelter.

Caroline came back wearing jeans and a dark blue sweatshirt. She had on white gym shoes. She had touched her lips quickly with pink lipstick.

'You do look miserable,' she said again, taking my arm and stumbling along the verge beside me.

I felt stiff and awkward.

There was pollen in the air and already my eyes were aching.

I didn't want to tell her about the interview.

I felt desperate about what was happening, as if a prison sentence was closing in and there was nothing I could do about it. I knew this was how friends at school had talked about national service, the misery of going away for two years and having no right to refuse, no say in what happened. I felt like that, even though I was signing the papers myself. I was free to do what I wanted, and I hadn't the energy even to think about it.

There was no way I wanted to say all this to Caroline.

We walked down to the village and went and had tea with Wilfred and Emily. He chattered amicably to Caroline, and took her off to show her round the orchard. I sat with Emily and she rocked steadily in her chair, her hands gently trembling, her eyes shining.

I must have been silent for a long time, because she suddenly leaned forward and touched me sharply on the knee.

I looked up.

'You don't have to do it,' she said very firmly, looking at me, refusing to lower her eyes.

I felt my own eyes fill with tears.

'I do,' I said, hardly able to speak.

'Why?' she said sharply.

'I just do,' I said again hopelessly, hearing Caroline and Wilfred laughing in the orchard.

111

Emily shook her head and smiled sadly.

She seemed impatient, and wanted to say something else, but then gave up. 'You'll be all right,' she said, as if she was making me a promise. 'You'll be all right.'

When Caroline came back, we went for a drink in the village, and then walked home to the camp, chatting about her progress with Pasternak, the Russian her father was still teaching her, the A level mock exams she would soon have to start sitting. I saw her home, and refused to go inside. I said I was tired, and needed to do some studying. I walked home, and told my father about the interview.

I did so badly in the exams that Cantor refused to give me a reference. I hadn't been working for weeks and the illness had lost me almost a month's study. I managed a sixty speed test for the shorthand, and a forty for the typing. I failed most of the other exams altogether.

My father went wild.

He came home and found the results on the kitchen table. He brought the envelope upstairs and threw it in my face.

I was reading *Ulysses.*

He ripped the book out of my hands and tore it apart.

When I tried to get up he grabbed the Ellmann biography of Joyce I had borrowed from the library and hurled it against the wall.

The book fell open at a picture of Joyce leaning in a doorway, peering obscurely into the camera.

'Is this how you waste your time?' he yelled, tearing the photograph out of the book and waving it in my face. 'Is this what you call studying?'

'That's a library book.'

'With this rubbish.'

'He's a famous writer . . . '

'You'll not go on doing it.'

'I like reading.'

'You'll not do it!'

He hurled the book across the room and slammed out of the bedroom.

I heard him ranting on the stairs.

He went out into the yard and shouted up to my window.

'Bloody twisted queers . . . '

I sat stunned in my room.

I Sellotaped the page back into the book, my fingers trembling.

In the morning, he said he had telephoned police headquarters and they were still prepared to accept me, provided I passed another simple entrance examination. They weren't as bothered about the college results as my father. Apparently shorthand and typing would be very useful, and the training inspector said shorthand speeds could always be improved with practice. It was the theory that was difficult.

My father seemed to want to apologise.

I took the biography back to the library and paid a fine for damaging library property.

On a warm afternoon, I burned what was left of *Ulysses* on a fire in the garden.

At the end of that week, I saw the fire engines racing across the runways, the clouds of liquid oxygen rising from Nemesis. It was supposed to be the usual Saturday morning testing.

The emergency telephone was ringing.

I ran from the house and got my bicycle. I cycled up the road and along the perimeter. The fire engines were racing towards the rocket. At the compound, three fire engines seemed to be on fire. Clouds of liquid oxygen filled the air around the rocket.

Matthew was already there.

We watched the fire engines wheeling towards the compound.

Sirens wailed and emergency staff were running in all directions, more fire engines and military jeeps heading from the hangars.

'My dad's out there,' Matthew said quietly.

When I got home, my father told me what had happened. There had been a spillage of liquid oxygen, six thousand gallons escaping and destroying the cast iron base on which Nemesis rested. The spillage had destroyed the fire engines standing thirty yards away. Civilian emergency services were standing by. That night, Matthew came round and told us his father was safe. He had been watching from the control office. The spillage had happened because at the fifteen-second firing stage, one of the Americans had forgotten to throw the switch for shutdown. Pressing the shutdown button late had caused the liquid oxygen to spill instead of evaporate. Another five seconds and the rocket would have fired.

'Don't be silly,' my mother said impatiently.

'I'm not.'

'They wouldn't let something like that happen.'

'Perfectly safe,' Matthew told her. 'It was only a dummy head. They keep the warheads in the hangars.'

EIGHTEEN

'A midsummer night party,' Matthew announced. 'It's obvious.'
'Is it?'

He quoted: '"I know a bank whereon the wild thyme blows, /where oxlips and the nodding violet grows,/quite over-canopied with luscious woodbine,/with sweet musk-roses, and with eglantine."'

'Round here?'

'Wilfred and Emily might let us use their orchard,' he suggested enthusiastically. 'Just imagine. You could take Caroline.'

My mother thought it was a lovely idea.

When Caroline arrived at the police house, she made her sit in the front room which we never used and told my father to make a cup of tea. Caroline was wearing a long white dress and she had her hair tied up behind her ears. She sat on the edge of the chair and listened while my mother told us about a party she had gone to on the farm where she was working.

'I was a child,' she giggled, touching my father's arm when he brought the tray of tea. He was in too good a mood to be irritated. He winked at Caroline and poured the tea clumsily, spilling some of it into the saucers. My mother fluttered round the room as if she was going to the party herself, and my father made some crude joke about the woods, making Caroline laugh unnaturally.

'Stephen says you're studying languages,' he said awkwardly, holding his tea and standing in the doorway.

'Music,' I said impatiently. 'We have to go.'

'I love music,' my mother said.

I knew she was going to start listing the records we had.

'I love Beethoven,' she said shyly, her eyes very bright, her hands dancing in front of her. 'Don't I, Norman?'

'Wouldn't know, love,' he replied. 'I'm tone deaf,' he told Caroline. 'I like a good dance, though.'

In the drive, Caroline took my arm and I could feel her body close to my own, her thighs brushing against mine as I opened the gate. She was warm from lying on the lawn all afternoon. The white

115

dress was soft like velvet and clung to her flat stomach, tightening underneath her breasts. Her hair was tied up with a white ribbon, and she had pale blue eyeliner round her eyes and a pale, delicate lipstick, pink shaded with white. Her eyes were shaped to points, so that she looked almost Chinese. She was wearing white ankle boots, and the dress had knotted tassels which swung around her long legs.

'I'm actually going to read mathematics,' she said suddenly, leaning on my arm while we waited for one of her father's friends to take us to the party. 'My father says I can always listen to music, and he reads constantly. He's read far more than most literature professors. He says reading should be a natural pleasure, an accomplishment, not a career. He admires you for trying to read.'

A white Oldsmobile pulled into the side of the road and Barbara and Matthew waved from inside, shrieking and laughing at my flannels and thick jumper. I crushed into the front seat beside Caroline and the driver turned round and shook my hand, saying he was pleased to meet me and hoped we had a good time at the party. He was a colonel who worked with Caroline's father on the fuel programme for the rocket.

'Ain't nothing like a party,' he shouted. 'Unless you reckon a baseball game.'

As the car bounced back into the traffic, he turned the radio up very loud and sang to the music. In the back, Matthew sat and pulled faces at Barbara. I felt hot and uncomfortable.

I shut my eyes and felt Caroline's body close to my own as we collided with the kerb.

With a blast of horns, we were swinging down the lane into the village.

'Right on,' the Colonel brayed to the night. 'Wow,' he bellowed at the wheel of his bouncing, walloping car.

I was already beginning to feel sick.

I went straight to the table where they had the cider and started drinking.

The orchard seemed to be full of voices.

Most of the youngsters on the camp had turned up for the party, and a radio was playing rock 'n' roll.

Between records, owls swooped low above the trees.

Caroline disappeared into the orchard, talking to her friends from the camp.

I wandered around until I found Matthew.

'I've been drinking,' he said, leaning against a tree trunk, his words slurred with the cider.

'It's a party,' I said.

'Before,' he said with a belch.

He drained his glass. He dropped the glass to the ground and bent down to pick it up. He rubbed his eyes with the back of his hand and peered at me.

'Fucking driver,' he said.

'What?

'In the car.'

I'd seen him flinch in the car when the Oldsmobile hit the kerb.

'I hate summer,' Matthew said abruptly.

I tried to take his arm, but he wouldn't move.

He was miles away.

'She died in the summer,' he said. 'My mother. She had an accident in the car. She was never much good as a driver. My father said she did it on purpose. She just wasn't a very good driver. He shouldn't have bought such a fast car. He couldn't expect her to know how to manage. She shouldn't have been driving on her own. I thought she'd gone to stay with my grandparents. She was away for days before he told me. I would have found out. On a small camp. Everybody else knew. I thought she was visiting. If he'd bought her a small car she could have got around the camp easily. I think she just hated always travelling. She hated never being in one place. She just wanted to settle down like ordinary people. She wanted a garden. I went to fourteen different schools, and none of them were any use. She just drove off the road and died.'

All around us, voices were calling.

I took him back to the cottage and left him asleep with Wilfred.

When I found Caroline, she was standing by the stream down at the bottom of the orchard.

'Are you really going to study mathematics?' I asked her.

She looked round and shrugged.

'Maybe.'

'Not poetry and music?'

'Mathematics is music.'
'Caroline . . . '
'My father says all music is mathematics.'
'Caroline . . . '
She was standing at the edge of the orchard.
'There was a fox here last summer.'
'Was there?'
'It came down to the stream to drink the water.'
'Did you see it?'
'Wilfred told me.'
'I like Wilfred.'
'It came down from the hills.'
'And Emily.'
She lifted her face to the moon.
The air was choked with blossom, pollen thick in the long grass, the invisible trees pulsing in the hot night.
She made me stand behind her and wrap her in my arms.
I could feel myself hardening as she swayed to the sound of the water.
'Is that you?
'What do you think it is?'
'I don't know.'
She put her hands behind her and stroked me outside the trousers.
'Don't.'
'Isn't it nice?'
'No.'
'Is that better?'
She started to unfasten my trousers, her fingers cold and clumsy.
I tried to turn her round but she refused, leaning her head back against my shoulder and squirming when I kissed her neck. Her skin was cold, and I could see she had her eyes open. She kept squeezing and pulling at me inside the trousers, and when I came she pushed me away, angry and upset, turning on me and then going and kneeling down beside the stream, washing her hands in the water and shaking her head briefly when I tried to kneel down beside her, pushing me away again and getting up abruptly to walk back through the orchard. I stood up to follow her, and then sat down again, my trousers and underpants

soaked and cold, my hands shaking and my head aching from all the cider.

At midnight, I got up and walked along the edge of the stream through the trees. I stumbled in the long grass and got my feet and shoes soaked in the deeper water. I could hear the music of the party booming in the distant orchard, and then suddenly the music stopped and there were shrieks and laughter among the trees, voices crying in the darkness. One of them was shouting, 'Caroline,' and then another called my name. I thought I could hear Matthew. Then there was a long silence and the nightjars filled the air, throbbing above the silent meadows. In the darkness, I heard an owl. I stood outside the crumbling eighteenth-century mansion, and watched the moon glide behind the clouds, the beech and ash woods motionless in the night air. Far away, a fox barked.

PART II

He Do the Police in Different Voices

NINETEEN

On my first morning, the training inspector was visiting one of the divisions and wouldn't be back until the afternoon.

'He said you should read the crime reports,' his secretary told me irritably, fiddling with her hair and staring at the letter she was in the middle of typing. 'Learn the definitions of felonies and misdemeanours. He's left a textbook for you.'

I waited for her to explain, and she looked up after a long silence as if surprised to see me still there. She sniffed and ripped the sheet of paper out of the typewriter.

'I suppose you don't know where they are,' she said, and led me out of the tiny room down a corridor to the back of the building.

County headquarters were in an old mansion not far from the cathedral. The main hall was oak-panelled and dark, and there were oil paintings of all the county's chief constables on the stairs up to the first floor. The long corridors were thickly carpeted and panelled, and ornate chandeliers hung from the high ceiling in the hall. I could hear telephones ringing, typewriters hammering in the offices. Dozens of police cars were parked at the front of the building, and uniformed men and women came in and out all the time.

The crime reports were filed away in a room next to CID.

'We call it the library,' Jaines's secretary informed me.

Her face was tight with wrinkles, and she held her hands together in front of her while she was talking, as if she was about to pray. She had withered, self-righteous lips and bitter eyes.

The radio in the information room boomed through the library walls. The big windows overlooked long gardens which sloped steeply away from the house. The windows were barred. There was a table and chair in the window, with a metal reading lamp. The walls were dingy green. I could hear men arguing in the information room, the blare of the radio, telephones ringing. The information room was in touch with all the divisions by switchboard and radio, and every patrol car in the vast countryside.

'I'm Mrs Berry,' the woman told me as she turned to leave the room. 'I'll fetch you when the inspector gets back.'

123

'Could you tell me where the toilets are?' I asked, and she let out another sigh of exasperation.

'You won't make much of a policeman, will you?' she said testily, and was out of the room before I could answer, slamming the door behind her.

I took some of the files and sat down at the desk.

A copy of the police common law manual, Moriarty, lay open on the desk, with a note from Jaines instructing me to learn the definitions of felonies and misdemeanours.

I flicked through the thick, black-bound book.

'Cadet training's largely a matter of learning from experience,' the superintendent from my father's division had joked with my father on one of his visits to the camp. 'Nobody knows what else to do with the buggers. You'll get a bit of marching about, Stephen, but, apart from that, if you learn anything it'll be from being out on the job. Only don't tell Charlie Jaines I said so.'

Jaines had been more precise.

'There will be lectures on police procedure,' he explained, 'and courses on Moriarty's *Common Law*. Once a week, you will have to attend classes on first aid. There will also be intensive physical exercise, work-outs and parades.'

'Yes, sir.'

'Apart from that,' he said, 'given that you will be in uniform and liable to get involved in any emergency that comes your way, it can be a haphazard and sometimes brutal process of learning.'

He seemed to enjoy listening to his own voice, savouring the words, leaning back in his chair and watching me with his cold sardonic eyes.

It was his eyes that were frightening.

Lifeless, grey.

In the CID library, I looked down at the first of the files and wondered when he would get back to headquarters.

I couldn't believe I was here.

The thing I had never wanted.

I couldn't concentrate.

I stared out of the window, watching a thrush on the lawn, sleek and alert after worms.

With surprise, I realised I was frightened, overwhelmed by the building, the spurious authority of the uniforms, the depersonalising of last names. Even the corridors seemed threatening with their ornate, drab blankness.

I forced myself to open one of the files.

The blue forms were the most important documents in a policeman's life. My father had already told me that. He had shown me some of his own forms one night when he was filing. In clinical, precise language, they gave the details and circumstances of any crime where there was likely to be a prosecution. An officer's notebook would be used for less significant incidents. The blue report forms were used for everything from a motor accident to a murder and, if the crime was serious enough, would come with photographs and medical reports attached. Because they were used for prosecutions, the forms had to be free of all emotion.

Now I was supposed to sit and read a whole library of the things.

I stared at the first of the files.

I knew the name immediately, Henry Taplin, recognised his weak eyes despite the grim institutional photograph.

He had been a teacher at my school, sent to prison for indecent assault not long before we left the coast. Three boys from my own class were mentioned in the file: Patrick Waller, Arthur Dodds and Kevin Drew, rancid, loutish hooligans, terrorising the playground, beating people up, white-eyed and acned from constant fingering. All three had given evidence at the trial. Taplin had been involved with them for years, at weekends and during holidays. For the first time, I was able to read the exact details of his crimes, or the things the court decided were crimes: his pathetic kindness transformed into dangerous guile, his unpleasant fumblings catastrophically redefined, his loneliness savagely ridiculed in the week-long trial.

He had been in the papers for weeks: Henry Taplin, child molester.

'He did it with his mouth,' Patrick Waller said in his statement.

'What did he do?' the police interviewer asked him.

'He put it in his mouth.'

I burst out laughing. I couldn't believe anyone would do that. Waller had the foulest imagination I'd ever come across. I wondered why the police accepted what he said.

He lived in a bleak redbrick terrace with lavatories out the back and infested walls. He spent his days reading comics, hiding them

125

at the back of the class, peering at the lurid cartoons. He spent his evenings on the pier wanking and giggling with anybody who could stand his odour, jerking off in the lavatories or the middle of the pier gardens.

I stared again at the photograph of Taplin. He was a gaunt, grey-haired man in his early forties, whispery, weak, tearful, swinging a knotted rope in the gym, falsely, dangerously aggressive. If you challenged him, his eyes would fill with tears.

They'd cut his hair in the remand prison and nicked the side of his face with the razor.

Sweating and breathing shallowly, he had only once gone near me, leaning over my shoulder during a maths lesson, correcting some arithmetic I couldn't finish. His breath smelt of cigarettes and sweets, and his skin was blotched and pock-marked. He must have known my father was a policeman. He never made any approach. He used to take us swimming and liked to stand and watch us getting undressed. He taught maths and sports. He took parties of boys away for weekends, and was accused of buggering eleven boys on a camping holiday.

At school, we heard that it was Dodds who finally reported him.

'I was painting the ceiling,' Dodds told us, bragging about how he'd finished Taplin's game. We always called him Henry. 'He put his hand up my trousers,' Dodds claimed.

He said he'd poured a tin of paint on Taplin's head.

The police reports said something different.

According to them, Kevin Drew's parents had actually complained to the headmaster and then gone to the police. An inspector in CID had done the rest.

Drew's statement was the worst.

He told the police that Taplin had tossed him off in the showers, and that it was the first time it had ever happened to him.

'What do you mean by "it"?' the detective asked carefully.

Drew said he had felt funny, and then his legs were all wet. He said it made him feel ashamed.

I stared at the words, carefully typed out, the typing making them seem real.

It was Drew who organised wanking sessions in the lavatories every lunch hour. He always watched for new boys at the beginning of the autumn term. After the trial, he sat next to me in the classroom, offering to pull me off if I would tell him what was happening to Taplin. He knew my father was a policeman, and wanted to write to Taplin in prison.

I read on, feeling embarrassed and disturbed.

Dodds and Drew had spent half their lives masturbating and having wanking contests with the rest of the fourth year. Dodds claimed he could shoot his spunk three yards minimum, and joked about Taplin's shrivelled-up penis. In the trial, he said he had never been touched until the teacher interfered with him.

Taplin got seven years in a maximum security prison.

Half-way through the morning, a policewoman fetched me for coffee and showed me round the building, introducing me to people in the traffic department, administration, the chief constable's office, the prosecution department, the information room and CID. We drank our coffee in the canteen and the women behind the counter joked about what would happen if Jaines found me wasting time smoking and drinking.

I went back to the CID library.

Another of the files dealt with a rape.

I remembered the girl from school, Christine Ellis. She had been a couple of years ahead of me. She was married now and had two children. The rape had happened before we left the coast.

She was notorious at school for the afternoon wanking sessions she ran in her parents' suburban sitting room. For sixpence she would pull you off and give you a glass of lemonade before sending you home. Some afternoons, six or seven boys would be lined up on her front-room carpet, waiting for her to unbutton their trousers and stare with mock amazement at their erect tools. I paid my sixpence once, and finished up with wet trousers and a sore cock, and I still remembered the girl's humiliating indifference.

'Isn't it little?' she said with mock surprise when she unfastened my trousers, making everybody in the room sit up and look.

She left school several months' pregnant, and then apparently started going out with a married man who was unlucky enough to be seen making love to her on the sands.

In her statement to the police, the girl gave deliberately vague details of everything the man was supposed to have said and done.

I read the accusations with a kind of stunned outrage.

127

'Then he took his thing out,' she said towards the end of her statement.

'What thing is that, love?' the policewoman doing the interview asked.

It seemed obvious to me, but I soon learned that vagueness was no good in a police statement.

'I don't know,' the girl said after some thought.

'You must have some idea,' the policewoman said.

'No, I don't,' the girl answered.

I snorted in the empty room.

I wanted to tell somebody, share the laughter.

I wanted an audience for her lovely invention.

The radio in the information room boomed down the narrow corridor.

'Then what did he do?' the policewoman went on.

'He asked me to touch it,' the girl said.

'Touch what?'

'His *thing*!' Christine shouted her irritation.

I noticed that the policewoman assigned to the case was a probationer.

She must have thought the girl was deranged.

I thought she was just a liar.

In the man's statement, he talked about his wife and children, and about the girl leading him on, telling him she was already pregnant and engaged to a filleter on the docks. He said he thought she was eighteen. She looked eighteen when she was in the infants. Some of the older boys called her tiger even then, though when I was ten I had no idea why. She loved pressing up against you in the corridors, and outstaring you with her slightly vague grey eyes, misty with some kind of lurid obsession.

The man got three years in Wakefield prison.

During the lunch hour I sat in the information room and listened to the radio operators chatting with the divisions and the patrol cars. A huge map covered the wall in front of the radios, and one of the policewomen kept moving cars around on the map as the reports came in. A long desk stood behind the radios, and several officers manned the telephones and handsets, taking details of incidents, giving instructions. A duty sergeant was in charge of the information room. Men were coming in and out all the time, bringing files, fresh reports. I could see my father's station on the map, and a red drawing pin that said he had last reported from the village and was going on to one of the farms where there had been an incident involving a dog.

When I'd eaten my sandwiches, I walked round the gardens on the narrow gravel path, and sat on one of the benches in the hot midday sun. I could hear the buzz of the information room from the open windows. There was laughter upstairs in the administration department where most of the civilians worked. One of the women in the canteen had asked me if I was a new civilian and I told her I was waiting for my uniform.

'Getting on all right?' Jaines asked brusquely when he came into the library after the lunch hour.

I stood up and mumbled something about knowing some of the people.

'What?'

He glared at me, his face inflamed, his eyes icy with bad temper.

'Nothing, sir,' I said quickly, standing straighter, touching the table where I had been reading.

'Speak clearly, Godard,' he snapped, and told me to follow him.

He walked down the corridor with his baton rigid underneath his arm, his neck stiff with tension.

He seemed to be in pain.

When he got to his office, he pushed the door open and dropped his baton onto the desk where a uniform lay neatly folded. He closed his eyes, lethargic, exhausted, and stood for a moment at his desk, gripping the back of his chair.

'I suffer from migraines,' he said tightly, not looking at me, staring at the window. 'Driving long distances aggravates the pain. I apologise.'

'Yes, sir.'

'Try it on,' he said, lifting his hand weakly and pointing at the uniform. I scrambled to undress and he stared at me with his cruel eyes, a contempt which made me stop, half clothed, in front of him. Balanced on one leg, I pulled my trousers off and straightened.

'In the lavatory,' he said very quietly, as if explaining something to a child.

The uniform was thick black serge, the shirt starched and painful

129

round the neck. It took me half an hour to fasten the collar with the gold studs. I had never had separate collars before. The shirt was stiff with starch, and I knew uniform shirts had to be starched at least once a week. The trousers were fastened with braces. The boots hurt my feet. The cap rammed onto my head made me look like a baby in uniform, round-faced and gormless because I had to hold my head back so that I could see.

Jaines walked round me, explaining about spit and polish, touching me with his baton. It was black and had a silver handle.

'Get your hair cut again,' he said.

I had just had it cut at the weekend. It was already cropped to the bone.

He went back behind the desk and sat down. 'You are your father's son,' he said wearily.

'Sir?'

'Just don't expect to be treated any different.'

'Sir.'

I lowered my eyes to his and he slammed the baton down on the desk so that my cap nearly fell off, jerking forward over my eyes. I lifted my hands to straighten it and he hit the desk again.

'Attention!'

I had no idea what standing to attention meant. I straightened up clumsily and he groaned. 'You've a lot to learn, Godard.'

'Sir.'

'Get out of here.'

'Sir.'

I left the room and Mrs Berry was waiting outside. She smiled at me frostily with her tight lips.

I was on the bus home before I realised I'd left my own clothes in the toilets.

TWENTY

My father was waiting at the bus stop, leaning on his bicycle and talking to somebody from the village, pretending to be surprised when I climbed off the bus.

'Here's my lad,' he said, raising his voice.

His face was tanned deep red from cycling round the farms and lanes and villages.

'Here's the future chief constable.' He laughed.

The man pushed his cap back on his head and rubbed his nose thoughtfully. 'Harvest's started,' he said.

I glanced at my father and nodded at the farm-worker.

'Gets earlier every summer, I reckon.'

'It does,' my father agreed. 'Must be summat to do with the rockets.'

He was loud, boisterous.

We walked to the house together.

He'd never met me off the bus before.

The journey had taken an hour. Sitting on the rear seats, I was hot and uncomfortable. I felt awkward in the uniform. The thick material itched. I was sweating. I was glad the pollen count had gone right down as the summer reached its hottest months.

He pushed his bike along the side of the road and asked me how I'd got on. I told him the uniform didn't fit.

'You got measured, didn't you?'

'Still doesn't fit.'

'They never do,' he said.

He put his bike in the shed and followed me into the house.

I wanted to get upstairs and get changed. I wanted to wear my jeans and T-shirt. I felt ridiculous, too big for the kitchen, sweating and dressed up in fancy costume.

'Wait till you've got a truncheon,' he said, taking his tea from my mother and sitting down in the doorway. 'He looks all right, doesn't he, Alice?'

My mother busied herself at the sink and ignored me.

'Don't you think?'

'He looks lovely.'

'Really smart.' My father nodded.

I took the tea and went upstairs. I stripped the clothes off and flung them on the bed. My back was soaked with sweat, the shirt sticking to my skin so that I had to unfasten all the buttons to get it off. The collar was cutting into my neck and I lost one of the collar studs, scrambling under the bed in the dark to try to find it. I sneezed and sat on the edge of the bed in my underpants. I could see a combine from the window, churning up the immense field. It was seven o'clock and they were still harvesting.

I could hear my parents talking downstairs, my father's bright enthusiasm. He seemed excited. I clenched my fists and ignored my mother when she shouted up the stairs.

'Dinner's ready, Stephen!'

'I don't want any.'

'What?'

I went through to the bathroom and had a wash in cold water. I got dressed and put my plimsolls on, going down the stairs quickly and out of the front door. I could hear my father on the telephone. I walked out of the gate without looking back and down the main drive towards the guardroom.

A guard stepped out of the entrance as I approached the gates.

'Come to join up?' he asked.

'No.'

'Your dad told us this was your first day.'

I walked straight past him, nodding and shouting back over my shoulder. I went straight to the Naafi and upstairs to the main bar. I ordered a beer and drank it back quickly, the cold numbing my throat. My hands were shaking. I felt as though everybody on the camp knew about my joining the police, and glanced angrily at the barman, who stared back with cheerful indifference, polishing glasses and coughing as he finished another cigarette. I drank another beer and walked out of the Naafi.

'Is it important?' Barbara's cousin said when I rang their doorbell, but I told her not to worry. Barbara was visiting friends in the town. I said I would come back. I didn't want to see Caroline. I couldn't face telling her about the day. I didn't want Matthew asking his stupid questions. I wanted to talk to Barbara. I walked across the green past the large detached houses and back to the main road. I cut across the fields towards the village, and then turned back, making for the beech woods at the bottom of the cliff. I walked through the woods, getting off the road as soon as I could and clambering down to the stream where I sat beside the water and bathed my feet among the pebbles and forget-me-nots. I drank some of the water, and it was icy and sweet.

I could live in the woods.

I could learn how to catch rabbits and pheasants and roast them over a fire. I could catch fish in the stream and steal from the big houses on the camp. I could live for months on what some of the Americans kept in their freezers and stacked in their garages. I could run wild.

An owl hunting early flew low over the woods.

I wondered how long it would take them to find my body if I drowned in the fast-running waters of the stream.

When the woods were dark with shadows, I went back to the house.

I felt humiliated.

Jaines was away again the following morning.

'You can continue with the files,' Mrs Berry told me.

She stood in the doorway, filing her nails, frowning with concentration.

'Not very pleasant, is it?' she said abruptly.

'Pleasant?'

'The files. They should be punished. Some people think they shouldn't, but it isn't up to us to judge. They should be sentenced and punished. The courts know what they're doing. The Lord would punish. You should forgive them, but the law has to have its way, the victims have to have their judgement. Do you go to church?'

'No.'

She finished her nails and smiled bitterly.

'Mr Jaines will be back soon,' she told me.

I sat at the oak desk and read about a murder that had happened recently in the north of the county. I remembered the newspaper reports. The little girl had been eleven. There had been a mob in the street outside the police station and extra police were drafted in from headquarters to protect the man who had raped and murdered her.

She was the daughter of a farm labourer.

She had gone walking through the woods near her home, looking for bluebells. The man who followed her also worked on the farm. He lived alone with his mother. He knew the girl, otherwise she would never have gone with him.

Her mother kept saying that: Betty would never have gone with him, she was a good girl. He took her for a walk, telling her he knew where there were some bluebells, the last of the spring, and when they were a long way from any houses, he forced her to the ground and tried to undress her. The pathologist said she must have struggled, judging by the bites on the man's arms and hands. He tied a scarf round her throat to try and keep her quiet and almost strangled her, making her pass out. The rape must have occurred while she was unconscious. He killed her by hacking at her face and neck with a broken bottle which somebody on a picnic had thrown into the long grass. He seemed to panic. The girl was unrecognisable.

I had to leave the room when I found the photographs.

I had no idea they were there, tucked into the back of the file.

They fell out onto the desk and I sat looking at them. The girl's cheekbone had been broken, the glass cutting through the flesh to the bone. The broken glass had caught the bottom of her mouth and torn the lip so that it was hanging loosely from the mouth, as if she was trying to smile.

I couldn't look away.

I closed my eyes and the face was still there in front of me.

I walked quickly to the lavatory and was sick in the bowl. My hands were soaked with vomit. I knelt down, my face hot on the cold enamel. I was shivering. I heard somebody come in behind me and a man touched my shoulder, helping me to my feet.

'I saw the file,' he said, gripping my arm, explaining.

He was a big man, wearing a checked shirt and loud tweed jacket. His loosely knotted woollen tie was bright yellow. He had a huge straggly moustache and darting, rheumy eyes.

'Godard, isn't it?'

'Yes, sir.'

'You look like your dad.'

I washed my face in cold water and he took me up to the canteen where he went behind the counter and made a pot of tea himself. He sat down opposite me and offered me a cigarette.

'You shouldn't be reading things like that,' he said.

'I was told—'

'You should concentrate on the non-violents.'

'Sir?'

'Burglary. Minor offences. How old are you, lad?'

'Seventeen.'

'You should concentrate on non-violents,' he said again.

I stared into the hot tea.

'He got seven years,' the man said suddenly.

I looked up. He was stirring his tea, looking round the room casually.

A sergeant came in, saw him, and left quickly.

'Seven years?'

'By the time he got out.'

I couldn't drink the tea.

He lit a cigarette and made me take it.

I thought about the crowds in the street outside the police station, chanting and spitting when the man was driven away in a van with an escort, hammering on the side of the van. My father never talked about it. My mother said he should have been burned.

'I should concentrate on Moriarty,' the man said when I tried to drink the tea.

'Yes, sir.'

'It'll come.'

'Sir?'

'The rest.'

I nodded.

At the end of the report, the mother had made a statement.

'I keep imagining what she was thinking,' she said. 'I keep hearing her voice. She wouldn't know what he was doing. She wouldn't know where I was. She must have wanted her mummy . . . '

In the afternoon, Jaines told me to report to the yard, and drilled me for two hours on marching, saluting, standing to attention and standing easy. The sun poured down on the yard, blistering the gravel. I stamped my feet and marched up and down in the sun. I slammed the hard ground with my tight boots until blisters burst on the soles of my feet. I felt sick with the heat and the pain. I refused to look at the inspector. I kept marching, and when he finally dismissed me I walked out of the yard and back into the CID library where

I had left my own clothes folded neatly under the table. I went home without seeing anybody. I could hardly walk when I got off the bus.

'That was Detective Chief Superintendent Hatherill you were talking to yesterday,' Jaines said the following morning.

I stood in front of his desk. I had plasters on both feet.

'Did you hear me?'

'Yes, sir.'

My father had often mentioned Raymond Hatherill. He had been on the force longer than anybody else alive. He knew every village and town in the county, and every villain. When a crime happened, he could usually tell you who had done it within minutes. He had refused to take promotion to chief constable because he preferred his CID work.

Jaines told me to sit down. 'Mrs Berry should have told you to concentrate on the files marked non-violent.'

'Yes, sir.'

'Did you learn the definitions?'

'Yes, sir.'

'Go on, then. A felony?'

'A crime which means you lose your lands and goods, sir.'

'Forfeit.'

'Yes, sir.'

'And a misdemeanour?'

'A crime which isn't a felony, sir.'

Jaines seemed about to laugh, glancing down at his desk. He crossed his fingers on the blotting pad in front of him and nodded calmly.

'Can you give me any examples?'

'Of a misdemeanour, sir?'

'If you like.'

I could feel my hands sweating. I clenched my fists and stared out of the office window. 'False pretences, public nuisance, and contempt of court.'

'Very good. And a felony?'

'Murder.'

'Yes.'

'Treason.'

'Go on.'

I stared down at his dark hair, a lump of Brylcreem caught on his collar.

'Child murder,' I said quickly.

He seemed awkward, embarrassed. He held his hands rigidly on the desk in front of him.

He looked up. 'I want you to spend the mornings in the library,' he said. 'I shall be seeing you in the afternoons. I have a training programme for the cadets, but at the moment you are the only one on duty. You have two colleagues here in headquarters. On training days, cadets come here from all over the county. Once the holidays are over, the training proper can begin.'

'Yes, sir.'

I had no idea why he was telling me all this. I couldn't have cared less. I was interested in my feet and getting back to the library, where I had a copy of *Macbeth* in my briefcase. I'd bought the briefcase for sandwiches and books. I had no intention of reading the files.

He dismissed me and I saluted awkwardly.

He watched me leave the room, my left foot swollen and bleeding.

I went to the toilets and changed the plaster.

I was determined to get through the day without telling him, or anybody else.

I sat in the library and hid *Macbeth* in a file of motoring offences, and read the whole play before lunchtime. I ate my sandwiches alone, and then went to the canteen to make some tea. One of the young probationers talked to me about the training, saying it was easy, you just had to keep your head down and do as little as possible.

'Keep out of Jaines's way,' he advised.

'He's all right.'

'He's a bastard.'

I shrugged.

I wanted to say something about my father being in the police, knowing Jaines for years. The probationer finished his food and wiped his mouth with a handkerchief.

'You play football?'

'No.'

'Mad on sport, the chief constable.'

I knew Needham was a cricketer. He had played for the county.

'I don't play.'

I sat in the information room again, and the young policewoman took me through to the lost property section for an hour to help label some of the items that had been in the cupboards for more than three months. The cupboards were packed with handbags and umbrellas and wallets. One of the wallets had a hundred one-pound notes folded neatly inside.

'Some happy millionaire!' the girl said, scribbling on a label and tying it to a huge handbag stuffed with newspapers. 'You could go on holiday with that lot.'

'Wouldn't take you far.'

'Far enough for me,' she said.

She was wearing a white shirt and black tie, and her hair was scraped untidily behind her ears, as if she was always having trouble with it. It was very thick black hair, and she wore no make-up. She had direct blue eyes.

'I'm WPC Stannard,' she said. 'You can call me Mavis. We'll be on the training course together.'

'Are you a probationer?'

'That's right. And a cadet before that.'

'I don't think I'm going to make it.'

'Course you are.'

I told her about the library and she nodded sympathetically. She had kind eyes and a brisk, warm voice.

'The library of nastiness we used to call it,' she said. 'I suppose they think if you can survive that lot you must be ready to face the reality.'

'I'd rather not.'

In the afternoon, I read the play again, and waited for the inspector to call me, but he left headquarters at half past three without asking to see me. I sat in the hot room, listening to the radio, the lulls in the conversation, the laughter from different parts of the building. When I finally caught the bus home, my head was aching from the heat and all the cigarettes I had smoked. I felt dirty with all the blood Macbeth had splattered around my imagination, the psychotic blankness of the blue forms. I sat on the crowded bus and went to sleep.

'It must be something in you,' Matthew said solemnly when I told him about my week's reading in the headquarters' library.

'How do you mean?'

'Something voyeuristic in your nature.'

'Don't be stupid.'

'Definitely voyeuristic.'

'I didn't ask to read the bloody files.'

'You didn't refuse.'

'I *had* to read them.'

'Probably means you're going to be a writer,' he said thoughtfully.

'Now what are you on about?'

'The voyeurism. Probably means you're going to sit by your wife's death bed and make notes about her cancer.'

'Bastard.'

Matthew lit a cigarette and handed me the packet. 'How's *Macbeth*?' he asked.

I said nothing.

I was too tired to talk.

I had had a letter from Germany from Liz saying she hoped I was all right and that the exams hadn't been too difficult, and promising to write me a good reference if I needed one for a newspaper. I wanted to tear the letter up but kept it hidden inside one of my books. I bought a new copy of *Ulysses* and pasted the German address inside the dust-jacket.

Like the particles in an atomic explosion, I felt as though the elements of my life were all heading uncontrollably for different horizons.

TWENTY-ONE

Matthew's exam results were good enough for him to go to university, but he told everybody he was not ready, 'not mature enough to face the temptations of academia'. He wanted another year off before leaving. He said he was going to be a student teacher, working in one of the nearby villages, and then go to university the following year. He said he still had some thinking to do, but I assumed his father was insisting on him being a teacher, doing something useful. He told me his father had stopped drinking.

I saw Barbara at the weekend.

'You look healthy,' she said, teasing me about my white face.

I had hardly had any sun all summer.

I hadn't seen Caroline since the midsummer party.

'She sends her love,' Barbara said.

'You've heard from her?'

'She sent a card. She's been preparing for exams,' Barbara told me seriously, as if she knew Caroline hadn't written.

'They're next year,' I pointed out.

'She's got to do well. It's important.'

'Yes.'

'She said to tell you . . . '

I didn't want to hear, at least not from Barbara. I didn't want what I thought about Caroline shared with anybody else.

In the evening Barbara, Matthew and I sat in the Plough and drank cider.

I told Barbara how I had spent my first few days at head-quarters.

I told her about the library of nastiness.

'I don't know how you can do that,' she said, as I explained about the crime reports, the blue forms.

'Do what?'

'Just sit there, reading about it.'

I blushed, angry, wishing I hadn't told them.

'Somebody has to do it.'

'Just *read* about it.'

'I have to know what happens,' I said. 'It's part of the job.'

'At seventeen.' Barbara laughed her derision.

She seemed upset.

Matthew fetched some more drinks and sat down between us.

'Stop arguing, you two.'

'I don't know how he can do that,' she said, ignoring her drink.

'He has to,' Matthew said.

Barbara was being awkward.

'Why?' she said, leaning forward and staring at Matthew.

'Because he has to do the job if he's going to do it. If he isn't then he refuses and they throw him out of the building.'

She laughed bitterly and sat back in her seat. 'You would say that.'

'I wouldn't say anything. It just happens to be the truth. I don't want him to do the damned job. I don't have any say. But if he's going to do the job, he's got to do what they tell him.'

I suddenly felt years older than Matthew.

I drained my glass and stared sullenly across the bar, listening to a group of lads arguing with the landlord. I lit a cigarette and the smoke smarted my eyes. I swallowed the smoke, sniffing and swallowing a lump of phlegm. I felt tired, aggressive. I wanted to go for a long run, and glanced at Barbara, thinking about our early-morning runs along the narrow lanes.

I bought another round of drinks and then walked home, leaving Barbara and Matthew arguing in the pub.

TWENTY-TWO

Each morning, I got up early to spend some time alone.

I unlocked the chickens and filled the food troughs. Pheasants fluttered and coughed in the fields. The sky throbbed with the birds chorusing from the woods. The sun paled the distant hills, the low crowded woodlands.

Sometimes I stood and watched the chickens.

They scrabbled for the food, fluttering on the damp ground, clawing at the feeding trough. I thought about Frank unlocking the battery. He was always first at the farm. He unlocked the huge sliding doors and left them wide open all day, whatever the weather. He wanted the birds to hear the dawn chorus.

My father made the tea while I fed the birds.

'I always worked the harvests,' he told me when they were finishing the barley and the spring wheat on the nearby farm. 'I liked that.'

I asked him why he hadn't wanted to work on a farm.

'Money was worse than fishing,' he said. 'All right for a bit of spare cash. Same as the fish docks. Plenty of casual work. But you can't live like that.'

I wanted to tell him about the girl in the photographs.

I kept waking up, her face watching me from the plastic sheet in the woods, her eyes alert and bruised, her lips moving, soundless, crying for her mother.

I told him I had been reading the crime reports and he shrugged warily, closing off, looking out of the window.

'You'll get used to it.'

'I don't think I will.'

'Course you will.'

He refused to talk.

I felt embarrassed, awkward at my own feelings, confused by his.

At headquarters, we spent a day each week listening to lectures on police powers and Moriarty's *Common Law*. Jaines paced backwards and forwards in front of us, speaking in a monotone, his black hair oiled back off his knotted forehead, his eyes yellow with tiredness or some dull fury. He always seemed to be irritated. He would turn suddenly and ask questions, glaring at a probationer or a cadet.

'You, Loundes, what's the answer? You're the only one who ever seems to know anything.'

Loundes jumped up to shout the answer. He loved standing to attention, leaping about. He seemed to enjoy saluting and saying, 'Sir.' He always said it very loudly, snapping it out, brisk, determined.

'He's a prat,' Mavis giggled.

Mavis sat with the other probationers, but was always ready for a laugh. She was nineteen, but looked much older, as if she ached to get married and never would and made up for her sleepless nights with endless jokes and good humour.

She detested the training sessions.

Cadets and probationers travelled from all over the county to hear Jaines lecture. Thirty or forty of us would be crammed into the lecture room, making notes, keeping our heads down, trying to avoid questions.

'I bet his wife sorts him,' Mavis said as we left one of the lectures. 'I bet she gives him a rough time.'

'Imagine him in bed,' another of the policewomen giggled.

I went to the canteen with three or four of the headquarters cadets and we sat at a table by the counter, eating steak and kidney pie and syrup pudding.

'How's your father, Godard?' one of the older policemen asked me when I was queuing up for the puddings.

I remembered him from the coast.

'Enjoying being a farmer?' he asked.

'We've got a few hens,' I admitted.

'Hens?'

'Rhode Island Reds.'

'That sounds like your mother to me.'

'Yes.'

'She keeping all right?'

'She's working.'

'She always was a worker, your mother,' the man said. 'Give your dad my regards.'

My mother had got a job on the farm. She was working with Frank.

'I don't like the way they treat the birds,' she told my father on the first day.

'Nobody asked you to work.'

'I don't think it's necessary.'

'Necessary?'

'I don't think they should put them in cages.'

She came home tired and dirty, and sometimes forgot to wash before doing the dinner. I would get home from headquarters and find her standing in the garden, staring at our dozen birds, flinging handfuls of food over the barbed wire. She brought a scabbed bird home one lunchtime and shouted at the farmer when he drove up to the house and complained. He said the bird was diseased but she nursed it in the garage, feeding it from a bottle and filling an old orange box with straw for the night. The bird died within a couple of days. My father yelled at her about stealing, and I could hear them arguing late into the night, shouting and banging about in the kitchen. She sat in the kitchen one afternoon, and when I got home, told me that when my father joined the police, the wives weren't allowed to work, weren't allowed to have any kind of job at all.

'We had to wear our dresses long.' She smiled, as if she was remembering. 'And no lipstick. And we weren't allowed to belong to a political party. Policemen aren't allowed to belong to any political party.'

'Isn't there any dinner?' I asked her irritably.

'Dinner?'

'Yes, dinner.'

I was shouting. I was hot and tired, fed up of a day spent marching up and down the parade yard in front of the headquarters building. I went upstairs and had a bath. I lay on the bed naked and listened to the radio downstairs. I couldn't be bothered to play any of my own records. I glanced at the books on the bookshelf and realised I hadn't read anything for weeks, not since the days I'd spent in the CID library reading *Macbeth* and the crime reports. I had words in my mind, about blood and havoc and violence, but I couldn't remember where I'd read them.

In September, I had to attend a rape trial at the quarterly Assizes.

It was an opportunity to use my shorthand.

'When you get back, I shall expect a complete record,' Jaines said with his icy smile.

I walked up to the Assizes with Mavis and Loundes. Quarter

Sessions were held in the castle every three months, the cases being heard by the Recorder, but at the Assizes you got the important cases and Circuit Judges.

The rape case had been in all the local papers for weeks.

The prosecution case was that the victim had gone for a walk with the accused, and that he had dragged her into a field and raped her. The girl bringing the charge worked as a casual farm labourer, lifting potatoes or singling sugar beet. Her complexion was red and angry, and she must have weighed eleven stone. Throughout the trial, the judge made sarcastic comments about the size of her assailant, a thin, bone-faced man with a tight, unpleasant smile. In his summing up, he instructed the jury to ask themselves what the girl thought she was doing, going for walks at night with a man she hardly knew. The girl said the man had threatened to strangle her with his tie, and the judge leaned forward and asked her caustically why the man had taken his tie off, and why she hadn't left the field when he started to undress. The girl cried through most of the trial, holding her breath, stunned by the questions, following the proceedings with a blank terror. I struggled to get most of it down in shorthand, but when the girl started sobbing, I sat mesmerised by the judge's withering indifference, the embarrassed faces of the jury.

'She asked for it,' Mavis said as we left the courtroom. 'She shouldn't have gone with him if she didn't want it.'

'That's right,' Loundes agreed, straightening his cap and glancing at his profile in a shop window. 'That's obvious. Wasting everybody's time.'

'I thought she was innocent,' I said bluntly, and Loundes laughed patronisingly.

'She wasn't the one being charged, Godard,' he explained. 'She *brought* the case.'

'I still thought she was innocent,' I said angrily, confused, upset, blushing bright red with embarrassment.

I walked away, telling them I would be back at headquarters after lunch, saying I had something else to do. I went across the cobbled square and up towards the cathedral. In the precincts, there was an old bookshop. I went inside and stood in the darkened room. The bookshelves went right up to the ceiling. The shop smelt of old books and beautiful paper. I stood in the silence and stared at the books. The man who ran the shop was a paraplegic, a tiny, friendly man who shuffled around and knew every book you ever mentioned, every volume on the shelves. He came through from the back of the shop and smiled when he saw me.

'I've got something for you,' he said excitedly, lifting his hand, shuffling back along the corridor. 'Delivered this morning. You'll be interested in this.'

He brought me a small blue volume, and watched as I opened the pages.

It was George Crabbe's *The Borough*, the Dent edition.

I'd bought Betjeman's *Collected Poems* when they came out, and ever since then the man had been showing me volumes of poetry.

I sometimes spent hours in the shop with Matthew.

I stared at the thick pages, the firm clear print.

I'd never heard of George Crabbe, but I was beginning to buy almost anything the man recommended.

'You've been at the Assizes?' he asked cheerfully.

'That's right.'

'I remember some of the murder trials,' he said disapprovingly. 'Awful affairs, dreadful. People have evil imaginations.'

'People?'

'The crowds. Wanting to hear the verdict. Wicked.'

I told him I liked the Betjeman, and he smiled, shaking his head.

'You'll find Crabbe much more interesting.'

'Why?'

'Much more *passionate*. You must know "Peter Grimes"?'

'No,' I told him.

'Not know "Peter Grimes"! That's a shame. That's dreadful. What do they teach them!'

I promised to tell him how I enjoyed the new volume. I left the shop and walked round by the front of the cathedral. I hadn't been back since the day I'd come with Caroline. I sat on the low stone wall and felt the sun on the back of my head, the heat rising above the shadows of the cathedral. I still hadn't seen Caroline. She had just got back, ready to start school in September. I could feel the autumn in the sun. I watched the people going in and out of the cathedral, and glanced through the pages of the new book. I could have sat there for hours, reading, listening to the bells. I could have spent my life in the bookshop. I got up, and walked back towards headquarters.

TWENTY-THREE

I went with Barbara to the pub most evenings, and we stood on the cliff road watching the stubble-burning ravaging the countryside, smoke rising in the distance, fires burning far away.

'Like a war,' Barbara said quietly.

Black ash floated for miles.

One evening, when we got to the Plough, I was surprised to find Matthew drinking with Caroline.

'I didn't know you were back,' I said, standing at their table and holding the back of Caroline's chair.

'Yesterday,' she said.

My stomach was churning.

I bought drinks for us all and sat down next to Barbara.

Matthew was fooling about, leaning across the table and whispering to Caroline, snorting with amusement.

'He's being childish,' Caroline explained, pushing him away.

'That's new,' Barbara said.

I finished my drink and smiled at Caroline.

She was tanned after the holidays, and her hair had grown long over her shoulders.

'You have a good time?' I asked her, and she pulled a face.

'I was studying.'

'You could still have a good time,' I muttered.

'Tell her about the library,' Matthew said, frowning at me. 'Tell her about the wanking.'

I felt myself going red straight away.

I wanted to punch Matthew.

Barbara got up and went to the bar.

'What about it?' I said angrily, glaring at him, sulking, furious, clenching my glass so that it nearly broke.

Matthew snorted. 'That girl. You *know*.'

When Barbara came back she stood at the table and listened to what we were saying. She blushed.

'The *girl*,' Matthew said impatiently, as if I was an idiot.

147

Barbara sighed and half shrugged, her eyes shining. 'I'm sorry. He's drunk.'

'I am not drunk,' Matthew beamed.

'I don't know what you're talking about,' I said, draining my glass empty.

'Misery.'

Barbara finished her drink and put the glass down on the table. 'I have to go,' she said.

'What!'

'I promised to be home . . . '

'Oh, do sit down,' Matthew said.

'I have to,' Barbara insisted.

'I was only joking,' Matthew said again.

I could see Barbara was nearly crying. She left the bar and I followed her outside.

She was standing by the door, drying her eyes with a handkerchief. 'I'm sorry,' she said.

'It's all right.'

'No, it isn't. He irritates me when he's like that.'

'It doesn't matter.'

She was crying again.

'For heaven's sake, Barbara . . . '

She reached out and touched my arm, shaking her head. 'I guess . . . ' She took a deep breath and crumpled her handkerchief. 'It's so unfair . . . '

'What?'

'Matthew, making fun.'

She touched my arm again. 'I'm hopeless. I'm not feeling well that's all . . . '

I felt surprised, sorry about my bad temper. 'Let's go home.'

'No, really . . . '

'I'll walk you home . . . '

'I want to go alone. You go back in. You haven't seen Caroline yet, you haven't had chance to talk. I'm fine, really.'

She walked back towards the church and turned and waved at the corner, saying she would see me in the morning. I watched her go.

I went back into the pub and got myself another drink. I sat down beside Matthew and emptied my glass.

'I'm sorry,' he said, embarrassed.

'Shut up, Matthew.'

Caroline came back from the lavatories. 'Did they really put all that down on a form?' she asked, straightening her hair in a hand mirror and smiling at herself vaguely.

'A statement.'

'Whatever.'

'They have to take statements.'

'As evidence, right?'

'Yes.'

'And you have to read them?' Caroline nodded. 'It sounds awful. Poor you.'

'Somebody has to do it,' I said aggressively.

Caroline heard the tone of my voice. 'How horrible for you,' she said quickly.

I said I had to get home, and Caroline stood up with me.

'I fancy a walk,' she said.

Matthew waved unhappily as we left.

We walked slowly up the hill to the main road. I felt better out in the night air, the darkness, the miles of silence. I breathed deeply, taking Caroline's arm. 'You never wrote.'

'Busy. I'm sorry.'

'You wrote to Barbara.'

'She's my oldest friend.'

She was speaking quietly, her voice seemed deeper, as though she had suddenly become older during the vacation. I couldn't tell what was different.

'Are the things horrible?' she said as we walked along the top road, the hawthorn hedges rustling in the soft breeze, the moon brilliant in the September sky, then hidden by rushing clouds. 'Do they upset you?'

'Some of them.'

'It must have been awful.'

'Just the first week.'

'I can't bear it. Poor you.'

She squeezed my arm again and we stopped at the edge of the road. She turned towards me and I could feel her face close to mine, her hair brushing my shoulder. I put my arms round her shoulders and kissed her on the mouth quickly, and then rested my head in

149

her hair. I wanted to stand there like that. I didn't want to kiss her. She held me gently, and then gripped tight, pulling me closer. I kissed her neck and then her mouth. A car turned up from the village, and we were blinded for a second by the headlights until it turned north and away from the camp. I kissed her again and she whispered something close to my face.

'I missed you,' I said, holding her close.

'I missed you too.'

'Did you?'

'Of course.'

'You didn't write.'

'I wanted to.'

I thought about the girl in the reports, the long afternoons when she'd knelt beside a row of boys in her parents' neat suburban house, a semi-detached on one of the estates on the outskirts of town. I felt myself hardening against Caroline and she giggled suddenly, burying her face in my shoulder.

'What's the matter?'

'Dirty thoughts.'

'No,' I jeered, 'not you!' but she pushed me away, still embarrassed. 'Not you, I don't believe it.'

We walked on towards the camp.

'Will you tell me?' she said, holding my hand and swinging our arms between us as we stumbled through the grass verge.

'Tell you what?'

'About the girl.'

'I thought you weren't interested.'

'Did she really do that?'

'I don't know what Matthew told you.'

'Sixpence a time.'

'I can't remember.'

'I wouldn't charge sixpence,' she said crudely, suddenly dancing away into the road, running along in the darkness and then spinning round, her arms held out awkwardly. 'I wouldn't charge anything,' she shouted after me. 'Honest.'

'I know,' I shouted back sarcastically, and she threw back her head in laughter, standing in the middle of the road, her legs apart, her hands swivelling on her hips as if she were doing exercises in a gymnasium.

'Naughty,' she said when I caught up with her, waving her finger in my face.

'True.'

'You shouldn't remember.'

'How can I forget?'

I could hardly walk in my tight jeans.

I stood in the road looking at her, and she pointed with her finger, shaking her head and pretending to frown.

'Not if you won't tell me,' she said, stepping back quickly when I moved towards her.

'Tell you what?'

'What it was like when she did it?'

'How should I know?' I said, blushing bright red.

'You were there.'

Her voice was suddenly quiet. She didn't move when I put my hands on her shoulders. I pulled her close so that she could feel me. She wrapped her arms round my waist and clenched her fingers, squeezing me so that I gasped at the pain.

'Yellow loosestrife,' she said suddenly.

'What?'

'In the woods. Yellow loosestrife, purple bellflowers . . . '

'For Christ's sake, Caroline . . . '

'In the woods.'

'What about it?'

'I want it to be like a Lawrence novel.'

'I haven't read any fucking Lawrence novels.'

'I want it to be like that.'

'Go and fuck him, then.' I laughed.

'He's dead.'

Caroline unfastened her blouse and bent my head down to her nipples while she fumbled inside my trousers and pulled me off, her fingers barely touching me before I came all over the grass, soaking her skirt and making her squeal with delight, instead of angry like she had been last time. She dried her hands on my handkerchief, and told me to stop worrying about the skirt. She said it would wash out in the handbasin in her bedroom.

'But you realise what we've just done,' she said as she handed me my handkerchief. 'Four hundred million sperm, wasted all over my skirt.'

'No wonder I'm tired.'

She giggled helplessly, leaning against my shoulder.

'We don't have to do it like that,' I whispered.

'Stephen!'

'Well . . . '

'Don't be naughty.'

'I thought . . . '

'Don't you think it's interesting?'

'What?' I said irritably.

'Four hundred million sperm. You can see the sperms fertilising the egg under a microscope. Only a few get through, of course. They die before they reach the womb. But you can see their tails wiggling, trying to get through to the chromosomes. Isn't it incredible? One sperm has to merge with the egg's nucleus and there you have a new human being. We might have lost an Einstein tonight. We might have lost the world another Shakespeare. All the times you masturbate—'

'I don't masturbate—'

'Don't be silly, all boys masturbate.'

'And girls don't, I suppose?'

'I wouldn't know.' She giggled again. 'You are funny.'

'I'm shattered.'

'That's what I mean.'

She went on, clinging to my arm, and kissed me until I calmed down, kneeling in the grass to fasten my trousers, touching the tip of my nose with the end of her polite fingers.

'You are *lovely*,' she said with her sweet derision. 'You are *ridiculous*.'

'Thank you.'

'*Delicious*.'

As we walked home, she talked about Pasternak, and said her father was still teaching her the language. She said the poetry didn't translate into English, none of it. She said it was impossible to understand without learning the language. It was that that had decided her to study languages. She wouldn't change her mind again. She would never be good enough to earn a living from music, and her mathematics were hopeless. Her father was arranging for her to study at Cambridge. As she talked, I listened to the sound of her voice, chattering and excited, girlish, young again. She seemed like a child, her hand still sticky in mine, as if she had been eating toffee apples. For a second, I thought about Sandra, the blue butterfly on her shoulder, clutching the microphone in her hand. Sandra had lived on toffee apples.

'You can teach me all about wanking,' Caroline whispered when we reached her house. A lamp was burning by the door, a nineteenth-century stable lamp but connected to the electricity inside the house. 'You can show me what to do.' She giggled.

I tried to kiss her, but her lips were cold.

She shivered.

'Good night.'

'Good night.'

In the woods, the last of the bellflowers were purple in the undergrowth. In places, the ground was blue with gentians.

I had never read any Lawrence.

I walked home, sick and sweating, determined never to see her again.

I could hardly sleep, thinking about her hot fingers, her clumsy, wet mouth.

TWENTY-FOUR

Her idea of passion was to 'make love' several times a day.

I sometimes ended up unable to walk.

'I want to do it,' I shouted at her, pushing her back into the grass, in the woods where she'd asked to be reminded of her favourite novelist, but she shrieked and shoved me away, hurting my shoulder and sitting up angrily to fasten her clothes.

'I'm a virgin,' she kept insisting, crying when I sulked or walked away, making me come back and lie down beside her in the tangle of grass and yellow loosestrife. 'I'm a virgin,' she whispered against my cheek, fumbling with my trousers.

She rubbed and jerked at me until my skin was raw and purple, and laughed hysterically when I told her I looked like one of the bellflowers, only not so beautiful. She said it was beautiful to her, and I lay back on the grass while she touched the bruised skin, surprised at my excitement, stroking me nervously as I flinched with the pain. She brought a bottle of ointment to massage the inflamed flesh, and gasped with shock when her massaging had the usual effect, telling me I had no self-control as she leaned forward and studied my wounds, her breasts loose and swollen inside her clinging black T-shirt.

I couldn't stop looking at her.

I closed my eyes and wished she would go away, leave me alone.

Each time we met, I ended up never wanting to see her again, promising myself I would avoid her. Within hours of saying goodbye, I was on the telephone. My eyes began to look frantic, yellow and bloodshot, bruised with exhaustion. I slept for hours on the bus. I felt tired and depressed, unable to concentrate, restless, haunted. I heard the birds singing every morning, and only slept with the dawn.

'It's not right,' I told Matthew when he asked me why I looked so tired.

'Sounds all right to me,' he said, pretending surprise.

'If she loved me she'd let me do it.'

'If you loved her you'd let her wait.'

'It's not natural,' I said vaguely, repeating myself.

'What's natural?'

Caroline called at the police house every evening.

As soon as she'd finished homework, she walked round to the house and chatted with my mother in the kitchen. She told her about the time her father had spent in Moscow, working on attachment at the embassy. She said he'd actually met Pasternak, shortly after the war, before things returned to normal. Normal, she said, meant evil. She said any state that imprisoned its poets was founded upon evil.

'Did you know Caroline's father was in Moscow?' my mother said excitely when my father got home.

'At the embassy.' My father nodded indifferently.

'He might be a traitor.'

'Don't be ridiculous, Alice.'

'He might be.'

'Jesus Christ.'

At headquarters, I was spending a week with each of the departments. I had worked in traffic and administration, and now I was answering the telephones in the information room. When I wasn't answering the telephones, I listened to the wireless operators talking to the crews in the patrol cars.

At the end of September, one of the operators got back from his honeymoon and spent the lunch hour showing the other men photographs of his wife. She had short black hair, and a skirt with an opening up the side. Seated on a car bonnet, she had her legs wide open, so that you could see the white lace of her underpants.

The wireless operator grinned and enjoyed his friends' reactions, turning occasionally to the microphone.

'You're too young,' he said, when one of the men handed the photographs to me, and they all roared with laughter.

I went to the CID room and sat down to eat my sandwiches.

There was rarely anybody in the CID office during lunchtime, and the girl on duty liked to chat. I opened my sandwiches and sat at one of the desks. I had a copy of the sonnets and flicked through to the last poem I'd been reading. Peggy went on with her typing.

'They're having a laugh.' She nodded towards the information room at a sudden burst of noise.

'Photographs.'

'I've seen them,' she said, shaking her head and taking the finished letter out of the machine. 'Funny sort of honeymoon.'

155

'Yes.'

'They're not very intelligent, policemen.'

'No.'

The telephone rang and I answered a routine call.

While I was speaking, the young sergeant in charge of the office came in and stood behind me. His name was Mellers. He was always making clever remarks about my father, saying I wouldn't have got in without my father's influence. He leaned on my chair, glancing at the book and then picking it up carelessly and flicking through the pages. When I finished the call, he flung the book back on the desk and sat down.

'You like reading that stuff?'

'It's my lunch hour.'

'I know it's your lunch hour.'

He glanced across the room at the girl but she went on working, deliberately ignoring him.

'You know anything useful?' he asked aggressively. 'You know the number of Scotland Yard?'

He laughed, as if it was a joke, looking at the girl again.

She still ignored him.

I closed the book.

I shook my head.

'You don't know the number of Scotland Yard?'

I shook my head again, staring at the desk.

'You seriously don't—'

'No,' I said quietly, still staring at the desk.

He slammed his fist down on the desk, making an inkwell vibrate and pens scatter across the smooth surface.

'Sergeant!'

'Sergeant,' I said.

He was sweating.

He had played county cricket with my father, and football for a couple of seasons. He was due for promotion to inspector. He was the only man in CID who never went drinking with the other men, the older detectives.

'Stand up,' he suddenly shouted, gritting his teeth, staring at me and going bright red. Flecks of spittle stuck to his lips and landed on the desk.

I was too shocked to move.

I could see his hands trembling.

'I said, stand up,' he yelled again, pushing his chair back and tensing with fury.

I stood to attention.

'Whitehall 1212,' he said abruptly.

'Sergeant?'

'Whitehall 1212.'

'Yes, sergeant,' I said helplessly.

'Say it.'

'Sergeant?'

'Say it.'

'Whitehall 1212.'

'Say it.'

'Whitehall 1212.'

'Say it.'

I stared at him.

I sat down and pushed the sandwiches to the back of the desk.

I could feel him standing close beside me, see his fists shaking. I could hear the men laughing in the information room, noisy, raucous laughter.

Across the room, the girl was staring out of the window.

In the afternoon, I found the wireless operator in the canteen, showing the photographs of his wife to the crew of a patrol car. The driver of the patrol car studied each with elaborate interest, holding the photographs out in front of him, puzzling over them before handing them on to his wireless operator, who whistled and said, 'Lucky bugger,' several times, winking at the women behind the canteen counter.

I sat down by the window and smoked a cigarette.

The girl in the photograph had dark hair, but it wasn't like Caroline's. Caroline's hair was long and soft, and it shone different colours in the light, auburn and copper, green and startling black. The sunlight changed the colour of her eyes.

I went back to the information room and spent the afternoon filing telephone messages.

'1212,' I kept hearing over the radio.

'1212,' somebody shouted down from the corridor.

I thought I could hear their laughter all over the building.

157

TWENTY-FIVE

My savage depressions responded to savage exercise. Each morning I ran miles before sunlight ignited the blue hills, shivered the ground into frosted rainbows. I ran for hours. I pounded the lanes, hammered the gravel, kicked through the spikes of rigid grass. I ran and ran, sweat pouring down my face and spine, soaking my underclothes and drenching the earth in a zigzag shower of water like hot rain. By the time I got home I was drenched and furious.

'You can't keep that up,' my father grumbled when I refused to eat the breakfasts he'd started preparing.

'Keep what up?' I snapped.

'Starving.'

'I'm fit.' I pounced at him, a hundred sidebends in the yard, a hundred forward bends, backward bends, swivels, swings, arm lifts, arm jerks, press-ups on the concrete ground, pummelling the air, dancing round the water butt, crouching up and down faster than the sergeant in the police gymnasiums, taking the cold morning air in gulping desperate gasps to force out the depression, flatten it, explode it with oxygen, get fit, get fit, get fit.

I walked down the streets near the cathedral as if I was looking for somebody to fight, somebody to start an argument. I felt safe in the uniform, aggressive, healthy, certain. I felt certainty. I told Matthew to shut up if he suggested there was something I ought to read. I bought Mailer's *Advertisements for Myself* and read it on the journey to work, ignoring the red-faced girls, the farm labourers ignorant with their smut and fumbling sex. I read about sex in Mailer and felt contempt for Caroline every time I saw her, obsession every time she was away for a weekend, white-eyed, treacherous, boggling.

'Sex should be dirty,' I told her when she got back from one of her school trips to Stratford.

She was trying to tell me about *Romeo and Juliet*.

'Dirty?'

'Pornographic.'

'In *Romeo and Juliet*?'

At headquarters, we drilled in the yard and I marched like a bone, nerveless, ramrod, slamming my feet into the ground, my boots shining with spit and polish and saliva, my collar shredding the skin at my neck, my lips white in a furious clench of anger. I marched better than anybody else. I cut the salutes through the air like a machine. My hand vibrated inches from my forehead. I swivelled on the order to turn like a demented chocolate soldier, erect on some fairground podium. I did the drills as if I had been rehearsing them in my sleep, and ignored Jaines's fury, his bitter temper.

He seemed to know what I was thinking.

He left me in the library when I answered all the weekly questions on Moriarty. He filed my top marks and told me to read the felonies marked for special attention. He asked careful, indifferent questions about murders and rapes, assaults and grievous motor accidents, burnings and torturings, accidents with tractors and threshing machines, industrial fires, chemicals flung into eyes, faces lacerated by flying glass and debris, children brutalised and burned and scarred by their parents, stepfathers buggering six-year-old daughters, step-mothers dislocating their sons' arms, an eleven-year-old schoolboy who had been tied to a tree by some acned maniac and had his penis amputated with a piece of filthy knotted string.

I wept at night, got up at dawn to go running.

I was seventeen, the age when Romeo and Juliet had already slept together, when Romeo and Juliet had already died.

In the farms round the camp they were lifting the potatoes, harvesting the sugar beet for stacking in the open yards.

I told my father about 'The White Negro'.

'It's rubbish,' he said when I suggested the courage of murdering a fifty-year-old shopkeeper.

'It's not rubbish.'

'It takes courage for thugs to murder a helpless old man?'

'A kind of courage.'

'There aren't *kinds* of courage, as you'd know if you'd seen a murder.'

'I've seen the photographs!'

His contempt was blinding.

The photographs turned my stomach, made me retch, left me sleepless for weeks afterwards.

'Photographs!'

He glared at the book as if it was a piece of chicken shit he'd found on the table.

'Filth.'

'What would you know?' I asked icily.

I was frightened of him.

I detested him.

'What's a white negro?' he sneered.

'It means—'

'How can you have a white negro?'

His voice lacerated, his pale eyes, coarse red face, clumsy hands.

'A black swan, a red melon, a blue cabbage . . . '

'Black *inside*,' I shouted.

He roared with derision.

'Black *soul*,' I yelled hopelessly.

I played *Kind Of Blue* alone in my room for hours. I read *Life Studies* and thought about suicide. I bought *The Adventures of Augie March* and devoured it, stunned by the jumbling language, the riot of words, the slanging, slumming fireworks of words. I borrowed *Howl* and *Leaves of Grass* and *The Scarlet Letter*. I read sometimes until the first chink of dawn, blue on the frosted windows, and then ran with the words in my head, and went to work to read about violence in the library. I dreamed about black swans and red melons and blue cabbages.

Matthew and I went for long bicycle rides at night and most weekends.

'I love this time of year,' Matthew told me, reading aloud from Keats and Cowper, wheeling drunkenly across the road and balancing no-hands on the lurching camber. 'I love autumn.'

It was a grey, lowering autumn, followed by an abrupt winter. Drifts of leaves blew across the roads. The hills glowered as rain shifted the horizon. Traffic thundered sullenly towards the coast. I hardly ever thought about the fairgrounds, the fish docks where the fishing season would be getting busy, the North Sea trawlers and the deep water fleet steaming for Norway and Iceland. Some mornings there was ice on the water butt, thin and transparent, melting at the first hint of sun. In the fields round the police house, sheep were out grazing.

On a freezing winter morning, I found my mother standing in

the garden with Frank, discussing the chickens and laughing about the way they pecked at the ground, their beaks darting at the hard earth, their round black eyes startled at any sudden noise.

'You've done wonders with these birds,' Frank told her in his flat, calm drawl. 'I wouldn't have thought it possible.'

'That's because I'm a country girl,' my mother cried gaily.

'How's the farm, Frank?' I asked unkindly, coming up behind them and resenting their low laughter, their easy familiarity.

He shrugged indifferently. 'Same as usual,' he answered. 'Nothing changes.'

In the warmth of the Naafi, I sat and chatted with Matthew. He was teaching in a primary school in the village.

'I spend my time writing plays and reading,' he said.

'I don't believe you.'

'I love the headmistress. She has a beard.'

'She has not got a beard.'

'She has a beard in my play.'

'She has a few hairs on her chin.'

'Isn't that a beard?'

'No, it isn't a beard.'

'Technically, it's a beard.'

He wrote his play about chicken farming, in which a student working for the vacation set all the chickens free and was shot by the farmer. It was full of lines by Tennessee Williams. He went on to write a play about a poet arrested by mistake by the police and beaten to death in his cell because they thought he was a rapist. Both plays used detail I had given him, and I read them straight through in my room while he sat and fretted, asking me why I found some lines funny, looked serious at others, didn't notice the ones that were important. If I criticised anything he ripped the play out of my hands and threatened to burn it. He said his work was important to him and I should only criticise if I knew what I was talking about.

'I know about chicken farms,' I protested.

'You don't know about plays.'

'I know about the police.'

'You haven't written a play, ever.'

'I know you don't get beaten to death in a police cell for raping somebody.'

'What do you get beaten to death for?' he asked, and we both

161

collapsed with laughter, irritating my father when he came home and found Matthew in the house. He kept telling me that Matthew's father drank, as if that was supposed to make a difference.

'You have to be careful about your friends,' he said pompously, and refused to explain.

When I told Matthew, he nodded and shook his head solemnly.

'I am going to write a play about the son of a policeman,' he said, leaning back in his chair and putting his hands behind his head. 'I think you ought to be written about. I think you could be the most marvellous original material.'

'Fuck off.'

'And are you still being infantile with Caroline?'

'Fuck off, Matthew!'

'Obviously, you are, or you wouldn't be *so* frustrated.'

I felt desperate for Caroline, ravished by her oblique beauty, her calm, remote appraisal, her sudden distaste, lurid fascination, her slow, stroking, tantalising refusal, her lips bruised with kissing, her tongue teasing and licking. I couldn't go to sleep without debauching her in my dreams, strange savage passions, bleak exhausting scenes, nightmares. I woke up ashamed and sometimes couldn't look at her. I started to get sties in the middle of winter, when normally they only came with the spring. I wanted to die.

'Your lusts for Caroline are adolescent fantasy,' Matthew went on. 'She's not really your kind.'

'Then why does she go out with me?'

'She lacks discrimination,' Matthew said with one of his sardonic smiles.

I stared at the pages of the book I was reading. Rain spattered at the bedroom windows.

'I'm writing a play about adolescent suicide,' Matthew answered after a long silence.

I closed my book and looked up reluctantly. 'Are you?'

'Naturally.'

'Let me read it.'

'Aren't you annoyed? Aren't you angry?'

'No.'

'With what I said?'

162

'You didn't mean it.'
'Aren't you *hurt* then?'
'I'm hurt so much these days, I can't tell the difference.'
We sat, drinking our Carlsbergs.
Miles Davis ached relentlessly on the turntable.

TWENTY-SIX

I would wake in the morning and each day was worse than the one before. I couldn't tell my parents, try to tell my parents. I told Matthew, and listening, he seemed stunned, worried, upset. There was nothing he could say. At headquarters, I got into a routine of exercises and reading that obliterated the most frightening thoughts, the dreams that kept waking me during the dreary nights: I was too exhausted to endure my dreams.

I was stationed by this time at the nearby divisional head-quarters, the area that included Nemesis and Fulnar, my father's own station.

'We can arrange it for you,' Jaines told me. 'We happen to have a vacancy. But it isn't normal. You can't rely on remaining in the same area as your father.'

I hadn't thought about it.

The station was a gloomy nineteenth-century building overlooked by an enormous engineering works. The windows were always filthy from the smoke of the factory chimneys. The walls were painted a dreary institutional green that always looked dead. Every station I visited used the same dead paint. I spent my days operating the switchboard and reading Robert Lowell and Kerouac. I loved the very idea of being on the road. In the evenings, when the office was empty, I telephoned Caroline and we talked for hours.

In the canteen, I chatted with the civilian girls or the other cadets, the policewomen who were vaguely interested in what I was reading. One of the policewomen sometimes sat in the switchboard room with me. She was studying for the advanced course at police college, and doing her inspector's exams a year early. I showed her the Lowell and some Ginsberg, and she laughed about the poetry she had done when she was at school. She was called Ruth.

'It's not like Tennyson,' she said.

I went to the library and borrowed a collected Tennyson, and was bored by the thumping lines, the luscious sentiment, the *characters*. I was too impatient to bother with heroes and heroines, narratives more complicated than *The Old Man and the Sea*. I wanted the fragmentary, intense moments of films or *The Waste Land*. I wanted immediate, romantic excitement. And I wanted it in a language and rhythm impatient as my own scrambled, greedy reading. After spending so much time on American poetry, I could hardly hear the naturally stressed lines of my own language.

I told Ruth I couldn't understand Tennyson.

She said she didn't mind.

She was dark-haired and stunningly beautiful, her eyes a faint, extraordinary blue, her lips slightly open, her neck astonishingly soft and pale. She stood in reception one afternoon, and unfastened her hair at the mirror, lifting her arms above her head as the hair cascaded through her fingers. She turned slowly on her heels, swivelling in the small room, smiling shyly into the mirror. When I moved, she blushed suddenly, and then smiled at me, as if she'd forgotten I was there.

'I didn't see you,' she said huskily, and then coughed, covering her mouth with her fingers.

The policewomen in the division dealt with all the domestics, the lost children and occasional rapes, the constant wife battering.

I was obsessed briefly with Ruth. I couldn't understand why she wanted to do such work.

She told me she had to get promotion before they threw her out, and smiled absent-mindedly when I asked her what she was talking about. She went on motor patrol and had been cautioned twice for not answering the car radio when she was on night patrols with one of the young drivers, Derek Corcoran. Corcoran was married.

'What were you doing?' I asked.

'Nothing.'

'His wife doesn't understand him,' she told me solemnly, and then burst out into helpless giggles, burying her face in the book I was showing her.

'Actually,' she said, when she recovered, 'he's a complete bastard.'

She asked me if I did anything else apart from read poetry, and nodded when I said I wasn't interested in sport. 'Me too,' she said seriously.

On a dreary March afternoon, the first men of the technical training squadron began to disembark for America. Transports thundered along the runways, and cars raced through the rain, lost in a cloud of spray. Matthew said the training was finished, the RAF officers on the station knew how to launch the rockets, the station was fully operational. We sat in my bedroom and watched the constant stream of traffic onto the camp, the lorries carrying furniture and equipment, the families queuing up for the aircraft.

'I shall miss them,' Ruth said sadly. 'They knew how to behave.'

On a freezing, bleak afternoon, the chief constable came to the division and we all paraded in the soaking rain, marching up and down outside the factory, the air thick with smoke and fumes, Jaines screaming his orders as if we were inside a concentration camp, rigid with fury when we made mistakes, when the older men not used to marching got out of step and stumbled into the men in front of them, when one of the cadets lost his cap as he turned the wrong way and collided with the men coming the other way. The chief constable watched icily, and took the general salute.

'What a waste of time,' my father grumbled when I went and sat down with him in the canteen.

He was drinking tea with some of the older men, a couple of sergeants who were near to retirement. They were all smoking. The canteen was like the inside of a factory chimney. I got my own tea and massaged my shoulder. I'd had an attack of cramp during the parade, and been forced to march at double time to break the agony out of my leg. My shoulders were aching from standing two hours in the rain.

'This your lad, Norman?' a sergeant from one of the remote villages said, stubbing his cigarette out on the ashtray and lighting another. 'He any good for football?'

'No,' I said.

'Don't follow your father, do you, lad?' another man laughed.

My father looked embarrassed, screwing up his eyes, pretending not to hear.

In the lavatories, I'd heard him talking with some of the other men, cursing and using foul language. 'Fucking aye,' he said repeatedly as one of the young men told a joke about the chief constable and what he did with his secretary during overtime. 'Fucking aye.' When he saw me at the wall, he turned away.

Back at the camp, late that afternoon, I found my father talking to a young black airman. The airman's wife was with him, a dull peroxide blonde, her eyes suspicious and cynical, her cheeks orange with panstick. She clung to her husband's arm, her voice brassy and Welsh as she chatted to my father, her eyes never resting anywhere.

'We're ever so grateful,' she told my father in her false cheerful voice. 'They wouldn't have bothered without you saying something.'

The airman had been posted to Louisiana, along with the rest of the squadron. In Louisiana, he would not be allowed to walk the streets with his wife. He had requested a posting to one of the northern sites, but somehow the request had got lost in the preparations for departure. Embarkation was well under way before my father managed to speak to the American commander and arrange a different flight. The couple were travelling together to Massachusetts.

In the steady rain, my father shook hands with the girl and then with the young airman. We watched them walk arm in arm up the drive.

'It won't last,' he said as I hung my greatcoat in the office.

'I don't see why not.'

'Never does.'

In the kitchen, he stood at the sink, scrubbing his hands for a long time, before he filled the kettle for some tea.

As spring arrived and the last of the training squadron departed, I attended my first post mortem. In the division, because the building was nineteenth century, the mortuary was actually attached to the police station, so that post mortems could be carried out on the spot. All modern mortuaries were built as part of hospitals.

'Under what circumstances is a post mortem required?' Jaines lectured me when he heard I was due to witness my first case.

'Where the doctor refuses to sign the death certificate, sir.'

'Isn't *able* to sign the certificate.'

'Sir.'

'And those present?'

'The officer in charge of the case, and his immediate superior.'

'Yes?'

'And sometimes a solicitor.'

'Yes?'

I fumbled for the words.

I couldn't think of anybody else.

The corpse, Matthew would have said.

'The pathologist,' Jaines suggested unpleasantly.

In a green room, I stood on the door guarding the body until the pathologist arrived. The body was that of a young woman, killed in a car accident. The car had skidded off the road into a dyke and she had been killed instantly. The pathologist was merely doing a routine examination. I stood at the door, staring at the body on the table. A white sheet was over it. I had never seen anybody dead. Outside, the factory siren hooted for lunch break, and I could hear them preparing food upstairs in the police canteen.

When the pathologist came in with the chief superintendent, I stood to attention and shook my head firmly when Watters asked me if I had ever seen a corpse.

'You'll be all right,' he said, as if it was an order.

He was in a hurry, impatient.

He nodded briefly to the pathologist, and they drew the white sheet back from the woman.

I felt the room steady around me, and then swing suddenly inside my head, lurching gracefully sideways. I felt my stomach tumbling like feathers in a cage-of-death ride on the fairground. I clutched for the door handle, and hit my head on the wall as I fainted.

In the afternoon, a man came to the counter and asked if we knew anything about a Mrs Hallam. I was working the switchboard and Joseph Midgley, an elderly constable, was on reception. He leaned round the door and asked me if I knew what he was talking about.

'She's the woman they cut up this morning,' I said in a whisper.

The man heard us.

He asked to see the duty sergeant, George Armitage, and then wanted to see an inspector.

I heard him shouting in the inspector's office.

I sat at the switchboard, my face wet with perspiration. I was terrified. I could feel my stomach clenching against the sides of my ribs. I could see the pulse thumping in my wrist. I stared at the switchboard and waited to be called into the office.

'That was his wife,' the inspector said when I stood to attention in front of his desk.

He didn't seem to know what to say.

He held a pencil in his hand and tapped with it steadily on the blotting paper, so that the tapping made no sound.

He looked up at me after several minutes.

'Dismissed.'

I went back to the switchboard and Joseph brought me a huge mug of scalding hot tea.

'Drink that,' he said brusquely. 'I'll take the calls.'

Absurdly, I kept wondering what Matthew would say.

I hadn't even seen the man's face.

I kept imagining him waiting outside, waiting until I'd finished work.

After a few minutes, Joseph sat down at the table and opened a packet of cigarettes. 'Want one?'

'Thanks.'

He lit the cigarettes and took a long drag. 'You'll get used to it,' he said.

'No.'

'Going to have to, aren't you?'

I went on smoking, ignoring him. I could hear laughter down the corridors, the cleaners downstairs scrubbing out the cells.

'Local doctors did it when I joined up,' Joseph said. 'Unless it were complicated. Used to carry the body to an old chapel. Lock it up overnight. We didn't have a mortuary. I was the only man stationed there. I had to help with the instruments, do the sewing up afterwards. I remember one old doctor, he used to bring a flask of brandy, stand it on the edge of the table. "I don't think she'll mind," he used to say, meaning the corpse. "I don't think she'll object." I used to go with him to the pub afterwards and have a drink. I can't remember his name.'

'It's as if you don't even like me,' I said to Caroline one night as we walked together outside the camp. 'It's as if you really hate me.'

'Of course I like you.'

'Then why don't we do it?'

'Do it with Barbara, you like her so much.'

'I never said I liked her.'

'You don't need to say anything.'

Across the runway, the security lights blazed round Nemesis.

169

Cars sizzled along the road.

'I don't know why you invite me round,' I said, confused, miserable. 'I don't see what you get out of it.'

'I'm doing my exams,' she said vaguely, and walked ahead without looking back, her dress occasionally lit up by the passing cars, her scarf brilliant blue as she turned and crossed the road to the officers' quarters, waving so quickly that I couldn't make out whether she was waving to me or to one of the cars going past along the road.

'You are a fool,' Matthew said when I told him.

'So?'

'Stop seeing her.'

'I can't.'

'Then stop complaining.'

'Thanks.'

'I've got my own problems.'

'You don't have problems.'

'I have problems,' he said nastily, and insisted that I let him teach me how to play chess. For several hours, I forgot all about Caroline.

TWENTY-SEVEN

Cantor commited suicide one suffocating June night. As far as the police enquiries could discover, he had visited the chemistry laboratories one afternoon and told the senior lecturer that he was concerned about the safety of any poisons they might have on the premises. The lecturer showed him the cabinet where they kept the prussic acid and a supply of potassium cyanide. The keys were under security lock. Later that night, the principal used his own keys to open the laboratory and swallowed enough prussic acid to kill him within seconds. The caretaker found the body the following morning.

The police pathologist said he had never seen a case like it.

'The man must have been demented,' he told the coroner at the inquest.

Alone in the laboratory, he would have choked on his own vomit, his disintegrating tongue and stomach.

I wrote to Liz and sent her a press cutting, telling her I didn't want her to hear about it from somebody else.

A few days after the funeral, I took some time off and visited the grave. There were flowers from several of the lecturers at the college, and a large arrangement from the local education authority. There didn't seem to be any flowers from family. There was nothing from Liz.

She never wrote back.

I thought about her all the time, even when I was with Caroline.

At the end of the month, the annual county show was held a few miles outside the cathedral city, and I was put on duty in the information caravan that the police used for such events.

Tannoy announcements spluttered through the heat all day.

I was supposed to attend the show for the full three days, but in the heat the pollen choked my throat and eyes and I was blinded by another attack of sties. I sat outside the mobile caravan on a bale of straw and wheezed desperately as one of the policewomen brought me a mug of tea.

'You'd better go home,' the sergeant in charge of the show grumbled.

'I can manage.'

'You can't manage,' he said angrily. 'You can't fucking see.'

A great shout went up from the beer marquee.

I thought my eyes were going to explode.

The doctor bathed them with ointment and then examined the inside of my mouth which was festering with sores. He looked grim-faced.

'You an only child?' he asked bleakly.

'Yes.'

He shook his head, peering into my eyes.

'In a state, aren't you?'

I was sent to the local hospital for tests, and had to give myself injections twice a week, plunging the needle into my left arm. It seemed impossible. The only way I could get the needle into a vein was to hold it horizontally along my arm and jab it underneath the skin, lifting it and plunging it into the vein once I'd broken the flesh. My mother couldn't stay in the house while I was doing it.

They were harvesting the winter wheat early.

'Your grandad had asthma,' my father told me, watching me plunge the needle into my bloodstained arm.

'I haven't got asthma.'

On the farm, the men ridiculed my mother because she talked to the hens, singing to them as she went round collecting the eggs, shouting angrily at the men if they lost their tempers and kicked the cages or threw broken eggs at the birds.

'Don't you dare,' she screamed, 'don't you dare.'

Frank came round one evening to tell us.

He knew my mother was in the village playing bingo.

'You have to admire her,' he said briefly. 'You have to.'

My father showed him to the door.

'Still doing the odd bit of poaching, Frank?' he said threat-eningly.

'I never poached in my life.'

'Not what I heard?'

'Then you heard wrong.'

Frank wasn't scared of my father. He banged the gate so that it shook on its hinges and rode off down the road back to the farm, not even bothering to turn his lamp on.

'He's my friend,' my mother said when she got home from the

bingo and my father started shouting about her working, making him a laughing stock and causing people trouble. 'He's my friend,' she shouted, slamming out of the kitchen and going down the garden to stand at the barbed wire, staring across the empty fields.

'Are you sure this is what you want to do?' Jaines asked me when I reported to headquarters for my annual interview.

It was a year since I'd joined the force.

It felt longer.

'Absolutely sure?'

'Yes, sir.'

He frowned, crossing his hands in front of him. He had exceptionally long fingers, white, almost delicate. He looked at me carefully. His face was pale and his eyes expressionless.

'You have another year before your nineteenth birthday?'

'Yes, sir.'

'How are you enjoying division?'

'It's very interesting, sir.'

'Is it.'

He spoke with his usual flat contempt.

He acted as if he knew I wouldn't stay the course, wouldn't be able to stand the pressure. He once told me that the training was designed to drive the wrong people out of the force.

'You knew Leonard Cantor, didn't you?' he said suddenly.

I could feel my face colouring.

'Yes, sir.'

'Unpleasant suicide.'

'Yes, sir.'

'His wife died while you were at the college?'

I nodded.

'Wasn't there something about a woman, one of the teachers at the college?'

'Sir?'

'One of the lecturers.'

'I don't know, sir.'

I spent an hour in the information room, chatting with one of the cadets, and then let myself into the CID library, checking quickly through the index and then reading the file on the suicide. I hadn't read it at division. I had refused to attend the post mortem. I sat in the library and read the brief report. I could find nothing about Liz Maxted, nothing about a suicide note.

'I wouldn't have thought one was necessary,' the coroner had said brusquely when he'd heard the evidence.

On the bus back to Fulnar, I felt as though the suicide lacked any meaning, as though there was something missing from the file. I couldn't understand how anybody could wait a year and then die in such agony. I was still waiting to hear from Liz, half expecting her to come back. I couldn't imagine myself not coming back.

'They were having an affair,' I told Caroline. 'They were lovers.'

'She has her children,' Caroline said. 'And a new job.'

'She should have come back.'

'She probably wants to forget.'

'She could at least answer my letter.'

Caroline yawned and rolled over onto her back, lying full length on the sofa, flicking through her last exam paper.

'She probably hates you for writing,' she said. 'She probably thinks you were trying to hurt her. Trying to get back.'

I dreamed about Liz briefly.

I tried to imagine how she felt, and shuddered at the thought of Cantor alone in the laboratory, swallowing the prussic acid. I knew the minute I posted the letter that she would think I was trying to blame her for Cantor's death, and the idea had never occurred to me. I lost my temper when Matthew made some sneering remark about my unconscious being more unconscious than most people's.

In my dreams, I was always lying in bed with Liz kneeling over me, her strings of pearls swinging down into my face, her breasts teasing my mouth. In the middle of the dream, the pearls would turn into stones, and she would swing them backwards and forwards, lacerating my face until the blood ran into my eyes, the pain made me shout out. If I tried to explain what had happened, she would punch me repeatedly in the mouth.

I had the same dream every night for weeks.

I felt ashamed when I woke in the morning.

I hardly ever saw Caroline now, avoiding her when she visited the house, telling my mother I didn't want to see her. It seemed to be what I wanted, and I mourned her like a sick animal, festering in my own grief, my eyes gunged and swollen in the harsh bright dawns, my left arm aching with the tearing jabs of the needle, my dreams plagued by Nemesis, erect on the blistering runways, violent with flashes of sunlight, pure white in the burning dust.

And in the division, things seemed to be getting out of control.

Watters no longer picked up the telephone when he wanted a number. He just shouted my name down the corridor.

In the admin. offices, the sergeant in charge had a nervous breakdown.

The switchboard was jammed with emergency calls after a series of summer fires. An arsonist roamed the town for weeks, incinerating rubbish tips and empty houses, setting fire to heaps of rags soaked in petrol. He was caught trying to burn his mother's wardrobe while his mother telephoned the police downstairs.

Early one morning, I went with a young policewoman to inform a woman that her son was dead. She refused to believe us. She stood in the doorway and when the policewoman asked if we could come in and have a cup of tea, she shook her head repeatedly, tears blinding her eyes, her lips pursed in fury. 'You'll not come in,' she kept saying. 'I'll not have you come in.'

We had to force our way into the house and fetch a neighbour. An ambulance and doctor came. The woman was given sedatives, and kept on shaking her head, her lips bleeding where she had bitten them, her neck rigid with refusal, her eyes a blank, wild desperation.

'Never seen one like that, George,' one of the ambulancemen said as they lifted the woman into the back of the ambulance.

'Takes 'em funny ways.'

The policewoman filled out her notebook.

'Did you notice the smell in her kitchen?' she said as we made our way back to the station.

I hadn't noticed anything.

'Fish, I think,' she said, 'rotting fish.'

'Maybe we should have looked.'

'Are you kidding?'

I was ordered to attend another post mortem, and fainted when the pathologist lifted the white sheet off the corpse. The body had been in a river for several days, and was bloated and white like an albino sausage, its eyes and nose already eaten away.

In a pub brawl, when I tried to help Joseph, I had a chair

unceremoniously broken over my head, and was reprimanded by the duty sergeant.

'You should have gone for help,' he said.

'He was in trouble,' I argued.

'I don't care if he was being murdered, you aren't trained to deal with pub brawls.'

I was told to read instructions, and then ordered to take my annual holiday early.

'You need a rest,' the duty sergeant told me wearily.

'No, I don't.'

'Well, I do.'

I signed off and took the bus back to America.

TWENTY-EIGHT

'It's the drinking,' Matthew said flatly. 'He can't go on with the drinking. His kidneys can't stand the damage.'

He had arrived at the house at dawn.

He looked as if he'd just got out of bed, not bothered with washing or shaving. His clothes were dishevelled, slept in. He was wearing socks that reeked of sweat, his shirt was stained dark brown underneath the armpits. His clothes stank, the seamy loutish squalor in which Matthew and his father lived.

The previous afternoon, his father had been transferred from the camp medical centre to the hospital in town.

'He finally collapsed at work,' Matthew told us. 'He's always held up before. Yesterday they found him comatose over the inventories.'

My mother brought some tea and fussed around Matthew.

'Shouldn't you get changed, Matthew?' she suggested nervously, touching his hair and shoulders in darting, urgent movements. Matthew ignored her, leaving the tea to go cold, staring out of the window up our drive to the white gates.

'There's no clean clothes,' he said.

'But shouldn't you be at the hospital?' my mother asked him, sitting down and touching his hand. 'Shouldn't you be with your father?'

'I can't go to the hospital,' Matthew said.

'Why can't you go to the hospital?'

'We had an argument,' Matthew told her.

'You had an argument?'

'My father doesn't want me to go to university.'

'Oh, that's just his way,' my mother said with bright relief. 'That's just his concern about what you're going to do with your life.'

'I don't want to be a teacher.'

'We're just as concerned for Stephen.'

'I don't want to spend my life teaching morons.'

'He's simply trying to do what's best for you.'

Matthew suddenly looked up at me as if he'd just noticed my mother. He looked as if he'd been up all night.

'She's lovely,' he said.

'What?'

'She's perfect.'

'Go away, Mother,' I said angrily.

'I'm only trying to help, Stephen.'

'Shouldn't you be at work yourself?'

'I hate that farm.'

'You can't just leave.'

'I hate it.'

'Not in the middle of the morning. How will Frank manage?'

'You left.'

'I had to go to college.'

I stood up and took the cups through to the kitchen.

I didn't know what to do about Matthew's father, and my mother's increasingly strange behaviour seemed to hang like a threat over the house, brooding and dangerous, flitting about us with a sort of delicate frenzy. I half expected her to set fire to the farm or assault the farmer. She hardly ever spoke to my father. She worked on the farm and then spent her evenings with Emily and Wilfred, talking to them about the orchard, her childhood on a proper farm. She insisted on telling everybody she met that she worked in a factory. My father told her she was making him look like a fool in the village.

I went with Matthew to the hospital and Matthew sat with the doctors for a long time, telling them what he could about his father's drinking habits. I sat in a corridor and watched the faces through the window. I couldn't hear what was being said. Mouths moved silently. The doctors asked questions and Matthew tried to answer, but he couldn't tell them very much because his father had always concealed his drinking, drinking alone or disguising the spirits in lemonade bottles, going for long rambling walks through the fields and draining bottles of whisky until he collapsed into the ditches. At the office, he kept a supply of whisky in the cupboard where the codes were filed, and only he had a key to the cupboard.

In brilliant afternoon sunshine, we walked up to the cathedral and sat and stared at the towering west front. Matthew said he was hungry, and after an hour, we walked back down the steep hill and bought a meal in a Chinese restaurant, special fried rice and sweet and sour pork in livid orange sauce. The pork was solid gristle, like sinews from a hundred-year-old sow, and the batter was inches thick, greasy and slimy from the sauce, which tasted like paraffin, and left a fluorescent orange film on our lips. We were both sick on the journey back to the camp.

'I've got some news about university,' Matthew told me. 'I'm going to Sheffield.'

I said I was glad.

'I'm going to read English,' he told me. 'The professor there's called Empson. You won't know him.'

I didn't.

'He's a poet.'

I said I still hadn't heard of him.

Matthew roared with laughter.

'He's also a genius,' he said solemnly.

A week later, while I was still on holiday, we travelled to the coast for the east coast jazz festival, and spent two days listening to Cleo Laine and Johnny Dankworth, Chris Barber and George Melly, Ottilie Paterson and Marion Montgomery, Acker Bilk and Kenny Ball. We slept on the sands and bought fish and chips and hot dogs from the stalls. We got autographs from Humphrey Lyttelton and Cleo Laine, and had our photographs taken with our heads through a wooden frame, a naked mermaid painted round us when the photographs were developed. The mermaid had enormous breasts, and nipples that looked as hard as barnacles.

On the Sunday, I took Matthew out to the fish docks. The heat was tremendous. The harbour was completely empty. We walked out on the north wall and stood and listened to the foghorns wailing, the bell on the buoy clanging at the estuary. A blue shine of oil glistened on the waters of the harbour. Heat rose from the sea, and a yellow fog drifted eerily from the estuary, hovering over the perfectly calm water, the slopping brown tide inside the lockpit.

'You used to work here,' Matthew said suddenly, as if telling me something I'd forgotten, something he'd always known but never before seen.

'I know that.'

'Isn't it strange?'

179

'I wouldn't want to come back,' I said flatly.

'You didn't want to leave.'

'I know.'

We caught the bus back through the deserted streets.

On the promenade, the fairgrounds were packed and noisy, the illuminations shining into the motionless sea, but I didn't want to go there.

'You aren't interested,' I said, when Matthew said there was no point coming to the coast without visiting the fairgrounds.

'Not really,' he said.

'Then why bother?'

'You can't visit the seaside without doing the fairgrounds!' he said.

But I saw nobody I recognised.

I was simply another stranger.

At the entrance to Wonderland, the tattooed man didn't remember me.

We got back to the camp and sat in Matthew's kitchen drinking tea.

'Do you realise,' he said, 'people like Caroline Strawson, they're doing Latin by the time they're seven.'

'They can afford it.'

'Precisely.'

'It doesn't make any difference.'

'It makes all the difference.'

'Why?'

'Things like *Piers Plowman*,' he said bleakly. 'Reading it in translation.'

'That doesn't matter, Matthew.'

'It matters to me.'

'Most people have never heard of it.'

'I'm not interested in most people,' he scoffed. 'I'm not most people. At university, I shall read it in the original.'

I walked home with him, and then I went back to the perimeter.

I'd never read *Piers Plowman*, in the original or anything else. I felt sometimes as though I'd never read anything. And the books I did read, I didn't understand. I never knew what they were about.

I was simply awed by their splendour. I was driven by my envy for my friend. I read them, and didn't comprehend a word.

'You don't have to *comprehend*,' Matthew said as though he despised me for trying.

'All you have to do is feel,' Liz had told me seriously on one of the afternoons in her overheated room. 'Understanding will come later.'

'Just read,' Caroline said.

I hated them all when they talked like that.

It was all right for them.

By now, Eliot was my favourite author. I read him all the time. I tended to concentrate on the yearning quotable fragments, what if she should die and the children hiding in the rose-garden, midwinter spring and the dahlias asleep in empty silence, but he was my author. I must have been his only illiterate fan in the whole country, and I cherished his remark that he would have preferred an audience who could neither read nor write.

But *still* I wanted to understand.

I wanted to *know*.

I wanted to join everybody else in their understanding.

And I resented them for not seeing how I felt.

On the last day of the holiday, I'd taken a photograph of Caroline sitting in our garden, her legs resting on a chair, her deep tan shadowed by the feathery leaves of the mountain ash. She was waving a piece of paper at the camera, her exam results for university. She had four A levels, and two distinctions at scholarship. Her special subjects were Russian, Greek and Latin. I hadn't even known those were the exams she was taking. She had never discussed them with me.

'I'm taking a year off,' she told me, 'before going to Cambridge.'

In our garden, she relaxed and enjoyed the sun, performing for the camera, drinking endless cups of tea with my mother, agreeing with her passionately about factory farming.

'We ought to sabotage the batteries,' she whispered urgently to me when I walked her home and she dragged me into the shadows behind the officers' mess buildings. 'We ought to poison all the feed.'

'That'll do the chickens a lot of good.'

'Set them free then.'

As I kissed her, she unfastened my trousers and touched me clumsily with her cold hands. As I came, she chattered about the batteries, perfunctory, passionate, absent-minded, saying it was horrible for my mother, having to work in surroundings like that, cruelty like that. I kissed her just to stop her talking. I bruised her shoulder against the wall and bit her nipples through the thin material of her dress.

'I love you,' I kept telling her, 'I love you.'

'But what about the chickens,' she said.

'Fuck the chickens.'

'Stephen!'

'I love you.'

Thoughtfully, she went on stroking my face, her hands still soaked with semen.

TWENTY-NINE

During the summer, our division was involved in an operation against the prostitutes working the town. Since the arrival of the Americans, a taxi operator called Peach had been running a brothel down near the old canal, and ever since Watters had been appointed to the division, he had been determined to stop the man working.

'The camp commander has complained several times about the incidence of venereal disease among his men,' Watters said in the briefing, 'and now this taxi bastard has started running a special service between the camp and the town. I'm going to have him. Is that understood?'

Late one night, as the pubs closed, a mixed unit of male and female officers got ready to raid the brothel, and traffic patrol started checking the taxis as they arrived in town.

'Bit of experience for you, lad,' the superintendent told me when I signed the roster for a night shift. Cadets didn't normally work nights. 'Bit of practical.'

I sat in the operations room and listened to the duty sergeant, George Armitage, telling the men what they were looking for. He was a huge man, his face mottled and red with broken blood vessels, his eyes lurid with a sleepy violence.

'He claims it's residential usage only,' the sergeant told us. 'Guest house or some sort of commercial accommodation. You'll be looking for evidence to the contrary.'

My father was working at the camp end of the operation.

'What kind of evidence, George?' he shouted out.

The men cheered and clapped and several of the policewomen told him to stop interrupting.

'We'll be the ones doing the interrupting,' Ruth shouted out.

Armitage shook his head, scowling good-humouredly and scratching the side of his battered nose. He'd once been attacked by a drunken crowd outside a pub and given a good kicking when they got him on the pavement, his notebook and half a dozen pencils in his jacket pocket saving him from a heart-attack.

'How'm I supposed to know?' he said. 'I'm a happily married man.'

After the briefing, Armitage stopped me in the corridor and told me to keep my eyes shut in the brothel.

'We don't want you getting into any trouble, Godard, whatever the superintendent says.'

'No, sergeant.'

'Don't want to be charged with corrupting a minor.'

'Sergeant?'

'Bum fluff still on his face.'

He beamed at his own good humour, ramming a dozen biros into his jacket pocket.

'And remember your powers of arrest,' he warned me.

I went through to reception and sat and listened to the radio. The switchboard was dead. Fluorescent lighting hummed in the room. The streets outside were dark. In the factory, they were working a late shift, the furnaces roaring, fires burning through the high Victorian windows which were built so as to let in the minimum of light. I made some tea for the reception constable and we sat waiting for something to happen, listening to the messages on the radio. There were patrol cars working all the roads from the camp, and occasionally I heard my father calling in with fresh information, giving car registration numbers and estimating the time of arrival in town, the number of male or female passengers.

In the operations room, men were playing cards or listening to music on the wireless. Some of the women were playing darts. A sergeant and three constables were down in the cells, preparing extra beds and bedding and making sure there was enough tea to get them through the night.

'Five-star hotel, this fucking place,' one of the CID sergeants grumbled morosely, coming through to reception to check the radio. 'Much happening?'

At three o'clock, as dawn began to filter through the grimy station windows, a message came over the radio that the taxi owner himself was driving into town followed by six Americans in a white Oldsmobile. I passed the message through to operations and the superintendent charged through to listen. Another message said that the taxi owner was driving at sixty miles an hour and seemed to be in a hurry. There had apparently been some kind of argument out on the road, and the Americans were following him, blasting their car horn, leaning out of the window and cursing.

'We've got him,' Watters yelled in the corridor.

An inspector and two sergeants with him began to get ready, calling down to the men to stand by. The superintendent took charge of the radio. Dozens of men were running up the stairs and out to the waiting cars. More set off through town to arrive at the brothel premises as silently as possible.

Over the radio, the patrol car suddenly warned us with a burst of static that the Americans had rammed the taxi vehicle. The wireless operator was shouting, and we could hear the squad car's brakes squealing across town as it raced after the other cars.

On the switchboard, the light flashed from one of the blue-lamp police boxes, and a constable reported that he'd seen the taxi and the Oldsmobile travelling down the main street and then swerving through the market as the taxi driver tried to get away. There appeared to be several women in the back of the taxi, and one of them had tried to get out as the vehicle was in motion, the door flinging back into her face as her friends pulled her to safety.

'Let's go,' the superintendent shouted, and I raced after Joseph out into the night and down along the road beside the factory. We were supposed to make for the alley behind the brothel, and join the beat officers who were already there. It was half a mile at least. Joseph was out of breath in minutes. I slowed down to his pace, and listened to the sound of tyres squealing in the darkness a few streets away.

'They're going round in circles.' Joseph grinned. 'Stupid buggers.'

By the time we got to the brothel, fourteen CID officers were already inside, busy interviewing the girls while forensic checked the premises. They found couples in every room. I stood on the stairs and listened to the raised voices, the arguments, the police wirelesses crackling all round me.

'Mind yoursen, lad,' one of the forensic men grunted, struggling down the stairs with a bundle of sheets, and a woman followed him to the landing, screaming and yelling abuse, waving her fist and clenching her dressing gown round her shoulders.

'Sordid bugger,' the woman shouted, and the forensic man grunted, raising his eyebrows and shaking his head.

There were loud shouts outside, and the front door burst open as the superintendent and two or three officers came in with the taxi owner, Peach. He was red-faced and sweating, his black moustache covering his thin lips, his eyes bright in the naked bulb of the hall. He glared at me and pushed me out of his way as he made for the stairs.

'This is a respectable hotel,' he yelled at the forensic men emerging from one of the rooms. 'These are private premises. Where's your warrant? I want to see your warrant.'

The superintendent stood in the hall chatting happily with the chief of CID. I could hear more screaming from rooms at the top of the house, and one of the women on the first landing leaned over and waved at me, her gold teeth shining in the dismal light, her thick lips smudged with purple lipstick.

'You want a quick hand job, love?' the woman asked me.

'Give over,' Joseph roared up the stairs.

'Pardon me for living.'

'You heard.'

'You want a quick suck?'

Up above us, Peach started shouting about his guests, what did we think we were doing to his guests, he was ruined, bankrupted, he would never be able to work in the town again, he would sue.

'Shut up, Peachey, for fuck's sake,' one of the girls yelled, and he flew into a rage.

'It's Mr Peach to you, it's Mr Peach to you.'

'Fucking barmy,' Joseph said, lighting a cigarette and immediately stubbing it out when the superintendent shouted his name. 'Fucking lunatics.'

Gradually, the women officers were bringing the girls downstairs, half of them refusing to get dressed, flaunting their bare shoulders and naked breasts as blankets and dressing gowns were hastily draped around them.

'Hello, darling,' one of the women said as she was marched past, poking her finger in my shoulder and blowing me a kiss. 'When am I going to see you again?' she asked, and the men on the landing sniggered. 'He's a lovely boy,' she called back up the stairs. 'Lovely little willy.'

'Never mind her, love.' One of the policewomen smiled. 'Have you got a lovely little willy?'

'You can see mine any day, pet,' Joseph boomed.

In the hall, the superintendent shouted his orders, cracking jokes with the women, telling the men they would be questioned down at the station. A call had already gone through to the camp commander, and he was on his way to the brothel. The rooms were being meticulously searched. The house stank of booze and cigarette smoke and a stale, festering smell of unwashed bedclothes. Most of the women being taken to the cars reeked of booze. Some of them looked younger than me. I recognised a girl from the camp who used to travel on the bus when I was going to the college. She had a diamond engagement ring which flashed in the light from the naked bulb. She seemed numb, dazzled. She stared at me vacantly as she was pushed down the stairs.

At dawn, when the girls had all been driven away to be interviewed, one of the CID sergeants told me to empty the dustbins in the alleyway and make a careful count of the contents. At first I thought he was joking, but when I searched the alleyway and found the dustbins full of rubbers, I knew he was serious. An ulcerous scenes-of-crime officer, he was famous for his lack of humour.

'Get it right,' Joseph joked, coming out into the yard as the sun began to shine down on the dustbins.

I blinked back into the light from the open door.

I had the counted condoms in one dustbin, and the rest to one side waiting to be checked. I had counted a hundred and eighty-seven so far, and there was half a dustbin left. Some were stiff and dried out. They all stank. The rubber was festering. A pool of slime lay at the bottom of the dustbins.

'Love,' Joseph said with his big lopsided grin. 'Makes you think, don't it?'

I wiped my face with the back of my arm. I could smell the semen on my hands.

'I don't know which is worse, the dried stuff or this lot.' I pointed to a pile of fresh rubbers that must have been thrown out that night.

'Did you know that girl?' Joseph asked.

'What girl?'

'The young one with the diamond.'

I shrugged.

'Did you?' he said carefully.

I glanced at him. 'I used to see her on the bus.'

'She claims she knows you.'

'I used to travel on the same bus . . . '

'She mentioned your name.'

I stared at him dumbfounded. 'She lives on the camp.'

Joseph shrugged. 'I suppose everybody on the camp knows your father . . . '

'She said she worked in Bellamy's shop.'

'They'll say anything,' Joseph grunted briefly, then went to fetch me some tea. I could hear men talking on the stairs. In the kitchen, they were smoking and waiting for orders. CID and forensic were still busy, sifting the evidence. Bedding and clothes were being checked and carted away. The taxi owner had gone to the station to be charged. In the town centre, I could hear the church clock striking the hour. I finished making the count, made a note on a sheet of paper, and took it inside to find the CID sergeant. He was sitting on the stairs.

'That's it, sergeant.'

He took the paper and winced.

'Must be animals.'

'Yes, sergeant.'

'I'm sorry, lad.'

I shrugged.

'You washed your hands?'

I glanced down at my fingers. 'Not yet.'

'Disinfectant,' he suggested. 'Anybody been round this lot needs disinfectant.'

It was breakfast time when I got back to the station. My father had driven in with one of the patrol cars and there were twenty or thirty squad cars parked in the street. The servicemen had nearly all left. The girls were being interviewed. The taxi owner would be charged with keeping a disorderly house and living off immoral earnings. The girls wouldn't be charged with anything. They would be witnesses, some of them quite happily, others reluctantly. Peach was not popular.

I went up to the canteen and queued for breakfast. The air was thick with cigarette smoke. Men were loosening their ties, unfastening jackets. They were beginning to tell jokes, thumping the tables, talking about the girls, comparing what they'd seen. The room smelled of sex, men on rut, heat. They were excited,

188

wild, celebrating. The women sat at the same tables. Several men from CID were drinking and emptying flasks full of whisky. There were calls for the duty sergeant and chief inspector, and one of the squad car drivers.

'They're all in the lavatories,' Ruth shouted above the din. 'They're all wanking.'

I got my food and sat down at Ruth's table.

As I was eating, listening to the racket, Ruth tried to explain the jokes to a young typist. She was excited, hot-faced. The girl giggled her confusion. Suddenly, everything went quiet and Watters stalked into the room, rubbing his hands, beaming with pleasure. He shouted for breakfast and then told everybody the operation had been a success, one of the finest the force had ever organised.

'A bloody credit to the division,' he said loudly. 'A credit to the division.'

He took his breakfast to one of the tables near the counter where the CID sergeants were checking notes, and then before he sat down came across and leaned on my table. 'You all right, Godard?'

'Yes, sir.'

'You heard about that girl?'

'Yes, sir.'

'I told Joseph to let you know.'

'I don't know her, sir . . . '

'Forget it, lad.'

'I used to travel to college—'

'I said, forget it,' he repeated, punching me gently on the shoulder. 'I don't let tarts slander men in my division.'

I stared at the food going cold on my plate. 'I used to travel with a friend,' I said. 'I liked her.'

The superintendent nodded, not really listening. 'I like her too, lad.'

'But we only talked.'

He shook his head ruefully. 'Don't tell me that, lad. Half the blokes we interviewed said that. You wouldn't believe the things that don't happen in a brothel. Enjoy yourself, Ruth?'

'How do you mean, sir?'

'You know what I mean.'

He went back to his breakfast and I left the canteen.

I caught the bus home, and slept on the rear seat.

189

I had a bath at home and went to bed, but I couldn't sleep. I kept thinking about the girl. I thought she'd said she was married when we used to talk to her on the bus, and she was. I wondered what her husband would do when he found out. I lay on my back and stared at the ceiling, listening to the birds in the fields outside. I had never tried to sleep during the day before, and wondered how I would manage when I had to work shifts, on duty all night and too alert to sleep during the day.

I went to sleep, dreaming about the girl, and in my dream she became Caroline, laughing and jeering, and then Barbara, standing sadly on a staircase, waving goodbye. I fell into a deeper sleep at the memory of Barbara, her wide friendly smile, her cheerful laughter. When I woke up, I had a strange sense of mourning, as though I had seen her for the last time. It seemed a terrible dream, and I wandered round the house all day with a weird sense of loss until in the evening I went round to find her, and we walked down to the Plough and had a game of darts and two or three glasses of cider. Even when I saw her home, I still felt numb with loss.

THIRTY

At the end of August, the government announced that Nemesis was going to be phased out early in the following year, and planning was initiated for the eventual disbandment of the whole of the operational complex at the camp. The technical training squadron had already gone. Operations were gradually wound down. The date for the closedown would be announced in Parliament in the new session.

'You realise what that means?' my father said, reading the newspaper over breakfast.

'You lose your job.'

'This job,' he pointed out. 'We'll get a transfer. Aren't you going to eat anything?'

'I'm not hungry.'

'You'll be ill.'

He shook tomato sauce onto his plate and poured some fresh tea. Every morning he had bacon, eggs, fried bread, fried potatoes and baked beans for breakfast, finishing off with toast and marmalade.

I went outside and watched my mother feed the hens. She always did this herself now. She prepared the slops the night before and carried the bucket down to the hens first thing in the morning, before cycling off to work at the farm.

'I like it here,' she said vaguely when I told her about the news in the papers.

'We can't stay.'

'I suppose not.'

The hens pecked and fluttered round her feet, scrabbling after the food, craning their necks backwards and forwards as they pecked at the dry earth. The garden was packed with vegetables my father had grown, lettuces and cabbages, peas and green beans. A climbing-frame shielded the bottom of the garden from the house so that we couldn't see the hens, only hear them when we were sitting in the kitchen. The area where the hens were fenced off was dry scrubland, thick with weeds and scratched bare round the wooden hut.

I walked round to Matthew's and let myself into the kitchen. He kept the key hanging on a length of string inside the door. I made tea and took the tray up to his bedroom where he was sitting up in bed, surrounded by books, a pencil stuck behind his ear, a notebook propped up on his knee.

'I heard you come in,' he mused, making notes on the book he was reading.

'What's that?'

'Chaucer. I've been up since five, reading. You should always read Chaucer to birdsong.'

'You hear about the rockets?'

'They always phase things out.' He yawned.

'You'll be leaving.'

'I'm leaving anyway,' he said, taking the mug of tea and peering at me over his glasses. He had taken to wearing them balanced at the end of his nose. If he hadn't been short-sighted, he would have worn gold-rimmed pince-nez.

'What's going to happen about your father?' I asked as we sat in his room and drank tea.

'He'll be discharged.'

'Can they do that?'

'Unfit for service.'

'What'll he do?'

'He's a good mechanic. He'll get something.'

I walked back to the police house and listened to records. I had sold all my old records and spent the money on American imports, Miles Davis and Dizzy Gillespie, Charlie Parker and John Coltrane. I played them very loud on the record player, the small bedroom booming with trumpets and saxophones.

On a clear September afternoon, I walked down to the village and found Wilfred in his orchard, examining the apples on his trees. He looked suddenly very old and tired, and had to hold on to my arm while he climbed back down the ladders.

'Got to get ready for storage,' he told me when he had recovered his breath, massaging his aching arm. 'Check the cellar's free from mice, get the trays clean for the fruit.'

I followed him round the orchard while he explained all about storing apples. You had to leave the new containers outside to absorb as much moisture as possible, otherwise they would take it from the fruit and cause the apples to shrivel. In the cool of the day, you

192

picked the fruit before it reached full maturity, at the moment when the apple parted easily from the spurs and the colour changed from green to yellow.

'Exposed fruit on the tops of trees will mature first,' he said, wheezing for breath. 'Inside fruit matures last.' If you were going to keep fruit in storage for a long time, it should not be too large, should be free from blemishes, and should have its stalk intact.

I told him he sounded like a textbook, and he smiled slowly. 'I never read any textbooks,' he said. 'I can promise you that.'

After picking, the fruit had to be wrapped in special oiled paper.

We stood in the late afternoon sunlight, the sun shimmering on the trees, the sound of the beck carrying up through the orchard.

He told me Emily was not too well, frail from last winter, weak after a recent cold. She had not come out to see how the apples were doing. She seemed tired and wanted to sleep. 'Not like her,' Wilfred said quietly.

I helped him with some of the containers, and then waved to Emily through the window, but she was asleep beside the fire.

At the station, CID were frantic with overwork, trying to process the evidence from the raid on the brothel. Inspectors came down from the prosecution department at headquarters, and seventeen charges were being prepared. The cases would be heard initially in the local magistrates court. Joseph kept joking about the girl who had spoken to me, but the case against her was dropped and when I asked my father what had happened he said she had flown back to America with her husband, a young serviceman from Wisconsin who belonged to one of the gospel groups on the camp. He used to go round with a choir and sing in local churches and chapels, handing out religious tracts after the services. He had asked for an early flight on compassionate grounds.

One afternoon, I sat in Caroline's house and listened to the slow movement of Beethoven's *Triple Concerto* while she finished reading Colette's *La Maison de Claudine*. Dark-eyed and nervous at my unhappiness, Caroline told me that she was determined to go to university. She was going to study ancient literatures. Her language results had given her a surprise, she hadn't realised her gift for languages was so serious.

'I have to use my talents, Stephen,' she said solemnly. 'Surely you can see that?'

Whatever happened, her family would eventually be returning to America. That was where all the most advanced nuclear work was being done, and they would need her father.

On the lawn outside, a pheasant stalked haughtily around the roses.

In the kitchen, Caroline's mother shouted down the telephone.

I bought a copy of Ezra Pound's *Selected Poems* and delivered them to Caroline's house at five o'clock one morning, meeting her father on the doorstep as he left for work. All he knew about Ezra Pound, he told me unhappily, was that the man was a traitor.

He drove off without waiting to see me push the package through the letterbox.

THIRTY-ONE

At the cold bedraggled end of autumn, the camp was put through a series of exercises, and the rockets were tested with a full complement of USAF forces and emergency services. Military police patrolled the camp perimeter, fire engines were left out at the rocket compound all night, and my father had instructions under no circumstances to leave the station.

A week later, the base was placed on full alert.

Sirens wailed at night. Jeeps raced round the camp perimeter. In the guardroom frantic orders were shouted and military police paraded in full riot gear, dozens of them patrolling the camp, questioning anybody who drove up to the main entrance. Aircraft droned over the countryside at night, giant transports delivering supplies which were quickly moved into the hangars. The Naafi and the American clubs were empty.

On television, the American president issued his warnings.

Aerial photographs had identified a series of offensive missile sites in preparation on Cuba. He talked of clandestine, reckless and provocative threats to peace. He called Cuba an imprisoned island, and announced a strict quarantine on all military equipment being moved there. As a necessary precaution, all military bases in the area were being reinforced and civilian dependants and personnel being evacuated. He told us our goal was 'not the victory of might but the vindication of right, not peace at the expense of freedom, but both peace and freedom'. He told us that, in an atmosphere of intimidation, a nuclear arsenal was being dumped on the shores of America.

'Farewell,' Matthew wrote melodramatically from university, and then proceeded to describe one of Empson's lectures, a poetic drama of Henryson and Dunbar in which the bearded poet recited the poems in a weird hypnotic chant and then gave precise and incomprehensible notes to accompany his own published writings. According to Matthew, *Seven Types of Ambiguity* was an under-graduate masterpiece but *The Structure of Complex Words* was the basis of his serious scholarly reputation. 'I am going through it a page at a time,' he told me, 'sitting up late at night with coffee and the dawn coming up over the treetops, a serious student in these serious times.'

I couldn't tell from his letters whether he'd actually heard about the missile crisis.

At the division, we were given urgent training in civil defence, and told what to do in the event of a nuclear attack. I thought the precautions sounded worse than the disaster. A locked cell without windows for the senior officers. The chief constable hurried away with key men from the army. All facilities to be directed towards helping the Americans at Fulnar. I tried to imagine being buried in a cell with Joseph for the rest of my life, and preferred the centre of the nuclear explosion, not that anybody told us what that would be like.

When Kennedy issued his ultimatum, reading the statement solemnly into camera so that half the world knew it was on the edge of extinction, extra police had to be drafted into town to deal with the drunks and street fight, the domestic quarrels that escalated into sudden vicious violence, the looting and suicides. A woman poured scalding water on her sleeping husband after he had beaten her senseless the previous night. Two six-year-olds were fetched to the station by a policewoman after she found them roasting a cat over a workmen's brazier, the workmen standing round laughing, the foreman drunk in the mobile cabin. A tramp, notorious in the town for her bags of cooked sausages and the stench of her hair, came to the station and demanded protection, saying she had survived the war and refused to be incinerated by a bunch of Communist foreigners.

On the camp, there was an eerie silence. The civilian and USAF personnel were all working on the rockets, maintaining twenty-four-hour readiness, sleeping in the hangars that had been converted for the duration. The wives and children stayed at home, watching television, waiting. There were hundreds of American cars parked outside the hangars, gigantic and colourful beneath the grey October skies, like a mobile rainbow, stunned and motionless on earth. The military police were the only people to be seen on the camp, racing around in their jeeps, patrolling the perimeter with a kind of furious alertness.

'They think they can stop the bombs just by being there,'

Frank said sarcastically when he called at the house to help my mother creosote the chicken hut. She refused to acknowledge the emergency. She said in the event of a nuclear attack, we would need all the eggs the hens could lay. Frank nodded glumly, and asked me how I was getting on with the police, how was the reading.

After days of not seeing her, Caroline suddenly called at the house, and when I was not there sat for hours in front of the television with my mother. She said she hadn't seen her father for days, and her mother spent all her time on the telephone, calling her friends in America, gasping hysterically and keeping Caroline awake at night. She came down one morning and found her mother asleep on the stairs.

Thousands of miles away, the Russian fleet steamed on, and freezing showers of rain kept us in the house for hours on end, staring out of the windows, restless in the hot rooms. My mother kept heaping coal on the fires. She polished the range and cooked shelves of meat pies and casseroles. On the radio, we listened to music and news bulletins, programmes of analysis in which politicians blamed each other for the crisis and agreed on the overpowering threat from the Soviet Union. In churches, priests talked about the end of the world, *Revelations* and the Judgement of God.

On the camp, all leave was cancelled, and security lights burned through the night.

I went to the Naafi and sat on my own drinking lager.

It felt strange, being without Matthew, and I hadn't seen Barbara for days. I listened to records on the juke box and watched as three or four young Americans argued at another table. They were drunk. As their voices rose, I could hear they were shouting about the British, about being here to protect the ungrateful bastards when they should be back home, looking after their families. I emptied my glass and got up to leave but one of the airmen saw me leaving and stumbled up from the table, crashing his chair into the wall. His friends tried to grab him but he came across the room towards the door. I turned and faced him.

'You know something,' he sneered, weaving and dodging in front of me, lifting his hands and jabbing at me wildly.

I could see his friends getting up from the table.

I kicked him hard on the shins, and slammed my fist into his face as he went over. I was wearing my boots. I hit him again in the kidneys with a clenched fist and walked out of the bar, running down the concrete steps and out of the main doors of the Naafi. I could hear them shouting upstairs, and a door swinging backwards and forwards on its hinges. I walked past the guardroom, massaging my hand. I walked straight past the military policeman who challenged me, and he stared as I walked up the drive, shouting something and then going back inside.

In divisional headquarters, Joseph read the newspapers and kept a bottle of light ale under his desk.

'You think I'm going to die sober?' he said when Watters caught him drinking from the bottle.

Watters ignored him.

'Unprecedented aggressive actions,' Joseph told me, reading from the paper, stabbing at the words with derision. 'An act of piracy, cynically flouting international standards. An attempt to strangle a sovereign country by American imperialist circles, taking a step towards unleashing a thermo-nuclear war.'

That was Khrushchev's opinion.

Joseph took a drink from his bottle.

I read the paper over his shoulder and saw the mention of surface-to-surface nuclear missiles.

Nemesis was a surface-to-surface nuclear missile.

'You're going to get it in the neck.' Joseph beamed delightedly. 'You aren't?'

'No, but you're a prime target, stands to reason, must be.'

He went on reading and drinking his ale. An old woman stood at the desk with her canary in a cage, asking us whether there was anything she could do to protect the bird.

'He was my husband's,' she kept telling Joseph. 'He still misses him. He belonged to my husband. He used to sing to him. He can still say his name. Say Arnold, budgy, say Arnold. He can. Good boy, then. He does it at home all the time. Say Arnold, budgy. Say Arnold.'

The American defence secretary announced that some twenty-five Communist-bloc ships were steaming towards the island, and intense military activity was reported from southern Florida, where large-scale concentration of troops, marines and air personnel was reported to be in progress.

'Did you hear about Bertrand Russell', Matthew wrote, 'sending a telegram to Khrushchev?' Matthew thought the philosopher was a great man. He was one of the leading campaigners for nuclear disarmament, and had appealed to the Soviet premier 'not to be provoked by the unjustifiable action of the United States'. He stressed that any 'precipitous action' might lead to the 'annihilation of mankind'. In his reply, Khrushchev expressed his sincere gratitude. 'Don't you think that's great?' Matthew said happily. He told me he was desperately trying to read through the whole of Shakespeare, because he didn't want to die without once in his lifetime having got through the entire works. 'I sit in my room and read *King Lear*,' he said, 'and it puts everything in perspective. I hope you are also using your time usefully.' A student union photograph was included with the letter. He ended by sending his love.

In the division, two officers arrested a man for soliciting in the public lavatories in the town square. The man had been under surveillance for weeks, and had been caught talking to a young boy in one of the cubicles. The man worked in the local library, and lived with his mother in one of the villages out of town.

I heard the beating when I took a blanket down to the cells.

'You going to tell us?' one of the policemen said very quietly.

The man didn't reply.

'You going to be helpful?'

I heard a chair move against a wall.

The man uttered something indistinct and there was a thump like rotten fruit hitting the floor.

'Don't, please.'

They hit him again.

'Don't.'

'Dougie . . . '

I left the blanket and caught the bus home.

In the morning, when I took the man his breakfast, he was lying face down on his bunk. I told him the tea would go cold and he turned and watched me leave the cell. He hadn't shaved and his eyes were black with tiredness. In the charge room, he trembled when the sergeant read out the charge, and then signed the confession he'd made the previous night. He refused to answer when the sergeant asked him if he wanted to telephone his mother before the hearing.

I went to see Caroline that night.

She telephoned the police house and said that her father was still working on Nemesis, her mother was down in London.

'I don't want to be on my own,' she said flatly.

She sounded nervous, tired.

I changed into my jeans and a shirt and plimsolls and walked round to the house. I took the letter from Matthew. She was waiting for me in the long sitting room.

'I think it's awful,' she said solemnly, pouring us both a drink of whisky and handing me the glass.

She walked to the french windows. They were wide open.

The room was cold and a shower of rain scuttered across the garden.

I went and stood behind her, and she leaned against my shoulder, holding her drink in both hands.

'You don't drink spirits.'

'I do now,' she said quietly.

I turned her round and looked at her face. She looked washed out. She smiled weakly. She was wearing a thick jumper and blue jeans. I took the glass out of her hands and put it on the oak bookcase. She watched me finish my own drink and smiled when I held her close, putting my arms round her shoulders. She was trembling.

I kissed her and turned to go to the sofa, but she refused to move, nuzzling into my shoulder, burying her face in my shirt. I held her close, listening to the rain in the garden. A few roses were still blooming, dull red in the dismal evening. I tried to get the cigarettes out of my back pocket but she clung to my arms, her body warm against my own, her hair damp from the cold garden.

'Can't we sit down?' I asked, but she shook her head and looked up at me.

'There's nobody in the house,' she said.

'So we have to stand?'

'Fool.'

She laughed nervously and took my hand. She led the way upstairs and took me into her own bedroom overlooking the garden and desolate countryside, wet, dripping mist over the fields and woods along the cliff road. The rain was coming down heavily by now, and I thought about the open french windows, but she said nobody was around, nobody ever came into the garden. The only way in was through the house. We stood at the window and watched the rain for a long time.

'Have you got anything?' she said, and I shook my head, saying no, my voice coming out in a whisper, my mouth and tongue dry. I couldn't understand the strange way she was speaking.

'Why should I have anything?' I said quietly.

'I'm sorry.'

'After all this time.'

'I know.'

She went to a white cupboard in the corner of her room and handed me a small packet. 'I got them off the camp,' she said nervously. 'One of the girls who works in the Naafi.'

I took the packet and we stood looking at each other, the room nearly dark in the twilight, the evening wintry and silent.

'Do you know what to do?' she asked.

I shook my head.

I fumbled with the slippery packet. She undid them for me when she saw my fingers trembling. She touched my hand as she gave them back. My hand was still bruised from the night in the Naafi.

I watched her, thinking about the dustbins at the brothel, the rubbers shrivelled and leaking, yellowed with stale sperm, the rusty bottoms of the dustbins awash with pale liquid moving like thick snot.

She unfastened her jeans and slipped out of the jumper, lifting it over her head so that her breasts were taut and bare, her skin freckled with goose-pimples. She came and undid my jeans and helped me pull them off. We got into the bed and shivered. The sheets were linen, cold. She rolled against me and started kissing my shoulders and neck. I could feel her hands between my legs. As I got harder, she kept whispering something about the time, and I glanced at my watch, making her laugh. I took my watch off and put it on the table where a pink rabbit sat and watched us, its china face white in the gloom, its eyes a piercing electric blue.

When I put my finger inside her, she was wet and writhing, clenching her fists behind my head and kissing me with her mouth wide open, her tongue licking my face, her teeth biting the inside of my mouth. She squirmed against me until my back was against the wall and I grazed my shoulder, struggling to push her onto her back, banging my elbow into the brass bedstead.

I could hardly get an erection.

I kept going soft.

She knelt up on the bed and touched me with the tips of her fingers, shy, solemn, awkward with her serious concentration. She sat over me and tried to unroll one of the rubbers, giggling as it slipped off my limp cock, her clumsiness making me hard again and her fingers slippery with excitement. As she touched me with her cold hands, she lay down and I climbed on top, leaning on my elbows, letting her guide me inside with her fingers.

She lay and watched me catch my breath.

I had never been so uncomfortable. My elbow ached from the knock against the bedstead, and my shoulder was grazed. I could feel Caroline beneath me, her breasts squashed against my chest, but I couldn't feel anything else. She had her hand down between us, doing something to herself, and came with a sudden shout, yelping as if in pain, her eyes wide open and frightened.

Outside, the rain spattered against the window.

I felt myself coming. I was so hard I could hardly feel the rubber, but the coming seemed to make no difference, I stayed hard inside her, rigid with pain, my groin aching as if I'd been kicked in the stomach. Caroline stared at me as I gasped for breath. I felt as though I was having an attack of asthma.

I stayed inside her.

I couldn't move.

I was still hard and my elbow felt as if it was broken. I began to come again, and Caroline flinched, surprised, her hands fluttering behind my head. When I started coming, she cried and dug her nails into my back, her eyes white and urgent, her teeth clenched tight, her lips wide open. In the cold bedroom, I started to cry. She held me locked inside her. She kissed me gently on the face, her eyes filled with panic. She kept telling me it was all right, she kept whispering something about the french windows.

PART III

By the Light
of the
Silvery Moon

THIRTY-TWO

The winter mornings stiffened with frost. I could feel the cold move in the fields.

I woke with Caroline on my mind, half expecting her to be there, curled up beside me, warm against my side. I felt like crying when she wasn't, as though I had been expecting her, as though her absence was a deliberate hurt. I could hear my mother calling to the chickens down the garden, but I didn't want to open my eyes. I didn't want to think about being in bed without Caroline.

'You getting up?' my mother shouted up the stairs, but she was not bothered, I could hear the humour in her calls. 'I'm doing breakfast,' she said, and I could hear her heaping coal onto the fire in the kitchen. Down the garden, the chickens squawked and screamed, fighting over the food, scrabbling in the metal feeders that must have been coated with a white rime. I looked at my watch and it was half past eleven.

'I'm going down to the village.' My mother chattered at the sink while I sat by the range and drank a mug of tea. 'You want to come?'

'In this cold?'

'It'll wake you up.'

'I haven't seen Emily and Wilfred for ages.'

'I know.' She nodded. 'They were saying.'

'Well?'

'You're busy,' she said quickly. 'I did explain.'

We cycled down to the village and left our bicycles leaning at the gate. The ground in the orchard was shining with frost. The apple trees were black and bare, hunched into the freezing weather.

Emily sat peacefully beside the fire, her hands crossed in her lap, her eyes gazing into the flames. 'They say the Thames froze one winter,' she said, Wilfred standing behind her, brushing her hair as if she was a child. 'That must have been something.'

'That must,' Wilfred said eagerly.

'They say you could skate for miles.'

205

A log cracked on the fire, showering sparks into the black grate, dazzling on the polished fender.

'We used to go skating in the country,' my mother reminded her.

'Did you?'

'On Black Fen. The field that froze. I told you!'

'Is the boy all right?' Emily asked abruptly.

'He's here, girl,' Wilfred told her.

'Apples were good this year, Stephen.'

'I told him, girl.'

'Apples were fine.'

I could see my mother crying.

We left and cycled slowly along the lane at the bottom of the cliff. The beck was frozen. On the cliff top, the oaks and beeches were bare, the sky pierced by Scots pine. The fields stood hard and empty.

'She'll die soon,' my mother said as we cycled up the hill back to the house. 'She'll die this winter.'

In the yard, I put the bikes in the shed, and watched her trying the tap on the water butt. It had been frozen for days.

'It doesn't usually get frozen this early,' she said, thumping the butt with the palm of her hand as if she could make the tap work. There was a dull thumping noise inside it, and the metal bands creaked. There were icicles hanging from the drainpipes and the ledge outside my bedroom window. Frost patterned the inside of the window every morning. I shivered, rubbing my hands together and going back into the kitchen. My mother was wearing her dress and flowered apron.

'You going to help me?' she said, coming and standing in the doorway.

'Leave it for later.'

'We can do it.'

My father had said he would break the ice on the tub.

'I need to wash my hair,' my mother said.

'You can wash your hair in water from the tap.'

'I like fresh water.'

'He said he'd do it.'

She scoffed. 'Wait for him we'll wait for ever.'

'He'll do it.'

She went to the shed and came back with a stepladder and the axe my father kept for cutting up wood. She propped the ladder against the water butt and began to climb up, holding the axe clumsily in one hand and slipping on the ladder.

'Come down, Mother.'

'Are you going to do it, then?' she asked, half turning on the ladder, looking at me defiantly, her eyes grey and teasing, her hair untidy and shining in the sunlight. 'Are you?'

'I said I would.'

'I know you're busy thinking about that Caroline.'

She came down the ladders and I got my duffel coat and boots from the cupboard.

I went to the shed and fetched the large wooden mallet we used for driving the stakes into the ground for the chicken wire. I told my mother to put the axe by the wall.

'It'd be quicker.'

'We're not using that.'

I told her to stand back.

I climbed up the ladder and peered down at the ice. It was inches thick, maybe a foot thick, solid and filthy, the surface cracked and dirty with grime. Leaves had fallen into the water and frozen with the ice. A feather stuck to the side of the water butt.

I balanced at the top of the ladder and lifted the wooden mallet above my head. I brought the hammer down as hard as I could in the centre of the ice and the head buried in the ice, the shaft breaking in two and my arm hitting the side of the water butt so that I thought it was broken, the skin taken off in a jagged cut, the pain making me lurch backwards and clutch at the drainpipe. For a second, I thought I was going to black out.

'You all right?' my mother said nervously, shivering in her dress and apron. 'Stephen?'

'Go and get a coat on, can't you?'

She watched me for a second and then went and got her coat from the hall. I massaged my arm. I could feel the blood on my shirt. When she came back she took the broken handle of the mallet and threw it down the garden as far as she could.

'You should have used the axe.'

I took the axe from her and climbed the ladder again. I stood on the top, staring down into the ice.

'Is this what you want?' I said, but my mother shook her head and wrapped her coat round her, waiting for me to go on, impatient.

'Get on with it.'

I thought briefly about Caroline.

I hadn't seen her since that last night of the missile crisis, when the fleet had turned back. I hadn't been back to the house and she hadn't telephoned.

I wrote a long letter to Matthew telling him what had happened, and then destroyed the letter.

'Stephen?'

My mother was looking up at me, shivering in the cold.

'Aren't you going to do it?'

'Yes, of course.'

'Be careful.'

I knew she was thinking about the farm, where she had grown up as a child. A water butt in the yard. They must have had to do this every winter, the men on the farm, when the water butt was the only water. I lifted the axe and felt the stab of pain in my left arm, my bruised arm already stiffening. I closed my eyes and brought the axe down on the ice with a savage crash, using all my force, tensing my arms and back so that when the axe hit the ice the shaft vibrated in my hands and I had to let go, the pain racking up my shoulders and sending me stumbling back against the wall, slithering awkwardly down to the ground. The ladder tilted and collapsed on top of me. I could hear the ice thumping inside the water butt. I wondered vaguely whether I'd broken both my arms.

Down the drive, we heard the gate clatter shut, and my father's bicycle, the chain whirring as he walked up the drive. He looked surprised, lost in his thoughts. 'You playing at soft buggers?' he said tiredly.

My mother said she was worried about the noise the ice was making in the water butt. She said she had to have some fresh water for her hair. 'He's hurt his arm,' she added, glancing nervously at me. 'I keep telling you this butt's not safe.'

My father frowned angrily. 'I said I'd do it.'

'You!'

'I said I'd do it!'

Leaving his bike against the shed, he turned off the lamp and stood

208

watching us awkwardly. His face looked frozen. 'You all right?' he asked me.

'Yes.'

'You sure?'

'He's all right!' my mother said impatiently.

For a minute, nobody spoke.

'Right, then,' my father said flatly. He shrugged, and without looking at either of us, went into the kitchen. We could hear him shovelling coal onto the range. A warm light shone out into the yard.

'I'll make some tea,' my mother said quickly, rubbing her hands on her apron.

In the kitchen, the kettle was already whistling, and loud dance music blared from the wireless.

An owl flew low over the police house.

'And muffins.' My mother giggled. 'I said I'd do some muffins.'

I went to see Caroline a few days later.

'I didn't think you'd come back,' she said.

She was sitting on the floor by the fire. Her parents were out. She was wearing a thick jumper and jeans and making notes for an essay. She was writing essays on Russian poetry which her father corrected.

I knelt down beside her and warmed my hands at the fire.

'I've been busy.'

She smiled, closing her notebook. She rested her hands on her knees. After a moment, she got up suddenly and went to the kitchen. She ran the tap and then came back to sit beside the fire.

'I missed you,' she said.

'Did you?'

'Yes.'

She didn't look at me. She seemed nervous, on edge. She was wearing her hair tied back off her forehead and behind her ears, and I noticed how small her ears were. She was wearing gold earrings for the first time, and they glinted against her cheek in the firelight.

'Barbara's leaving soon,' she said suddenly, and I thought she was talking about Matthew, not hearing the words properly, not really listening. I stared at her and then rubbed the side of my face quickly. My arm was agony.

'Barbara?'

'In December.'

I thought about the letter I'd written to Matthew. I wanted to stand up and go through to the study and use the telephone, call Matthew at university, talk to him, tell him Barbara was leaving the camp, would soon be leaving the country. But why should he be bothered about Barbara?

'Everybody's leaving,' I said, and Caroline laughed, a sudden bright ridicule, her eyes shining fiercely, then looking away, embarrassed, awkward.

I felt stupid.

She got up again and went to the kitchen, and I heard the tap running for a long time. When she came back, she sat down at the opposite side of the fire.

'Stephen,' she said carefully.

'Yes.'

'I've been thinking about you.'

'Oh.'

'I don't think you should go into the police.'

She leaned forward, folding her arms across her knees.

I could see the water on her lips, her mouth thin and white, the tip of her tongue touching her teeth nervously.

I got up and went and sat next to her. I leaned forward and tried to kiss her but she looked surprised, lifting her hand to her cheek suddenly, her eyes alarmed and flinching. She shook her head very quickly. I touched her shoulder and then stared into the fire.

'I hurt my arm,' I told her.

'How?'

'Breaking the ice in the water butt.'

'Don't you have mains water?'

'Yes, but my mother likes fresh water to wash her hair.'

'Your mother's strange.'

I kissed her again and the same startled look flickered through her eyes. I thought for one brief weird second that she didn't know who I was. I tried to hold her face and look into her eyes but she moved my hand gently, and rested her chin on her knees, folding her arms round her long skirt.

'I shall miss Barbara,' she said flatly, as if she was trying to explain something.

'You weren't that close.'

'She's my friend.'

'I miss Matthew,' I said bleakly, the pain suddenly filling my eyes, the idea of him working somewhere a hundred miles away, sitting in a room completely silent, reading his books or preparing one of his essays, awful. I shook my head and stood up. 'I have to go,' I told her.

'I'm sorry.'

'What?'

'I'm busy, that's all it is. These exams.'

'Yes.'

'I'll see you at the weekend.'

At the door, she kissed me on the mouth, her lips cold from the water she'd been drinking, her hand shaking on my shoulders. I held her close for a second and then stood back. As I walked away across the huge open green, I could see the light from the doorway shining in the frosted grass. I turned and waved, and she shouted something about going to the cinema at the weekend. I went back home and told my father I needed to do some studying for the common law exams. He was working in the office. A single-bar electric fire hummed from the green wall. He wanted to talk about when I was going to make my decision about going to Wakefield for the next stage of my training.

'You'll have to decide sooner or later,' my father persisted.

'I know,' I agreed.

I went upstairs, and sat in my cold room.

THIRTY-THREE

'I'm going to get rid of the chickens,' my mother said one morning when we were eating breakfast.

Music blared from the radio in the kitchen.

In the office, my father was shouting down the telephone, angry about some equipment that hadn't been delivered, furious with the civilians in headquarters who didn't seem to know where Fulnar was.

I waited for her to explain.

'If you get moved to another division,' she said, buttering some toast and then leaving it uneaten on her plate. 'That's why I'm worried.'

'I don't help so much.'

'You help.'

'There's my father.'

She shook her head. 'He's too busy.'

I felt as though she was getting rid of them because of me, because I was leaving home. Somehow she was blaming me, though she kept saying she wanted me to go, wanted me to make the application. She couldn't see herself going on feeding and caring for the hens without me.

I had never been that interested.

I hadn't taken the eggs to the village for weeks. I lay in bed in the mornings, thinking about Caroline instead of getting up. I could hear my mother going down to the garden at six o'clock every morning, but I never wanted to get up. It was warm in bed with Caroline, dreaming about Caroline.

My father immediately said it was a good idea, and went round the village asking people if they would like to buy one of the hens for their Sunday dinner. A week later, all twelve had been ordered.

I sat in the garage and took the first of the birds on my knee. You were supposed to form a crook with your fingers and break the neck with a sudden jerk backwards. On my knee, the bird sat patiently. It was one of the birds that used to come up to the kitchen during the summer, pecking at the ground round the door for food, sitting on my shoulder so that my father could take a photograph. It sat on my knee, familiar with my voice, trusting. Its head jerked from side to side, the bright eyes black in the dark garage.

Tears poured down my face.

My father went and asked Frank if he could help us.

'I thought you grew up on a farm,' he said nastily to my mother, making a fuss as he got his bike to go and fetch Frank. 'I thought you knew all about farming.'

Frank cycled up to the police house, and left his bike at the gate.

He told me to go and get a cup of tea.

In half an hour, the birds were all dead.

We sat in the kitchen and talked about the weather, the early frosts, the hard grazing for the sheep.

'You can sell the hut at the next farm auction,' Frank said as he left the house.

'I've thought of that,' my mother told him.

She walked with him up the drive to the gate and I watched them from the front room. My father had gone off on his rounds. He was due to meet his sergeant in one of the villages, and was irritable at being made late. When my mother came back, she got her coat and gloves and said we ought to take one of the chickens down to Emily and Wilfred. I went with her, cycling along the slippery road, laughing as she skidded and wheeled into the rough hedges, balancing the enormous chicken on my handlebars. Now that they were dead, the hens all looked alike. I had no idea which hen I was carrying down to the village for Wilfred and Emily to eat.

When we got to the cottage, Emily was still in bed.

'She won't mind,' Wilfred told us. 'She wouldn't want to spoil anything.'

'Is she all right, Wilfred?' my mother asked.

'Just tired.'

We sat round the fire and drank mulberry wine while Wilfred plucked the chicken.

'You have to do her in front of a fire,' Wilfred said slyly, and my mother flicked him lightly with her fingers, telling me to take no notice and holding her glass up to the firelight so that she could look at the flames through the coloured liquid.

'We used to sit round the kitchen and pluck the birds at Christmas,' she said excitedly, her cheeks glowing from the cold and now the wine and fire. 'We used to tell stories and sing carols.'

'Get 'em from the deep freezer now.' Wilfred nodded solemnly.

'And a lot easier it is too,' my mother said.

'Now, girl!'

'You wouldn't get Norman bothering.'

'He'd do it if you asked him.'

'You don't know him, Wilfred.'

'No romance, these women,' he said to me darkly, flicking feathers into a cardboard box and holding the naked bird up so that we could see the fine flesh on the bones. 'No romance at all. Now isn't that something. Like a turkey, this bird. Like a real turkey.'

I took my mother to the Plough after we left Wilfred and Emily's and we sat in the corner by the fire and drank cider and ate beef and mustard rolls. I had never seen my mother so excited or proud, her cheeks flushed, her eyes shining. She had green eyes. She smiled and leaned on my shoulder, and told me she couldn't wait for me to finish with the cadets, start doing the job properly.

'You know, when your father joined,' she said, 'I couldn't use lipstick and I had to wear long dresses.'

'I don't believe you.'

'It's true, Stephen. I had to wear long dresses. We were supposed to be respectable in those days, after the war. We had to be decent, good living.'

'You're making it up.'

'No, I'm not,' she said with a firm shake of her head, pursing her lips and holding her drink in front of her. 'This is nice. I'm not making anything up. I didn't wear lipstick until quite recent. You couldn't get it in the war anyway, but I wouldn't have worn it without your father saying.'

'Like you didn't work in a laundry, and he didn't do odd jobs on the docks?'

Policemen were not supposed to do part-time jobs, and their wives were not supposed to work at all.

That was another yarn she'd told me.

'They got more relaxed about that,' she said. 'After the war. So you needn't think you're being clever. They just started not to take any notice. Because the pay was so poor.'

214

'You get a free house,' I said sarcastically, but she always took me seriously, always thought I was being straight.

'It's lovely, isn't it?' she said. 'I shall be so proud, and your father's really excited. And they'll look after you. They'll see you all right.'

I drained my glass and felt the buzz inside my head.

I walked back to the camp, my mother cycling up the road ahead of me, singing and wobbling into the grass, shrieking as she almost fell off. I felt sick and hot from the drink. I felt as though the chickens were lucky, having somebody to break their necks. In the darkness, my mother's voice carried over the fields. The lights round Nemesis twinkled. I stood at the gate for a long time, watching the blaze of lights that shimmered from the camp, the miles of surrounding darkness. I put my bike in the shed, and my father was shouting at my mother in the kitchen, telling her to grow up, telling her she never thought about anybody but herself. I went to bed, and listened to them arguing.

In the morning, my father looked as if he hadn't slept.

'You'll get the papers soon for a transfer,' he told me as he rushed through his breakfast. He was due to meet Watters, and didn't want to be late. The superintendent sometimes arrived at checkpoints, just to make sure the men on the isolated stations were keeping to their routines.

'How do you know?' I asked him.

'It's about time.'

'You asked Watters.'

'So what if I did?'

'It's none of your business.'

'You're my son.'

'You don't own me.'

'Somebody has to make a decision.'

'And you think you can make mine?'

'Somebody has to,' he shouted.

He banged his fists on the table and slammed out of the room, coming back immediately and crashing his chair into the wall.

'You won't,' he yelled. 'You won't. You aren't capable. All your reading. All your cleverness. You aren't thinking.'

My mother stood in the kitchen doorway. She was trembling.

'It's a good job,' he shouted furiously. 'It's a good job.'

215

'Norman . . . '

'You ought to be grateful . . . '

'Norman . . . '

'You ought to be thankful you've got something . . . '

'Please . . . '

'You ought to beg them to take you on, because you can't do anything else, you can't even kill a few hens, you're that fucking useless.'

He walked out of the house, slamming the door behind him.

THIRTY-FOUR

I went to the Naafi and sat with Matthew drinking double whiskies. He was back for the Christmas vacation. He was thinner than ever. He carried a shoulder-bag full of books. He talked endlessly about Empson and the students he was sharing a house with, the parties and all-night studying, the bright lights of the library, the curries and rich stews they cooked in their tiny kitchen, the muffins they toasted on proper forks over the fire.

'If you go ahead with your father's plans,' he told me, 'you'll go mad, like the Duchess of Malfi.'

'They aren't my father's plans.'

'Your own plans then, what's the difference, you'll still go mad.'

'Is it anything to do with you?' I shouted angrily.

'I'm supposed to be your friend.'

'Then shut up.'

'How many writers do you know who are in the police?'

'Who said anything about being a writer?'

'Journalists, then?'

'Or a journalist!'

'You won't survive. You'll have a nervous breakdown. How can you *stand* such people?'

'You mean I should prefer people who are interested in books?'

'I think you should respect yourself,' Matthew said quietly, draining his glass and banging it down on the table.

'And what's that supposed to mean?'

'You know what it means.'

'Because nobody else will?'

'Because you won't *yourself*.'

'You don't know what you're talking about.'

'You won't because it isn't your decision, you haven't *chosen* to do this job, it's been chosen for you because you feel guilty about hurting your father. But you know it won't work, so why go on lying to yourself? Nobody else cares.'

'Except you.'

'That's right, except me, you arsehole.'

In the cold outside the guardroom, Matthew sighed and stared up at the darkness. The sky was blistered with stars.

'It's making you unhappy,' he said as we walked across the grass. 'It's making you cynical. Despising everybody's motives. You're losing all your innocence.'

I shivered and pushed my hands deep into my pockets.

'You're losing your mind.'

In the darkness, I felt sick with loneliness.

'You get all your knowledge from books,' I said. 'You get all your experience from reading.'

'You think Tolstoy knew nothing about lust? You think Dostoevsky didn't understand gambling? You think Shakespeare never lost a child, never suffered sexual infatuation?'

'You get it all from other people.'

'Absolutely.'

After a long silence, he shrugged and touched my arm, shook my hand and walked away.

In the cold, I could hear his footsteps for a long time.

'I have to go,' Caroline said when I got upset about the vacation. 'I can't help it if my parents have friends in Paris.'

'You're going to *Paris* for Christmas?'

'What's wrong with that?'

'What about me?'

'What about you? We aren't married or anything.'

'You might at least . . . '

'I might at least what? I can't come and stay with you. I don't want to spend my Christmas with your parents.'

'Thanks very much.'

'I didn't mean it like that.'

'Yes, you did.'

'Well, we could hardly be making love all the time could we, not with your mother hanging around?'

'It's their house,' I started to shout irrationally, and she leaned forward and gripped my hand firmly, talking straight into my face.

'Exactly.'

I sat back against the wooden seat and glared into the pub fire. I could feel my face burning from the drink and the heat and the argument. I saw Caroline's hand next to mine, her knuckles white as she clenched and unclenched her fingers, her fingernails bitten back to the quick.

'I didn't know you bit your nails,' I said after a long silence.

I could hardly control my voice, embarrassed, resentful.

'You don't notice much, do you?' She sighed.

'You didn't used to bite your nails,' I said angrily.

'Didn't I?'

'No, you didn't.'

After a pause, she shook her head and tried to pick her glass up from the table. Her hand was shaking. 'I'm sorry,' she said quietly.

Her hair was parted down the middle. She was wearing a tweed skirt and a blue jumper with a string of her mother's best pearls shining round her neck. She had faintly pink lipstick and pearl earrings. She looked grown up.

I sat beside her, stunned at the thought of her being away at Christmas. I couldn't imagine the holiday without her.

I told her I might be moving to a new division after the holiday.

'Where?'

'I don't know. Could be anywhere.'

'How will you get home?'

'On the train, at weekends.'

'Is it definite, then?'

'Yes,' I told her, though nothing had been decided.

I walked her back to the house and went with her inside. Her parents were at a party. I followed her upstairs and in the small fluffy bedroom she undressed and lay down on the bed naked. I could never understand her wanting the cold, liking the cold. She flinched when I touched her. I knelt in front of her and kissed her face and neck until she started unfastening my jeans and smiling at me in her vague, distracted way, solemn as she watched me harden. I went inside her urgently and came straight away, her eyes watching me as I shouted out to the empty house, her hands resting lightly on my shoulders, as if she was being careful not to scratch my bare skin.

I lay down beside her and listened to her steady breathing. I could hear the boiler roaring for the central heating, and the voices of the party coming from one of the big houses across the green. I turned my head on the pillow and stared at Caroline.

'I shall miss you,' I said, and she flinched, as if thinking about something else, as if I hadn't been there. 'Did you hear?' I said, and touched her arm, squeezing her elbow.

She turned slightly to face me and smiled. 'I'm sorry.'

'I just wanted you to know.'

On the night before Christmas, I walked to the Catholic church with Barbara and we sat on the back row, making the responses and listening to the stumbling voices of the choir, watching the altar boys in their white surplices, the midnight candles burning round the Host, the consecration of the bread and wine, flame shining on the silver chalice.

'I believe,' Barbara whispered at my side, kneeling before the flickering candles. 'I believe.'

I didn't believe anything.

I resented her quick responses, her prayers and rosary, her sense of belonging.

I wanted Caroline, and she was with her family in Paris.

In the morning, I would be opening my presents with my parents.

As the priest intoned the words for the mass, I knew that soon I would be completely alone, the only person left on the camp, listening to the skylarks or the circling crows, the absolute silence of the frozen countryside. As they left, one by one, I would stand in the fields like a scarecrow, frightening the birds, watching the grim patrols round Nemesis. At midnight, I remained seated, counting the hairs on the back of the neck of the American colonel in front of me. Barbara walked with the rest of the congregation to the front of the church.

On a cold January morning, Barbara came to say goodbye.

'I'll write from America,' she told me, but she knew I would soon be leaving myself, and wouldn't come back to the station. 'I'll write through Matthew,' she added, squeezing my arm and shivering. 'It's cold.'

I walked with her to where the car was waiting.

She held me very quickly and kissed me on the cheek. 'I'll miss you,' she whispered.

I shook my head, unable to speak.

'Stephen.'

'I'm all right.'

'Sometimes people get caught,' she said. 'Trapped into things they don't want to do.'

I nodded.

'Isn't that right?'

'Yes.'

'I'm so sorry. I have to go.'

'I know.'

'They're waiting.'

'You'll miss the transport.'

'Just *do* something about it.'

'I will.'

'You promise?'

'I promise.'

As the car drove off, I stood in the road and waved.

THIRTY-FIVE

My father seemed closed off from us. We talked late at night, sitting round the range, my mother's laughter bright and girlish, electrical because of his stubborn refusal to join us, his anger lost in the work, the patrols, the endless watching. He would cycle for hours through the frozen countryside. 'There's going to be snow,' he told me abruptly one morning. By late afternoon, a thick cloud of snow was drifting against the house, obliterating the windows, gathering at the back door. The fence we had erected for the chickens collapsed under the weight of snow. The chicken run looked ruined and desolate. The lanes were deserted. We had to go down to the village each day to help Wilfred get wood for the fire, carry food from the village store. On the main roads, the Americans used their enormous snow ploughs to shift the worst of the drifts, and made jokes about the kind of snow they got back home. For a week, I couldn't get through to the division, and sat in my room reading, or helped my mother in the kitchen. I spent hours with my mother.

After two days, the road into town was frozen and treacherous.

On his heavy Rudge bicycle, my father had difficulty getting through the narrow lanes, but he was determined to keep contact with the village. He fretted all the time in case anything went wrong. At breakfast, he wouldn't speak.

His restlessness disturbed my mother.

'If it goes on much longer,' he said, 'I shall have to get to the village across the fields.'

'He's excited,' my mother said to me, laughing, watching him.

He ignored her, frowning at his plate.

'I don't see why you have to go,' she grumbled half jokingly when he set out each morning. 'They don't thank you.'

She told me I ought to stay in bed, and frowned when I brought her a cup of tea. Drinking her tea, she sat propped up against the pillows with the curtains open, the bedroom ceiling dazzling with the reflection of the snow.

My father stood in the doorway, fastening his heavy coat. 'We'd best be off,' he said.

'Is Stephen going with you?' she said resentfully, her eyes shining pale green in the light from the snow.

My father's eyes were a cold blue, calm and level as he looked at her. His hair had gone almost completely grey since we moved from the coast.

'We've got our duty.' He smiled.

'Showing off.' She yawned, pleased. 'Go on then, the pair of you.'

Cycling to the village, we skidded through the ruts of snow. We made straight for the Plough. The Plough had no lounge. It was open all hours. In the freezing weather, some of the old people sat there all day, drinking cider and gossiping about the snow. As I went past late some nights with my father, the lights would still be burning in the bar. My father said he got too much information from the drinkers to bother about the licensing laws.

In the village, we dumped our bicycles outside the post office and went inside to get some tobacco. The graveyard was opposite the post office. A cold wind blew scurries of snow across the graveyard, banking it against the blackened tombstones.

'You hear about Mrs Starr?' the woman in the post office asked my father when we walked into the shop.

'Emily?'

He looked frightened, alarmed. He shook his head and listened tensely while she told him about the ambulance.

'They come all the way from town,' the woman said, 'and then they got stuck at the bottom of the hill. Somebody should complain about that lane. There's been no gritting since we had this weather.' She measured out my father's tobacco, frowning as she concentrated.

'We'd better get round there,' my father said, handing her a pound note. 'Is Wilfred all right?'

A man coughed outside the shop, struggling with the door so that the bell rang jerkily. He stood in the door, kicking the snow off his boots.

The woman counted out the change and banged the till shut.

Several men from the pub had come out to try and help, she said, but there was nothing they could do. They found Wilfred standing in the garden in his slippers, shouting at the ambulancemen to hurry up. By the time the men got through to the cottage with the stretcher, he was frozen, shivering with the cold. 'He'll die of pneumonia,' the woman said irritably, as if it was his own fault.

'He's a tough old sod,' the man said, ignoring her sharp glance. She frowned triumphantly at my father.

'I don't suppose you could get through,' she said spitefully.

'I could get through,' my father said. 'If I'd been told.'

She shook her head. 'That'll be another funeral,' she said, pursing her lips.

'What?'

'She died.'

'Died?'

'Yes, died,' the woman said, emphasising the word as if my father was thick-witted.

My father pushed his tobacco into his pocket and went back outside. He looked shocked, white-faced.

The road was thick with snow, and he slipped on the pavement. The villagers had given up throwing salt onto the pavement. One of the farmers came down the main part of the village every day spreading grit, but it froze as fast as the snow. He pushed his bicycle past the vicarage and round the narrow lanes to Wilfred and Emily's cottage.

I followed him, struggling in the snow.

'She was nearly a hundred,' Wilfred told us when we were sitting in the tiny front room, watching him stuff tobacco into his pipe. 'She wanted to make a hundred.'

His eyes were pale blue, grey in the bright firelight. The brass fender shone with polish. A row of slippers stood in the hearth. Wilfred sat in the oak rocking chair, his pipe clenched between his teeth. Photographs lined the mantelpiece.

Wilfred and Emily were the first people in the village my father had got to know, making friends easily and gently with Emily, joking with Wilfred about the poaching he had done as a boy.

'We were hungry then,' Wilfred always said self-righteously, ignoring my father's laughter.

'I told everybody she would live longer,' he said. 'I told her she had to let me die first. I said I'd have nothing to do without her to chase after.'

As he joked, there were tears in his eyes.

My father sat and unwrapped his tobacco.

We drank camomile tea, and my father and Wilfred smoked their pipes in silence. Wood crackled on the fire. A pear tree creaked and groaned at the window, growing up the side of the house. The earth of the garden was almost level with the tiny windows.

'There's not much for the boy,' Wilfred said vaguely.

'He's all right, Wilfred.'

'He'll be wanting to be off.'

'He's all right.'

We stayed in the cottage most of the morning.

At the funeral, we stood with Wilfred in the cold church, coloured light from the windows like a rainbow on the stone, candles flickering on the altar.

In the small churchyard, we helped him drop the petals of some wild roses onto the coffin. He had kept the wild roses in a box, because Emily always said they were her favourite flower.

Trapped in the house, my mother cooked enormous meals and fretted about Wilfred. She said there were rats coming in from the fields, looking for food, and she was worried they would find a way into the house. Bored with the snow, unable to get into town, she sat by the fire in the evenings, relaxing on the floor and watching the television. When my father told her he ought to do night patrols, she lost her temper and, for a few nights, moved into the single bed in the front bedroom.

My father cycled down to the village most nights and spent an hour chatting in the pub. Because there was nothing else to do, I usually went with him. The clock on the church still chimed the hours, and at closing time, my father left without saying a word, not wanting to bother the landlord. The lights went on burning in the pub windows. Walking round the village, we could hear the televisions in front rooms, wirelesses booming with music. Most of the old people went to bed early, trying to keep warm. Smoke rose from several chimneys.

At Wilfred's cottage, we could see the lights burning in the windows every night. My father thought they were lamps, flickering through the thick curtains, but when we went into the garden, we could see that they were candles. Our boots creaked in the snow. I knocked my head against the branches of the pear tree.

Wilfred didn't answer the knock on his door.

My father walked round the cottage, and there were candles in every window. For a moment, he couldn't remember whether the house had electricity, and then laughed briefly when I said of course it had, every house in the village had electricity. Wilfred must be burning the candles to keep warm. Or to save money.

'He can't have much money,' I said.

Getting back on his bike, my father said he would have to come back in the morning and tell Wilfred he must be careful of fire.

In the intense silence, we pushed our bicycles back up the lane. The immense sky seemed to be full of stars.

In the morning, Wilfred refused to answer the door.

He waved from the window that he was all right, and shook his head angrily when my father rattled the letterbox. At the post office, the woman told us he had his milk delivered, and groceries from the village store. Nobody had seen him since the funeral. We went back, but all the curtains were drawn, and we could hear the wireless playing in the parlour. A thin trail of smoke rose from the stone chimney.

My mother was sullen and unhappy. She watched television for hours and complained about the time my father spent in the village. He came home one night, and she said she could smell the cider on his breath. She accused him of seeing another woman.

She stood for long hours, watching the snow out of the window.

One afternoon, she saw a rat underneath the water butt. She was screaming by the time we got home, flailing at the tub with a broom handle. Her hands were bruised and frozen. The rough wood had chafed her skin.

We found the rat, lying underneath the water butt, its back broken.

My father made a pot of tea and we sat drinking in the kitchen, talking about Wilfred and eating toasted muffins. My mother spread thick strawberry jam on the muffins. When she heard my father telephoning the division, asking if there was any way they could get into town, she flew into a rage and slammed the telephone out of his hand.

The snow stopped after a couple of weeks.

The gritters cleared the main road to the town.

226

Frank came and laughed at my mother's bad temper, building a huge snowman in the garden and pelting the house with snowballs.

In the graveyard, clusters of snowdrops suddenly appeared around Emily's grave.

One morning, I went with my father to Wilfred's and watched him hammer on the front door. Nobody had seen him for almost a week, and there were two milk bottles outside his door. The curtains were all drawn. With the force of his shoulder, my father heaved at the front door, and it gave immediately, only the latch holding the door closed. Inside, the key was hanging from a doornail.

Wilfred was sitting beside the fire. He had been dead for several hours, his eyes open, his face locked into a frown of concentration. He was staring at a photograph of Emily on the mantelpiece.

While my father checked the room, I stood by the fire and looked at Wilfred. After a few moments, my father closed his eyes. His cheeks were still warm from the fire.

Slowly, we checked the house.

There were candles burning in every room.

Even in the pantry, thick curtains were nailed up to the window.

A blanket had been draped across the window on the landing.

At first we didn't notice but, despite the dozens of candles, every light in the house was turned on.

We locked the door and went to telephone for an ambulance.

As we walked up the garden path, I felt as though somebody was watching us, or that we ourselves ought to be watching, alert in the house full of light, waiting for the sound of a visitor.

THIRTY-SIX

At the end of the month, I was told to report to an isolated, bleak division about eighty miles away on the east coast.

'You can come home at weekends,' my mother said quickly while she packed my things. 'You can get the train and we'll pick you up from the station.'

'Leave him alone,' my father said testily, standing on the landing, getting in the way, watching us, helpless.

'I'm just telling him he can come home.'

'He knows that. He'll want to stay with his friends,' my father said, and I felt my heart lurch, a dull, empty ache that made me want to stay in the room for ever, never leave the flat fields, the frozen landscape. 'He'll be too busy chasing lasses,' my father said, and went downstairs.

When we were alone, my mother went on with the packing and told me about a young American who had called at the station one afternoon for no particular reason and sat drinking black coffee in the kitchen for nearly two hours, telling her all about his parents in Illinois, his sister who had just finished college.

'I'm not going to Illinois,' I pointed out.

'I know.'

'Well, then.'

'He was just a boy, feeling lonely.'

In lodgings, I shared a room with a cadet called Toyne who slept with a swastika underneath his pillow.

'It's a joke,' he said when I asked him about it, always good-humoured, always cheerful.

'But where did you get it?'

'Off my father.'

Toyne played football and cricket and went running each evening after work. He had thick black curly hair cut very short, and a long, chiselled nose. He made fun of everything, polishing his boots and spitting carelessly so that the phlegm landed on the carpet or on the chest of drawers. His father was a superintendent in another force.

'Where did he get a swastika?' I asked him derisively.

228

'Off a dead German,' he said. 'Where else?'

'At an auction?'

'Clever.'

The woman running the lodgings was a Christian Scientist who served us undercooked meat swimming in pools of blood, and chips she counted out from the frying pan. 'Seven each,' she would announce, counting the people at the table, and then counting the chips in the frying pan. 'Seven each tonight.'

Her husband worked for the council. They were both massively overweight and bilious with greasy food. She spoke as if we were deaf or stupid, explaining the rules of the guest house. Her husband darted around the house in a frenzy of unfinished jobs, waddling down the narrow corridors, mending fuses and taking things to pieces, scattering the floors with bits of wire and broken electrical parts. He ate everything that was put in front of him.

After every meal, we walked into town for fish and chips.

The landlady spent her evenings in front of the television, eating her way stolidly through pound boxes of chocolate while she read her religious pamphlets.

The only other person in the house was the daughter. 'I'm Madeline,' she told me when I met her on the landing. 'I'm their daughter.' She nodded briefly downstairs. She was immensely fat, and wore brightly coloured flared frocks and ribbons in her hair. She was sixteen.

'You mustn't disturb me,' she said confidentially. 'I'm doing my exams this year.'

'What exams?'

'Hairdressing.'

'I didn't know you could do exams for hairdressing.'

'Can't know everything, can you?'

Late one night, Toyne got all of her dresses and underwear out of her bedroom and pegged them to a washing line which he trailed down from the attic landing to the main landing below.

We heard the shriek in the middle of the night.

'What if there had been guests in the house?' the landlady said furiously when we came down for breakfast and found her serving the eggs and bacon. 'What if there had been guests?'

'We're guests,' I pointed out.

'What if I came down to the station this morning and saw your

229

superintendent?' she went on in the same hectoring voice, as if we hadn't heard a word she'd said. 'What if I did that, eh, eh?'

She banged a plate down in front of each of us and nodded firmly, standing at the head of the table, her arms folded across her electric green apron.

I caught the train home on the first weekend and went straight round to see Caroline. Her hair had been cut very short, making her face seem white and her eyes much larger than before. When she opened the door and saw me, she threw her arms round my neck and then held my face in both her hands, kissing me urgently on the mouth and pulling me into the house.

'I hate that uniform,' she said, unbuttoning the jacket and loosening my tie. She couldn't manage the collar stud.

'Let's go upstairs,' I said.

'No.'

She kissed me again and buried her face in my shoulder. 'My parents will be home any minute.'

She was shaking. In the lounge, the television was turned up to full volume and I could see books and loose papers scattered all over the floor where she had been working. On the television, they were announcing the football results. The only train I could catch from the division was at twelve o'clock, and I'd had to run from the station, leaving several minutes early to be sure of catching the train. There wasn't another until Sunday. The journey had taken all afternoon.

'You aren't interested in football,' I told Caroline.

'Yes, I am.'

'You never used to be.'

'I am now.'

She made some black coffee and brought through a plate of ginger biscuits. Sitting by the fire, she refused to speak until the results were finished. I drank my coffee and spilled some in the saucer. My hand was shaking. I got up and straightened my tie, and told Caroline I had to go home just to let them know I was back. She jumped up quickly and kissed me again on the mouth, holding my face, half turning to watch the television. I gave her a quick kiss on the nose, but she was standing with her arms folded, staring at the television as if she hadn't time to see me out of the house.

I told my father I hated the division.

'It's your first week,' he said.

I told him about the lodgings and he said I could always change them.

'I lived with a real bitch my first lodgings,' he said, making the tea and glancing out of the window for my mother. She had gone to the village because one of the old people was ill. She would be back any minute. 'She used to say I reminded her of her son, God help him, I don't know what he was like.'

'I can't stand it,' I said abruptly, interrupting him, watching him pour the tea.

He glanced up and shrugged. He didn't want to talk about it, didn't want to bother. 'Talk to the duty sergeant,' he said.

'I don't want to,' I said hopelessly.

I wanted him to telephone the division.

I wanted him to understand.

'Leave, then,' he said quietly, and walked out of the room.

I could hear him whistling in the hall, and then his office door closed.

I sat down and listened to the flames licking up the chimney.

I felt as though the house was surrounded by animals, scampering in the dark furrows, shivering in the deserted lanes.

A car roared past on the main road.

I stared down at my boots, the toes shining in the flames from the fire, the laces knotted in a tight bow.

I had to learn how to tie the knot when they gave me the boots.

'You don't do it like that, lad,' Jaines had sneered. 'Didn't your father teach you anything?'

I wanted to take the boots off and drop them on the fire.

I got up and went upstairs as soon as I heard my mother.

THIRTY-SEVEN

At the end of March I was instructed to report to Wakefield for a month of intensive training.

'It's good experience,' my father told me. 'It'll help you decide.'

He was driving me to the station. He never took his eyes off the road.

Digs were found for me and another cadet with a woman who fed us on onions fried in thick batter. My bedroom overlooked the rugby ground. At night, I could watch them practising. The landlady was frail and elderly, and kept asking us if we liked the onions.

'It was my husband's favourite,' she smiled when I told her I loved them.

The training was mainly physical. We went for forced marches and cross-country runs, stood for hours on parade in the cold and rain, were taught judo and self-defence. On a mat on the lawns, we threw each other hard against the ground and kicked and flailed in bare-knuckle fights. In ferocious sessions, two sergeants showed us how to use a truncheon to disable with maximum pain and minimum damage. In lectures afterwards, all the nerve centres of the human body were carefully explained.

'But you never draw the truncheon without orders,' the sergeants insisted, nodding at each other, echoing each other's words. 'Isn't that right, Sergeant Crosby?'

'It's right, Sergeant Vallance.'

'What happens if you get cornered?' I asked my father when I got back.

'You fight,' he said.

'But they told us on training you can't use the truncheon without orders.'

He looked at me as if I would never learn anything. I knew he was thinking about his friend from the fairgrounds who had been beaten up. He was determined that would never happen to him.

'You use it,' he said flatly.

During one of the sessions with the truncheons, the older sergeant pretended to be a drunk, and then caught me with a savage punch to the kidneys that left me stunned for several minutes.

'Sorry, lad,' he said afterwards. 'You have to learn.'

Every morning we paraded at dawn, and a grey-haired chief inspector spat and yelled into our faces, inspecting our gear with abrupt contempt and deafening us with his foul-mouthed abuse. He was a tall, thin man called Vessey and walked with a limp, holding himself stiffly and scowling with pain. He had worked in a munitions factory during the war and been injured in an accident. The side of his face had been badly burned, and his nose was pockmarked with scars. When he caught me wearing unpolished boots, he made me march for three hours round the parade ground, wearing full uniform and the greatcoat that was meant for extreme weather. After two hours, he strolled out of his office and screamed at me to increase the pace to double-time. At the end of each week, he inspected our finger nails, smiling nastily if our hands shook.

On the first night, the landlady's granddaughter came round with a friend. 'You want to go to the pictures?' she asked.

'Great.'

'Will you wear your uniforms?'

'Can't.'

'Go on.'

'We're not allowed.'

'Spoil sports.'

We took the girls to the cinema and sat on the back row. The girl I was with wore a white cardigan and plastic raincoat which creaked in the darkness. She told me she was an orphan and lived with foster parents who wanted her to work in the cotton mills.

'I hate factories,' she said, munching through a packet of sweets. 'I hate common girls.'

She had a thin colourless face, uneven teeth. She fidgeted all the time, her voice a reedy whine. She finished the sweets and held my hand, her fingers sticky and cold.

'You can see me again, if you like,' she said politely when I saw her home.

She held out her hand for me to shake, clutching her raincoat to her neck.

I told her I had studying to do most nights, but she came round

233

the following afternoon and told the landlady I had promised to take her out.

In the final week, the chief inspector screamed at an Irish cadet who was one of the most popular in the group, and the cadet suddenly turned and walked off the parade ground, going straight to his lodgings and catching the train before any of us had chance to speak to him. He left his uniform in a heap on the floor of his bedroom. The sergeants went round to the lodgings and then told us that he was a good lad but not cut out for the life, not the right temperament.

The girl was waiting at the house every evening. She let me kiss her but kept her lips tightly closed, her hands on my arms. She wore a perfume that made me want to sneeze. I told her I liked rugby and wanted to watch the practices from my bedroom window. 'Best chance I'll ever have,' I told her.

At the end of the month, when we were asked to write a report on the training, I produced a clumsy imitation of Hemingway, and grinned stupidly when the chief inspector told my parents it was 'most interesting'.

All forty of us were photographed after the passing-out parade.

My face was completely round underneath the peaked cap.

My cheeks looked red and swollen, although the photograph was black and white.

My eyes were expressionless.

At the reception, my mother was wearing a new dress and my father shook hands with the sergeants as if it was the proudest day of his life, joking and saying I would have to make more of the job than he had done, listening attentively when they talked about the work I still needed to do before I made my decision about joining properly.

'When is he nineteen?' Sergeant Vallance asked cheerfully, punching my arm as if I'd done really well.

'August, isn't it, Stephen?' my father said.

'Don't you know?' I said coldly.

They all laughed.

When we got back to the lodgings the landlady had done us tea, and my parents sat and chatted in her front room while I packed my things. The girl had come round. She stood patiently on the landing, leaning in the doorway, biting her fingernails.

'I could come and live near you,' she said.

'I don't think so,' I said.

I turned and looked at her. I hated her. I hated the old-fashioned cardigan and frizzled hair. I detested her job in a department store. I felt terrified, as though she was going to be my future if I didn't get away. I kept thinking about Caroline. I kept hearing her voice, seeing her at the piano. I kept imagining her reading a book, scribbling her urgent notes, telling me about Pasternak and Rimbaud. I thought suddenly about the cathedral, and the evil faces of the gargoyles, and the excitement with which she had shown me the passages from Lawrence. I wanted to go home and never leave her again.

'I have to go,' I said, and walked out of the room, pushing past the girl on the landing. I went downstairs and told my parents we ought to be on our way. I let the landlady kiss me briefly on the cheek and climbed into the back of the car without bothering to wave.

'It was wonderful, Stephen,' my mother said as we drove through the darkening countryside. 'It was wonderful, wasn't it, Norman?'

'It was,' my father said emphatically. 'Best day of my life.'

On the back seat, I closed my eyes and tried to go to sleep.

THIRTY-EIGHT

In the spring there were daffodils everywhere and the grass around the camp was overgrown with speedwell. The skies seemed to vibrate with skylarks out of the blue, remote hills.

When Matthew had finished revising for first-year exams, we travelled down to London and spent a week going round the galleries. Matthew was helping to organise a national tour of student art and preparing a play for the Edinburgh Festival, and he said he needed some fresh ideas. We stayed in a bed and breakfast place near Kings Cross, ate cheap curry in a restaurant in Leicester Square that offered meals from every country in the world, and sat for hours in the cool corridors of the Tate and the National Gallery.

'You can't be an expert on everything,' I told Matthew.

'Why not?' he said, looking genuinely puzzled.

One afternoon, while Matthew wrote notes on Van Gogh, I wandered along Tottenham Court Road and down Oxford Street and ended up in the Marquee listening to Tubby Hayes. He played without stop for two hours, standing on the edge of the stage, leaning into the hot darkness and the smoke, and when I stumbled back out into the sunlight, the dusty roar of the traffic, I couldn't imagine how I was going to go back to the division, to the bleak house near the camp.

'Then don't go back,' Matthew said simply.

'You know it isn't that easy.'

'Yes, I do, but it doesn't change anything. You still have to do it sooner or later. Nobody else can. Don't go back.'

That night, we went to see *West Side Story*, then lay awake on our beds, the couple in the room next door making noisy, exhibitionist love, the man urinating frequently into the sink.

'It makes it better,' he said loudly. The walls were paper thin.

'I bet she's a prostitute,' Matthew whispered.

'It makes it agony.' The man shouted his excitement.

'He's probably got the pox,' Matthew said.

'Why?' I whispered back urgently, trying to suppress my laughter.

'Why what?'

236

'Why do you say she's a prostitute?'

'Would you do it without money?' Matthew hissed.

'Not with him.'

We both buried our heads under pillows as the man and woman rocked backwards and forwards on their bed, the ancient iron bedstead crashing into the grimy walls, the woman singing hysterically between the man's grunts.

'You have to be a journalist,' Matthew told me when we went down to breakfast and watched the couple at their table by the window. The girl was wearing a wedding ring. She had her hair tightly permed and her flat-heeled shoes were brown suede. The man wore a pale blue suit and open-necked shirt.

'Why do I have to be a journalist?' I asked.

'With instincts like yours? You knew it was the real thing. You knew it was genuine. You're a natural. I thought she was a prostitute.'

'I think you're right.' I choked into my cereals.

At the weekend, we walked happily through the London parks. A vast crowd marched ahead of us, and we joined them to see where they were going. At Hyde Park Corner, we stood and listened to the speakers, Vanessa Redgrave and then Bernard Levin, ridiculing the idea of Civil Defence.

'You've got four minutes to get half a ton of sandbags into your kitchen,' one of the speakers shouted, and the crowd cheered happily at the nonsense.

'And brown paper,' the speaker reminded us. 'Don't forget the brown paper and vinegar.'

The immense crowd roared their approval.

Nobody ever brought a protest to Fulnar.

Without speaking, Matthew and I must both have been thinking about Nemesis, and the exercise when they had taken seventeen minutes to get the missile out of the ground.

'Better buy you some brown paper.' Matthew nodded solemnly as we made our way back to the hotel.

'I'm going to live like Henry Miller in *Tropic of Cancer*,' I told him as we jostled and sweated on the Underground. 'I'm going to rent a room and live on cheap wine and curry.'

In a dingy restaurant behind Kings Cross station, we wrote postcards we had picked up at the Tate Gallery. I sent one to Caroline and to my parents. I kept a dozen cards for myself, to pin around my room. I bought several by Francis Bacon and imagined sending them every week to the girl in Wakefield. Since I'd got back, she had telephoned my mother several times, crying down the line that I had promised to write to her.

We sat together in Russell Square and read the advertisements in the *Evening Standard*. We had no idea most of the advertisements were from agencies, but Matthew insisted on telephoning several of the numbers, and after an hour in a call box, told me that I could get a bedsitter in Kensington for three guineas, and could be guaranteed a temporary typing job that weekend. Even with my typing speeds, the agency said there would be no problem.

'So there's nothing to stop you,' he said, folding the newspaper and dropping it into a rubbish bin as we walked round the gardens, following the ghost of Prufrock who still worked in the square, with his bowler and folded umbrella.

On our last day, I stood with Matthew and watched the crowds swarming across London Bridge to work.

' "So many, I had not thought death had undone so many," ' Matthew recited melodramatically, waving cheerfully to the crowds.

I could have hated Matthew.

I resented his freedom.

But I had already decided that I would leave home and find a bedsitter somewhere in London.

I would become a journalist.

One afternoon in Russell Square had decided me.

When I told Matthew I was going to resign from the police cadets, he was as excited as I was myself.

All I had to do was find the courage to tell my parents.

When I got back, my father was dismissive.

My mother said it was all because of Matthew.

'You're eighteen,' she scoffed when I said I wanted to rent a bedsitter and get a job in London.

'I'm old enough to be in this lousy job,' I shouted back.

My father was furious. He was obviously thinking about what his friends would say at headquarters. 'Don't talk like that,' he said, white-faced and confused.

I told them I wanted to be a writer. They must have thought I was mad.

238

'Nobody'll ever publish anything you write,' my father sneered.
They seemed to hate Matthew.

I felt diminished that they couldn't take the decision as my own.

'I have to decide this summer,' I told them.

'No, you don't.'

'I have to decide when I'm nineteen.'

'You can do the probationary period,' my father said furiously. 'You can do the two years.'

'Two years!'

'You'll have a better idea by then.'

'I know *now*.'

'At least wait until you're nineteen.'

Pathetically, I gave up and agreed with them.

I would wait another few months and decide when I was nineteen.

I felt as though those months would last for ever.

I walked round to Caroline's house and her mother told me she was in town shopping.

'We may be leaving soon,' she told me brightly, her face blotched with make-up, her eyes shining and over-excited.

'Leaving?'

'The government are phasing Nemesis out,' she said bleakly. 'We're going back to Washington. Didn't Caroline tell you? Well, no, I don't suppose she would. We're going back as soon as my husband gets his orders.'

She turned and smiled at me brightly, patting her elaborate hair.

'Not that I'm surprised. This government hasn't a *clue* what they're doing. I'll tell Caroline you called by.'

I walked back to the police house.

They were drilling spring wheat again in the fields that surrounded our garden.

I chatted with my mother about the closing of the camp, and then went upstairs to pack my bags. I had to return to the division in the morning.

THIRTY-NINE

In July the camp and its associate sites was declared non-operational. The missile squadrons were disbanded. The munitions squadron responsible for supplies returned to the United States. The camp was almost deserted.

'Just a few families left,' Caroline wrote in a letter to my lodgings. 'The green seems quite empty.'

I attended first-aid classes during the week and did hardly any reading. There was no time during the day, and at night Toyne wanted to go out drinking or lie on his bed masturbating, chanting remarks about the landlady's daughter to the pink ceiling, wailing as the bedsprings screeched and howled.

'She's got fat tits,' he groaned into his snotty handkerchief. 'She's got huge fat tits. I want to come all over her tits. I want to rub my spunk on her tits.'

I lay in the heat, listening to his rancid monologues, his foul imaginings.

'You've got a mouth like a lavatory wall,' I told him.

'Summer visitors,' the landlady said to him one morning, holding his sheets up in front of him and then ramming them down into the laundry basket. 'Summer visitors.'

At the station, I was asked to take notes during interviews.

A man suffering from acute depressions was brought in for questioning about a series of assaults. Six children had complained to their parents about the man fiddling with their clothes, touching them inside their underpants. The man was brought in and left in a waiting room for two hours. He was unshaven, his shirt collar grimed with sweat, his stubble grey and filthy. He glanced at me nervously when I took him a cup of tea, and stood up when one of the sergeants walked into the room to begin the interview. The man's wife was kept waiting in the corridor.

He was charged with eighteen separate offences and taken down to the cells. His wife went with him, weeping, hysterical, a plump, flat-nosed little woman in old clothes, her face lined with dirt and tears. She kept brushing her skirt down over her knees and touching

240

her mouth nervously. She watched her husband all the time, asking him if he was all right, calling him love. He had been having treatment for depression for years, hadn't worked for as long as she could remember. He liked to go fishing. He smoked twenty Woodbines a day.

'I can't stand bastards like that,' the CID sergeant said bleakly when the man had been taken downstairs. 'I can't stand them. They smell. I know it straight away. They mess with themselves. I reckon he should be castrated. Save him bothering.'

He saw me watching him, and slammed the file closed.

'I hope you've got it all down right,' he said, and walked out of the room.

A week later, the man's daughter called at the station.

'Can you tell us anything?' the sergeant asked her.

She sat and stared at him, tired, insolent, her eyes glancing round the room. She wore a tight yellow dress that needed washing, and sat with her legs crossed, the dress riding up her thighs. 'Why should I?' she said aggressively.

'To help him?'

'Why should I help him?'

'I don't know, love.'

'Bastard.'

She had a black leather shoulder-bag which she held on her knee all the time she was talking. Her fingernails were bitten to the quick. A strip of sticking plaster round one finger was black with grime.

'I wouldn't do owt to help that bastard,' she said bitterly, staring at me as I made notes of what she was saying. 'What's he doing?'

'Just a record, love.'

'What's he doing that for?'

She lit a cigarette and started crying. Her hands were shaking. Her mascara ran down her cheeks, smudging the rest of her thickly daubed make-up. She had a thin, tight mouth. She blew her nose noisily and told the sergeant to sod off, walking out of the interview room with her bag slung casually over her shoulder.

'Can't fucking credit it, can you?' Jukes said.

'What?'

'Tart like that.'

'She's upset.'

'He's been banging her twenty years, bet you.'

'You don't know that.'

'Don't I?'

He got up and slouched out of the room.

I sat reading my notes, staring out of the window. In the heat, the Woolworth's sign opposite blinked on and off, two of the letters missing.

I hurried home every weekend.

After the appalling winter, the warm days were airless and enervating, skylarks and terns wheeling above fields the colour of mustard, the busy roads around the camp suddenly empty.

I went for long walks with Caroline and talked listlessly about going to London.

'You could get a job,' she insisted.

'How do you know?'

'There's lots of work down there, you could get a job easily.'

'How do you know?'

'You said so,' she reminded me gently.

We lay in the fields and made love, and said nothing about America.

Some days, I could hardly get an erection.

'It doesn't matter,' Caroline said quietly.

'It does.'

'Don't be silly.'

She was kind, unhappy. She said nothing mattered. She held my hand and touched my face.

At night, in my silent bedroom, I could hear Nemesis singing, a low throbbing hum, a metallic whine across the wheatfields.

The military police still patrolled the perimeter.

The police and a few scientists were the only ones left.

I missed Barbara.

I read *Life Studies* all the time, lost in some deep anguish.

At the station, the fluorescent lighting in reception hummed against the green ceiling. Midges darted round the lights. On the dead switchboard, a red light glowed, and the radio jarred with static, like a thunderstorm, crackling and erupting a long way away. A man cried in one of the cells, dreaming of some lost love. I imagined it all. I imagined the ghosts of the corridors weeping, the dead imprisoned in their ghostly cells. I touched myself, thinking of Caroline's cold fingers.

One hot summer night, attending a suicide on some railway embankment, a sergeant jokingly told me to go and look for the dead girl's eyes, and I passed out, grazing my face on the rusty track.

When I came to, the sergeant was kneeling beside me, resting my head on his knee.

'You all right, son?' he asked kindly.

I couldn't speak.

I stared at him, blinded by the torchlight.

Voices were crying down the track, a car radio whistled with static.

'Stephen?'

They never called you by your first name.

I went home and handed in my resignation.

FORTY

Caroline lay by the open windows.

A pheasant stalked across the lawns and rustled into the overgrown flowerbeds. A dog barked in the distance.

'I can't bear it if you go back.'

'I know.'

'I can't bear the thought.'

We lay for a long time, listening to the garden, the bees in the honeysuckle, the birds racketing in the trees.

Caroline lit a cigarette and swallowed the smoke, closing her eyes briefly. Her parents were away.

My eyes filled with tears. 'I can't live without you.'

'Stephen . . . '

'I keep saying these things.'

'Don't.'

'I keep saying them.'

She went on smoking.

She no longer wore earrings or make-up. She kept out of the sun as much as possible and her face was pale and exhausted.

'They're harvesting the spring wheat,' she said quietly as we heard the huge combines in the nearby fields.

The machines seemed relentless.

'Yes.'

'You taught me that.'

'It was Matthew really,' I said. 'I didn't know anything about farming.'

She pushed the hair out of her eyes and leaned up on her elbows.

Her breasts touched my arm. She was naked, her long legs pale as her face, her flat stomach pressing on the carpet. She smiled when I touched her face with the tip of my finger. I was lying on my back. She leaned forward and kissed me very gently on the nose. As we made love, I could hear the fridge in the kitchen humming, the faint rattle of bottles every time the motor sprung to life. I closed my eyes and felt Caroline lean over me to fit the condom. She held

244

me with one hand, and giggled when I opened my eyes, frowning, urgent. She bit her lips when I leaned up and started touching her. I came inside her, and she kissed me hard on the neck, her arms wrapped behind my head, her body clinging to mine.

She called my name for the first time when we'd been together.

She kept saying my name, as if it was something she was trying to remember.

Late that night, her parents came back.

We could hear them moving about downstairs.

I got out of bed and dressed quickly, dropping my shoes on the floor, knocking into one of the chairs. I pulled my T-shirt over my head and tried to straighten my hair.

Caroline sat on the edge of her bed and watched me.

She held her head in her hands, rocking backwards and forwards, chewing her lips.

As I got dressed, she didn't speak.

When I looked down at her, she was crying, shaking her head from side to side, tears pouring down her face. She looked terrified.

In the hall, her father stood tiredly in the doorway, his grey hair iron in the light from the lamp in the sitting room, his gold-rimmed glasses reflecting the light.

His wife stood behind him, her hands hanging loosely at her sides.

I let myself out of the house without speaking.

She wrote to me a few days afterwards, saying that her father had been posted to Washington. She would be travelling with her mother, once they'd seen some friends in London. She hoped I could get back before they left. 'I am going to university in Cambridge,' she joked, and told me to look it up on an east coast map. She promised to write as soon as she knew where they would be living. Her parents, she said, weren't angry. Just upset.

'I do love you,' she wrote at the end of the letter, 'but you put me under such pressure. You're so angry all the time, so upset. I can't seem to help you. But I won't forget. Take care. Love you, Caroline.'

In my frenzy, I burnt the letter.

FORTY-ONE

I didn't wait for the final day.

I left the division a week before my notice was due to expire, and thumbed a lift up the coast. I was wearing my jeans and T-shirt, and a pair of new plimsolls. I travelled in a lorry, trying to concentrate on what the driver was saying, thinking about the things I had left in my lodgings. I had hung my uniform behind the door. I had nothing with me but a copy of *The Rainbow*.

By the time I arrived home, the roads were deserted, the night was black and moonless. I walked out onto the runways and stood watching the clouds, great banks of blackness scurrying across the moon. There were no stars because of the cloud.

I walked straight across the runways and out towards Nemesis.

In the silence, I thought I could hear the sea, carried on the breeze across the hills, but when I stopped, all I could hear was my own blood pumping through my head. An owl hooted above the village.

I reached the site and looked up at the barbed wire.

Nemesis had gone, but the site was still surrounded by high wire fencing.

I scrambled up the rough grassy bank and stared down into the compound.

The bunker was wide open.

In the darkness I could see the massive steel ramp on which the rockets had been fired.

The grass around the bunker was blackened by fire.

The bunker was completely empty.

Late in the summer, a swarm of flying ants settled on the house. For an hour, my father and I sprayed them with boiling water. The rubber of the garden hose began to swell. The metal nozzle burned our hands. Scalded ants crawled in heaps round the garden, rotting in piles at the bottom of the walls. Hundreds of them got into the house, squirming under carpets and into cupboards, nesting underneath the stairs. For days, we kept finding them. One morning, as we sat at breakfast, dry wings fluttered in the lampshade and a huge ant fell from the ceiling onto the yellow tablecloth. My mother carried it out into the garden, and threw it as far as she could into the fields. 'There,' she said, coming back and sitting down at the table. After a long time, my father went through to his office and closed the door.